Praise for Other Books
By
Howard Weiner

"This is such an interesting read! I found it really exciting and compelling, with lots of detail that pulled me in, right from the start. It is definitely a book that keeps you on your toes and guessing just what in coming...I found the characters really were created well. They had a lot of depth and personality, which meant they were easy to get to know and really decide who you liked and didn't, though it may have been hard!...Overall, I liked this read, and am excited to read more from this author. I recommend giving this book a go and keeping an eye out for future reads!"

One for the Price of Two
Amazon, April 10, 2018

"Great character development...I really enjoyed this book. He really developed all the characters. He reminded my of Elmore Leonard in his characters. I couldn't put the book down."

Serendipity Opportunity
Amazon, February 12, 2018

"A Good Read After All!...a very enjoyable crime thriller with well crafted characters and a fast moving easily readable plot. The details provided throughout the book shows great attention to detail and greatly enhance the storyline. Recommended for those readers of the genre of crime thrillers. A fun read by all accounts."

It Is Las Vegas After All
Amazon, May 8, 2017

"Having just completed the first book in the series (*One for the Price of Two*), itself a very satisfying experience, I was pleased to find this one a significant step up. While the characters continued their evolutionary development, the presentation of their experiences and the intricacy of the plot were compelling on a much more engaging level. I found myself not wanting to stop reading despite the intrusion of real-life demands. I rarely give a 5-star review, but this book earns it...."

THE BIG LOWANDOWSKI

Howard Weiner

Triple Play Series

THE BIG LOWANDOWSKI

By

Howard D. Weiner

i

Copyright

Library of Congress Control Number: 2018903196
ISBN: 978-0-9998619-2-9 (paperback)
ISBN: 978-0-9998619-3-6 (ebook)
ASIN: B07CVPQ16Y

Cover design by Howard D. Weiner
Edited by Wendy F. Weiner

Version_1

Books by Howard Weiner

FICTION

THE TRIPLE PLAY NOVELS
It Is Las Vegas After All[1]
Serendipity Opportunity
The Big Lowandowski

HAIR ON FIRE NOVELS
Bad Money
By Any Other Name[2]

THE BLOOD RELATIONS NOVELS
One for the Price of Two
Deadly Walkabout
If At First

ACADEMIC

Introduction to Structured COBOL: A Programming Skills
Approach

[1]Also available on audiobook
[2]Forthcoming, Fall 2019

DEDICATION

To my Bride,
You were right—again.

TABLE OF CONTENTS

CHAPTER 1

A Prologue

"ARE YOU SHY?" SHE ASKED, a sly smile transformed her face. The all-business, no nonsense attitude she struck at the beginning of their discussion softened somewhat. He immediately saw the change and exhaled. Either he complied with her request, or she was gone, and he didn't want her to leave despite the tone she'd adopted from the outset of their discussion.

He couldn't believe he was about to do what he was going to do. How did he lose the power in this bargain? He knew the answer. He liked her. He wanted her to stay, to take the job. So, he loosened his belt and stuck the fingers of both hands under the elastic waistband of his underwear. He took one more look at her face—and then the rest of her.

Then, as his high school gym teacher used to say, he dropped trow.

"You know," she started, "nothing looks sillier than to see a man standing with his pants down around his feet. Why don't you finish what you started with some style and step out of them altogether?"

He still couldn't believe he was standing there with the fresh island breeze ventilating the lower half of his body. What did he have to lose by kicking his pants to the side? He weighed the issue carefully, but quickly, and despite that he was in very foreign territory, he complied with this request as well. Now he stood before her with his pants several feet from where they would ordinarily be.

They stood an arm's length apart. Looking at the full-length mirror behind her he constructed her composite view which, if he was totally honest, was incredible. What wasn't impressive was his reflection in the mirror. Pretending someone else—not him—was standing there, made it easier for him to admit how silly he looked. Either he put his pants back on, or he took off his shirt. With the former off and the latter still on, he thought he looked ridiculous.

He removed his shirt as well, and in an exaggerated manner, extended his arm, opened his hand, and the shirt dropped atop the pants. The breeze had a calming effect. Which was good, because if he thought too much about his current circumstances he might—he knew—bring further embarrassment to himself.

Her gaze temporarily shifted to the growing pile of clothing and then back to him.

"Normally," she said in a business voice, "I applaud initiative, especially stylish initiative."

He smiled thinking, at least I gained some measure of respect in this conversation.

She caught his smile.

"I said, *normally*," she continued. "This, however, is not one of those times. Instead, taking off your shirt smacks of impatience. Like you're trying to get this over with by forcing us to the next box on the tick list."

She clucked several times in disapproval.

"Is that what you want, Charles? Are you trying to move this negotiation along? Because, if you are, I need to remind you we're still negotiating. Nothing has been settled, yet."

His face flushed. She was right. He was desperate.

"I'll keep in mind that one of the things I'm supposed to do—if I accept this assignment—is to bring you along, to make you successful in your other interpersonal relationships. To help you build your self-esteem and confidence. But it appears to me that you might have a tad more confidence in your abilities than circumstances warrant. What I see before me is an overconfident, self-impressed, man-child. The type of man a woman of quality wouldn't give a second look let alone a first."

She continued the clucking sound as she walked slowly around him, appraising what stood before her.

"Muscle tone could stand some improvement," her appraisal finding the first flaw. He wondered, actually feared, how long, how specific his list of faults and shortcomings she could summon forth. His disappointment and concern were immediately reflected in his posture.

"So," she sniffed, "in addition to everything else, you're a sloucher, as well. Yet another unattractive trait."

"*Everything* else," he thought to himself.

He watched her movements reflected in the mirror as she made her way behind him. She leaned in to sniff the areas behind his armpits.

"Hygiene, while not terrible, could use some additional effort," she opined. "It's clear you use soap—hardly a foregone conclusion these days. What deodorant do you use?"

"Stuff I buy at the local market," he replied.

"*Stuff* is it? 'Stuff' implies you see hygiene as a requirement—which is good, I guess. However, it smacks yet again of 'ticking the box' rather than a calculated assessment of need and purpose."

She was once again standing in front of him.

"Let me offer one more comment and then a question."

"Shoot," he said.

"*Shoot*, you say? My, aren't we the erudite conversationalist."

He wasn't certain of the meaning of "erudite," but from the context of her remark it probably trended in the same direction this entire negotiation was headed.

"You are at the very beginning of adulthood. You might be a fully formed man—more about that in a minute—but your comportment strikes me more typical of a teenager. Hasn't any woman taken you in hand before this?" Realizing the answer to her own question, "No, of course not. You are what someone with a wicked sense of humor might term a 'self-made man.'"

"Is that your question?" he asked.

"What's that?" she replied with some irritation. "Oh no, I was thinking aloud."

"What then *is* your question?" he responded with some irritation of his own.

3

She scanned his body from top to bottom yet again before answering, "Why exactly do they call you the 'Big' Lowandowski? The use of the adjective isn't apparent, or fitting, from where I stand."

He was officially mortified. In fact, he was miles beyond that.

"Next," she started.

"There's a 'next'?" he complained.

"Sloucher and a whiner," she clucked. "Aren't you a bundle of surprises."

He self-corrected his posture, exhaled deeply, searching for a mindful moment.

"Well, I'll give you a few points for the attempted recovery—"

He grew hopeful.

"—but you lost too many style points in so exaggerated a tactic."

He felt lower than his pile of discarded clothing beside him.

Charles Lowandowski—née Big Lowandowski—adopted the best business demeanor possible under the circumstances.

"Excuse me," he started. "I advertised for the 'girlfriend experience.' I'm uncertain what that means to you, but I can tell you without reservation that this," he said gesturing to the room, her, and himself, "isn't that."

She chuckled.

"Oh my, you've never had a real girlfriend before," she was now standing almost nose to nose. "Have you?" She smiled. "Be honest?"

Having failed miserably with his other tactics, perhaps it was time to try honesty—anything that might result in her approval. Hell, he'd settle for a lot less than her approval right now.

"No, I have not."

"Have not what?" She countered. "Hmmm?"

"'*Hmmm*?'" he mimicked. "Aren't we the erudite conversationalist?"

"Very good, 'Big.'"

He thought this might be a taunt, but his hope sprang eternal. Sooner or later things had to improve between them.

He smiled.

"Mockery," she said, "has seldom lured a reluctant woman into any man's bed." She continued, "Mockery is the domain of a shrewish mother-in-law whose child rearing skills are vastly overrated, judging the end product." She paused. "In case you are uncertain," she stubbed her index finger into his solar plexus, "You are the end product."

There was now an even more awkward silence between them before she broke her soul crushing stare.

"Now, let's move on to the questions of, shall we say, a *personal* nature."

Christ, he thought.

"Are you a virgin," she asked.

He regretted his answer as the words tumbled out of his mouth, "Technically."

She stepped back presenting him with a look of incredulity.

"Technically?" she asked, and before he could respond, "A woman can answer 'technically,' but not a man. No man is ever *technically* a virgin."

"I guess we'll have to disagree on that point.," was his clipped response.

"A sloucher, a whiner, and now, snippy. There is no end to your prodigious talents."

He endured another painful silence.

"Where is the bedroom?" she asked.

"Bedroom?"

"The bedroom," she emphasized.

"Why?" he queried.

"You cannot be serious," she responded. "It's time to assess the state of your skill level."

He was speechless.

"The bedroom?" she asked, yet again.

"I don't think I can. In fact, I know I can't."

"What? Find your way to your own bedroom? Surely you can. Even I believe you can do at least that. Go on, now, show me the way."

She gave him a light tap on his rear end like an equestrian might use a riding crop.

CHAPTER 2

EDDY O'CONNER DREADED THIS meeting. The "Affair Lowandowski," as her contacts in the Director of National Intelligence's Office referred to it, was hardly her firm's finest hour.

She took her assigned seat in the conference room. Thankfully, she was relegated to one of the seats not at the center table. Instead, she sat inconspicuously along the far back wall. If she could crawl under the carpet, she would. Better still would be skipping the meeting entirely. Unfortunately, her firm, Triple Play, had a contract with the DNI's Office that was central to the topic at hand.

Slowly the room filled with the people who mattered. They arrived in their respective order of importance. The final two were the DNI and the FBI's Assistant Director for Counterintelligence.

The DNI opened the meeting with a short greeting and launched into the heart of the matter.

"Charles Lowandowski represents an ongoing threat to the Homeland.

"Over these many months, and thousands of hours of interviews, our colleagues have constructed an enlightening timeline and set of interesting profiles we are here to review today.

"I want to take a moment to introduce Ms. Eddy O'Conner. Eddy's firm, Triple Play, assisted this office initially serving as a fresh set of objective eyes on the assassination of one of our FBI special agents, and much later, Mr. Lowandowski himself.

"Eddy, please stand for the benefit of those in this room who may not know who you are."

O'Conner briefly stood—the only woman in the room. All faces turned away from the DNI to appraise Eddy, no emotion showing on any faces. Other than the DNI, she had no other friends in this room.

The DNI continued.

"Eddy and I go back—way back into the Cold War days. There aren't many of us 'Cold Warriors' left in government. The skills we acquired to do battle with the Soviets fell into disuse after the fall of the USSR in December 1991.

"Most of the people in this room were still in the public school system in December 1991. But Eddy and I are relics, brought back from the brink of extinction, because Mr. Putin has, in many ways, transformed the 'New Russia' into the old USSR—and he's not done, yet.

"So we two dinosaurs are in a unique position. We know the old methods and practices of the KGB and the GRU. Everything old is new, again.

"My own operational experience includes some of the current principals in both organizations. We would formally meet—and parry—at Embassy events here and in Moscow. When circumstances warranted, we could meet for a walk around the Reflecting Pool on the Mall. Sometimes those chats proved worthwhile. Often, they were disappointing moves in a frustrating draw in an international game of chess among the Grand Masters.

"Eddy, on the other hand, was, shall we say, more operational in her service. She worked as an undercover agent for the CIA behind enemy lines during the coldest years, metaphorically speaking. She lived every day in a danger that none of us in this room can possibly imagine.

"Over the years, and without breaking her cover, Eddy taught the occasional course for us at the Farm in Camp Peary. She also agreed to serve as mentor for a whole generation of women operatives at a time when the number of plausible role models was few and far between.

"More recently, Eddy broke her cover to establish her own firm, Triple Play. Along with two former agents from the CIA, Triple Play, was critical in apprehending two physicists playing with low level radiation in the form of dirty bombs. Without Triple Play, there's an excellent chance much of the most valuable real estate in Las Vegas would still be in quarantine for radiation exposure, and our two young perps would have escaped to Canada and beyond."

When he finished with Eddy's work biography, everyone turned to take a second look and a more informed appraisal. What they saw the second time was different. She wasn't some functionary in the back of the room. Eddy O'Conner was a hero, a Cold Warrior.

The DNI continued.

"Many of us Cold Warriors came from all walks of life. This is the USA after all.

"Eddy O'Conner came to us from a life of privilege and wealth few of us can imagine. Even today.

"Eddy could have remained in the warm embrace of her large, extended family, started a family of her own, and undoubtedly become the matriarch of a current day family still considered to be among our elite.

"She didn't do that.

"Instead, Eddy took an oath of poverty, and joined a religious order. She became a stranger to her own family while dedicated to our national security. And, as alluded to a few moments ago, she maintained this cover for almost fifty years.

"Colleagues, let's have Eddy speak a few words."

O'Conner had not expected a central role in this meeting. Nor had she prepared any remarks. And she certainly did not expect the embarrassing introduction the DNI provided. Always adept at improvisation after a lifetime in the business, Eddy O'Conner did the only thing she knew how.

She lied.

She wove elements of the truth in with the lies. That's what her training taught her to do: Just enough of the truth to be credible with enough of the falsehoods to avoid calamity.

Eddy stood while everyone seated pivoted to provide an audience.

"First, I want to acknowledge my old friend and mentor, the DNI. Today, he showed the critical skills for a Cold Warrior: He can still spin a credible yarn and dissemble when circumstances call for it."

Those in the room understood Eddy's point. There was always truth—and falsity—in anything a Cold Warrior had to say. They wouldn't be worth their weight in salt otherwise.

They chuckled.

The DNI laughed heartily, "I told you she was good."

Eddy launched into a short chat she constructed as she spoke.

"We—my two colleagues and I—met Charles Lowandowski quite by accident. He was passing as a developmentally challenged young man, with a safe government job, doing the work that most of us fail to acknowledge, fail to really see. He took out the trash. Much of that trash represented some of the best intel the FBI gathered on domestic crime involving the dark web.

"Lowandowski's performance was, in retrospect, entirely and utterly believable. Why? Because we—all of us—have little contact with the developmentally challenged. Their challenges *challenge* us. We become uncomfortable in their presence, a 'There but for the grace of God goes us,' reaction.

"Next, we'll hear from the colleagues and profilers who delved into Lowandowski's past."

O'Conner paused and scanned the room.

"All of us here have earned the right to be here. Each of you has compiled a record where failure is scant. After all, everyone loves a winner."

More laughter from the group.

"Unfortunately, without the opportunity to confront your failures, to learn from your mistakes, means we are all far less than our brilliant records of achievement would otherwise suggest.

"Make no mistake about it. I failed. Charles Lowandowski beat me. He humiliated my firm, Triple Play, and my two gifted colleagues.

"We burn for a second shot at Mr. Lowandowski, one where he is totally and unequivocally unprepared for us.

"That will come at a price. Some of us will pay more than others to be sure.

"But second chances aren't handed out like candy to children. Second chances involve confronting our failures—my failures—and that is why we are here today. Today is all about what we did wrong. You, me—all of us.

"We will be embarrassed. I am already mortified. A 'brilliant' Cold Warrior laid low by an untutored teenager who, lacking our powerful security apparatus behind him, nevertheless kicked our collective asses from one end of Washington, DC, to wherever he is today."

She looked around the room one last time and reclaimed her seat.

CHAPTER 3

THE YOUNG FBI SPECIAL AGENT was well beyond his comfort level as he stood before this group.

"Good morning, everyone," his voice breaking on "everyone."

No one laughed, but most feigned a cough or a yawn as their raised hands covered their smiles. To his credit, the young briefer understood.

"You are all too kind. Please bear with me."

He took a deep, shaky breath and launched into his presentation.

"Charles Lowandowski, a high school dropout, secured a protected position reserved for the developmentally challenged in a local FBI field office. Lowandowski was many things, but not developmentally challenged."

The FBI's hot wash of the scandal laid out a perfect storm of events. Responsible for a one-person juvenile crime wave among his peers, state and local laws prohibited expulsion. The mandated programs to keep unruly juveniles in school, but separated from their classmates during punishment, were well intended by policy makers. More often than not the policy was not always a success in practice. Lowandowski spent more time in segregation than any two, three, or four of his unrulier peers, yet failed to thrive academically—even when he was the sole beneficiary of instruction and counseling.

It wasn't fashionable among public education policy makers to admit failure. These were people who believed there were no failing students, only schools failing those students. Lowandowski's principal took bitter issue with such sentiments. He had one murdered vice principal and a broken sports coach who paid the ultimate price for their efforts at Lowandowski's rehabilitation.

According to the agent briefing the room, the FBI re-opened the investigation of his parents death just to be certain Lowandowski hadn't engineered their demise as well.

"The death of his adopted parents was a transformative moment in Lowandowski's life.

"The probate court assigned him to a private wealth management firm where he met several developmentally challenged young adults the firm sponsored *pro bono*. The firm set the young heir's financial affairs in order. In visits to the firm's offices, Lowandowski met and befriended one of their young clients. We determined he took note of the young man's federally protected position and lifestyle. He set about establishing a similar opportunity for himself."

The agent looked up from his briefing notes to offer this summary: "It is from this point 'the system' didn't work as intended. In retrospect, there was an absence of effective internal controls."

The agent continued with his slide presentation.

"Under the mistaken impression Lowandowski was injured in his parents' vehicular accident, and without the benefit of an examination, the family physician signed an affidavit attesting to Lowandowski's alleged developmental impairments. The subject leveraged the affidavit to receive an endorsement for a protected position with the federal government. The local FBI office, in need of custodial services, avoided a prolonged commercial procurement process by the expedited hire of someone in Lowandowski's situation in accordance with OPM's administrative procedures.

"All parties involved wanted to do the right thing.

"The field office assigned Lowandowski a temporary security clearance to permit him access to secure spaces to perform his duties. The system-wide backlog of background investigations extended for more than a year. Lowandowski's request was pushed back in the queue several times to facilitate higher priority investigation requests, undoubtedly, because of his developmental challenges and the nature of his custodial work.

"Ironically, no one saw the handling of classified documents by a developmentally challenged custodian as a security risk."

The DNI spoke up, "That's no longer the case. I can assure you."

The agent waited for permission to continue.

"Resume, please," the DNI finally said.

"Lowandowski's tests, administered by the high school and ordered by the juvenile judge assigned to handle one of his appearances before the court, tell us Lowandowski is of above average intelligence. His psychological profile—again courtesy of the public school system and the juvenile court—suggest he was a typical, lazy teen. His foster care placement and subsequent adoption by wealthy parents who indulged his every whim, who protected him throughout his encounters with school administrators and the juvenile authorities, did not serve him well."

The agent looked at the audience, "Not the experience provided by my parents. Probably not yours either," drew a smattering of chuckles.

"We suspect Lowandowski read the confidential case summaries and advisories circulated within the local office. We further suspect these reports provided Lowandowski with both the initiative and roadmap to begin his efforts in cybercrime activities.

"These reports were electronically distributed. They were intended to be read electronically. They were never intended to be printed. Lowandowski should never have had access to these reports."

The DNI rose to face the group to offer this summary.

"There are digital natives and digital immigrants. Old folks, like myself, are digital immigrants. We embrace paper documents, even prefer them. Our younger agents and employees prefer digital documents and avoid paper.

"A digital immigrant in the local office, his preference for paper in violation of policy, made some of this problem possible. This whole damned situation was a cluster fuck of things that weren't supposed to happen."

He paused to let that sink in.

"But they did. And a lazy teenager put us in the position we now find ourselves."

The FBI Assistant Director of Counterintelligence spoke next. "Thank you, Agent.

"Next, we asked our profilers in Quantico to give us a better picture of Lowandowski. I didn't see the value in taking more of your valuable time to share their results—which were unexceptional. I'll just hit the high points.

"Lowandowski was a lazy, sullen teenager with low self-esteem. A teen who preferred to play video games rather than pursue young girls, or drugs, or alcohol, or fast cars. He was a loner, an introvert, who resented authority and his parents' success. Despite his preference for violent video games, he avoided any violent act involving face-to-face encounters. He was prone to seek anonymous acts of retribution on his aggressors—practical jokes embarrassing his victims. At least that was the case, until he mastered the possibilities of the dark web. At that point, his acts of retribution became quite real and quite violent with catastrophic outcomes. Still, he conducted these acts of revenge at a distance by third parties—like playing a video game.

"His financial cybercrimes followed the playbook circulated by our financial crimes unit to the local offices. Again, typical of a gamer, his acts never involved face-to-face encounters and his various bank accounts functioned as an electronic score board.

"He didn't need the money he harvested from these crimes. And again, using the FBI's playbook, he moved the proceeds through a labyrinth of off-shore banks where much of it vanished into thin air. We have reason to suspect his continuing involvement in this type of criminal enterprise."

The DNI interrupted one more time, "Provide some background on his disappearance."

The counterintelligence chief responded per the request.

"Remember, we were clueless. We had no idea Lowandowski was active while in our employ. However, we did take notice of other suspicious activities.

"For example, toward the end of Lowandowski's employment, we noted an increase in GRU activities. Operatives normally based out of the west coast suddenly appeared here in Washington, DC.

"Next, one or two GRU operatives exploded into teams sufficient to mount continuous surveillance activities. Surveilling whom was unclear, and we didn't realize until it was too late that the local field office figured prominently in their activities."

The DNI interrupted yet again.

"Much of what we know today came to us from our own surveillance of a 'meet and greet' the GRU uses on the west coast. While the FBI was trying to solve the puzzle of GRU agents flooding our zone here in DC—pardon the use of the football metaphor—we noticed a similar uptick in activities at the 'meet and greet.' Activity there escalated from the occasional reporting of subordinates to superiors to an almost daily who's who of GRU executives.

"We rolled up one of their high-ranking folks: A person who operated in our country for years. Much of what you're hearing today comes courtesy of that individual. He's proving to be a cagey character. He feeds us a little information at a time, knowing how long it takes us to confirm the truthfulness of these revelations. We keep him in a suitable lifestyle as long as he proves useful. It's a classic game of cat and mouse, one that is likely to continue for years.

"Part of what we suspect of Mr. Lowandowski came to us from Eddy O'Conner.

"Eddy?"

O'Conner stood and began to speak.

"We met Lowandowski while conducting interviews on what we now know was a related matter. 'Met' is the wrong term, actually. He moved through the spaces we shared with a squad from the local office. He collected the trash, did some clean-up, and then he'd disappear. We'd see him once, twice a day. Always in the background. Never attracting attention. Just doing his job. A sullen teen, earbuds playing God knows what, not slovenly, yet not well-dressed. He was just there.

"One day, my colleague noticed a bandaged head wound. She took an interest in his well-being. Tried to engage him. She wanted to know more about his injury.

"Personally, I've had little experience with the developmentally challenged. I'm guilty as most, maybe even more so, when it comes to acting stand-offish in their presence. My colleague wasn't burdened by my biases. She engaged.

"My colleague—Alice Linda—had a sense there was more to this young man's injury. Like a dog with a bone, she tried to pay him a visit to his home. He didn't react well to her interest. I grew uncomfortable with her efforts and even encouraged Alice to leave the young man alone.

"She wouldn't.

"Alice was convinced something was amiss. She found he owned the big beautiful home he lived in. This suggested he had financial resources atypical of someone in his circumstances. She suspected a person, or persons, unknown were harassing him.

"Just to be clear. Alice did not suspect the GRU. At that point, she believed Lowandowski might be experiencing unwanted attentions from other teens.

"Regrettably, I pushed her back to our case work—the reason we were in DC. In retrospect, I'm haunted by the belief Alice would have blown the Lowandowski matter wide open had I not interceded."

She sat, deferring to the DNI.

"Where is he now?" came from the audience.

The DNI responded, "We followed him to Miami and then Key West. Then he fell off the grid."

"GRU?"

"Our source insists not. But as I stated earlier, he's a cagey character dragging out the debrief. It may be years before we know everything he has to tell us. For now, we can rule that out. We might want to revisit this possibility in the future," the DNI authoritatively stated.

CHAPTER 4

THAT DAMNED MOISTURIZER, he thought.

The wounds from his plastic surgery long healed, Charles Lowandowski faithfully applied the high SPF skin moisturizer recommended by the plastic surgeon in Key West. When he perspired heavily, something in the crème wicked down his forehead and into his eyes. The burning sensation was unpleasant and blurred his vision.

He tried bandanas, hats, and all manner of head covers to help with the problem. Nothing worked. It was hot and humid in Vanuatu, and the effort to get in shape came at a cost.

He stopped at the convenience store at the end of his run. Purchasing ice and water, he hardly drank from the cup, preferring instead to slowly pour the cold water over his eyes while looking into the bright blue sky.

Lowandowski's year of working on his physical conditioning paid handsome benefits. His energy levels improved, and he resumed sleeping through the nights. The sleep was the most welcomed benefit. He was hardly at his best when tired and irritable. For the first time in his life, he was deeply tanned. Even his hair was bleached lighter by the sun. He wasn't beautiful in a classical sense, but he was handsome.

He was fifteen pounds lighter and stayed his distance from his once steady diet of junk food. Lowandowski's new diet consisted of smoothies morning, noon, and night along with his new culinary staple, the fish taco. As a reward, he did permit himself the occasional order of fries.

Lowandowski found part-time employment opportunities where no one was interested in his past. He mostly worked the docks as a laborer for the ferry operators hauling freight to and from the local islands. The work paid poorly, and most of the freight was from Port Vila to the outlying islands—not the other way around. So, there wasn't much to do, and little was expected of him, on the return trips. He could stare at the brilliant blue waters of the Coral Sea forever.

He was always paid in cash. He used the funds for walking around money—most of which found its way to the nearby smoothie and fish taco stands.

He lived in a room above a garage fashioned out of an old steel building with origins back to World War II. The price was right, although it was light on the amenities. Cold water only, limited electrical outlets, no kitchen, combination shower and commode reminiscent of a budget recreational vehicle.

Most notably, there was no heat and no air conditioning. The former wasn't a problem. The latter bedeviled him.

Internet access was the sole saving grace of his otherwise miserable living conditions.

Lowandowski made productive use of his time on Vanuatu. Working in the overnight hours when competition for satellite bandwidth was at a minimum, he mined the directory of internet service providers in the U.S. maintained by the FCC.

He took a particular interest in the smaller, community-based providers. Small companies and cooperatives emphasized stringing cable to provide access. He avoided larger outfits. They had technical staff who obsessed about cybercrime and took the time and expense to mount defenses. Instead, Lowandowski preferred the weaker, undefended providers.

He maintained a Willie Suttonesque attitude when it came to these small internet operators: That's where his money was—or would be, once he stole it.

It was his experience people on the fringes of society, the locus of small internet providers, were dependent on firms like Amazon and Walmart On-line. They paid by credit card for everything they purchased, and surprisingly, they purchased a lot.

Lowandowski's *modus operandi* was simple: Find the internet operator, install a compromise on a key switch or router, collect and sell the credit card numbers on the dark web, get out, and cover his tracks before he was discovered.

He was maniacal about limiting his exposure.

Lowandowski believed law enforcement wasn't lurking around these small spots of internet activity, trolling for criminals. He was right about that, but he no longer had access to the intelligence reports produced by the FBI to confirm his suspicions. Anyone familiar with his business model would describe it as exceptionally risk averse. He faced a very small risk which he nevertheless regarded as his Achille's heel. Lowandowski, preferred to exercise an abundance of caution.

Originally, he took his compensation in bitcoin. That worked exceptionally well as the exchange value of this cryptocurrency skyrocketed. Truth be told, he made more income in bitcoin speculation than he did in trafficking stolen credit card numbers. So much so that his business paranoia took hold and he cashed out his bitcoin for a more stable currency using on-line access to some shady banks in the Caribbean. Those banks were only a brief stopover, however. He was careful to transfer his funds to accounts he established in more traditional banks. Even then, he limited activity and balances at each one to avoid the thresholds where auditors and regulators took an interest.

He made it a point not to withdraw any of his funds on deposit in the U.S. and managed on his behalf by his private wealth management firm, Kennedy Financial. Lowandowski had a longer-term plan—many years down the road—when he would re-enter the U.S. to live a quiet life in the obscurity of some remote wooded locale in the Pacific Northwest. Until then, he would let his U.S. holdings accumulate.

In the immediate future, Lowandowski decided to rent something a bit more suitable, more civilized. If anyone was following him, they were doing a damned good job. With all of his physical changes, he doubted it was probable. Besides, he had assembled a complete legend using the vast resources of the dark web. And, it was a pretty good cover story at that.

Officially, he was a citizen and passport holder of the Philippines. Not the mainland, but one of the more remote outlying islands. His parents, now deceased, were ex-pats from Australia who moved off the grid to pursue a bohemian lifestyle.

He was home schooled by his mother and had the accreditation documents to prove it.

For additional cover, he episodically worked as an English speaking, customer service agent for a subcontractor to the official airline of the Philippines. Between his occasional gig at the docks and as a customer service representative, he appeared to be a productive member of Vanuatu society.

For all his efforts, there was one challenge he hadn't addressed.

Charles Lowandowski was lonely.

CHAPTER 5

THE GENERAL MEETING AND brief completed, the DNI and Eddy O'Conner met privately.

"Bring me up to date on Triple Play's progress"

"Joe McRory is in Key West now," O'Conner shared. "He had some initial trouble with housing."

"Hurricane Irma?"

"Yes. But he found a family in need of the extra cash. They agreed to rent him their sleeping porch. It's not ideal obviously, but it is working for the time being."

"Alice Linda?"

"Linda has healed nicely. Her broken nose required reconstruction and she took the opportunity to make a small number of additional changes, enhancements. The bruising and swelling are gone. With a change in hair color, she's unrecognizable. Quite frankly, I wouldn't have believed the overall change in her appearance could be so dramatic."

"Is she ready to participate in the search?"

"Linda is always ready. Getting her to lay low during the convalescence was a problem. She's been in the gym non-stop. Probably in the best shape of her life. The surgeon wants to limit her sun exposure for several more weeks. After that, there'll be no stopping her."

"Does McRory have any leads?"

"Maybe. We're uncertain, actually."

"Tell me more."

"Linda's surgery prompted us to ask whether Lowandowski might have done the same thing?"

"And?"

"The hurricane brought everything to A standstill in the Florida Keys. There are only a half-dozen or so plastic surgeons in Key West. Some temporarily relocated to the mainland and points north. All the practices are just now resuming operation—mostly limited."

"I'm surprised Key West had so many plastic surgeons. Any likely suspects?"

"They're all board certified, none with anything in their background to suggest a willingness to do anything illegal. Apparently, business was good before the hurricane."

"Why do you like the plastic surgery possibility? Why spend your time chasing that angle?"

"We did get a close look at Lowandowski before he skipped town. He wasn't an ugly kid by any means, but he did have some scarring from acne. Linda's focus on her own rhinoplasty led her to believe Lowandowski was likely to have some work done."

The DNI stood and walked over to the large window before resuming.

"Eddy, I want to put a fine point on what I say next. While we know about some of Lowandowski's financial crimes, there's a lot we don't know. For example, what else did he pass on to the Russians? Quite frankly, I was hopeful rolling up Alexi Kaledin would provide the answer to that question. He did run the GRU's entire U.S. operation."

"I gathered from your earlier comments General Kaledin isn't cooperating."

"The General was quite a catch for us. Like landing a whale in a row boat, unfortunately," the DNI chuckled. "He knows what we know—and then some."

"He's been in the game for years," O'Conner offered.

"True, that. He's proven adept at feeding us just less of the information we need to keep us coming back for more. Using that as leverage, he has us keeping him safe and comfortable. A lifestyle I'll never experience. It's costing us millions."

"Is the funding a problem?"

"No, the money is a round-off error, given our financial resources. But the expenditure is growing to the point where congressional oversight will become a problem. When the House and Senate intelligence committees get involved, there will be difficult questions for which we won't have the answers."

The DNI shook his head in distaste.

"Politicians, you'd think they'd understand a professional liar, like General Kaledin, better than your average citizen. Given enough time, and confirmation of whatever Lowandowski might know, we can gain some leverage, some control over Kaledin. When that happens, then he'll start singing for his supper."

"Until then?"

"Don't focus on that. It's my problem. What you need to do is find Lowandowski."

"Do you want him in custody, too?"

"Yes and no. Part of me still wants to believe the vast security apparatus of the federal government can wring young Lowandowski like a wet rag. However, I can't overlook the success he's enjoyed at our expense. And I certainly don't want to have two minimally cooperative detainees when our friends in Congress call me to the Hill."

"Just to be clear," O'Conner pressed, "what do you want?"

"Get someone close to him—as close as necessary to get him to talk. If he's like most teens and young adults, he's probably dying to tell someone—especially a very attractive someone—everything he's done."

"Then what?"

"'Then?' We'll decide what's next based on what you can tell us."

"Do you think we can turn him?" O'Conner asked.

"First, we need to know how deep the Russians are into him. At the end, they certainly threw enough of their resources following him to Florida. Maybe they found him, and that's why we can't. Hell, he could be in Moscow right now, and we wouldn't know."

"What if they didn't?"

"You mean, what if this young American managed to give the mighty GRU the slip?"

The DNI chuckled, again.

"Then I'd like to meet him and shake his hand. We could find a way to use someone like that. Don't you think?"

"What about his financial crimes? Would Justice let those go?"

"Justice will do whatever we tell them to do. As for his crimes, in the larger picture, he was a gnat. I'm sure he thought he was making good money. But in the context of financial crime in this country, he wasn't worth our time and concern."

"Eddy, find Lowandowski. We must know what he knows."

* * *

MCRORY WELCOMED THE cooler temperatures and breezes of the winter months. When he first landed in Key West, the sun burned through his skin right into his bones. Working all day in the heat and humidity took its toll. His sleep suffered without air conditioning. He wasn't working at his usual pace.

It didn't take him long to understand the laid-back attitude of the island's residents—especially the old-timers. Nothing moved quickly in the summer sun. That included the clean-up after the hurricane and repair of the battered electrical system. A lot of shops and restaurants were still closed, although fewer of the storefronts had plywood where shattered glass made looting a possibility. The city was slowly coming back to life.

McRory was going through sun screen like water. He no longer had Eddy ship it to him. The open shops were fully restocked and charging outrageous prices for the stuff.

Sitting in the examination room wearing only his underwear, McRory was trying not to freeze. "Now they have air conditioning," he muttered. "Who needs Siberia in Key West in January?"

There were two knocks on the door as it swung open. Two women entered.

"Mr. McRory, I'm Dr. Evans," gesturing to the other woman, "and this is Rhonda, our Physician's Assistant. Let's give you a good look, shall we?"

"I think there's been a misunderstanding," he said. "I'm interested in having some work done, not an exam."

"Mr. McRory—can I call you Joe?—this is the Florida Keys. We check everyone for skin damage when they come in. You're no exception. Why don't you jump up on the examining table where we can get a better look at you? After that we can discuss what sort of 'work' you have in mind."

McRory was caught off guard by the exam. To the plastic surgeon, he appeared to be reluctant. She patted the tissue paper covering the exam table. An offer of encouragement.

"I won't hurt you, I promise, Joe. Come now, jump on up."

McRory moved to the exam table, albeit with some ambivalence.

"Right off the bat, I can see some precancerous growths, here, here, here, and here," she reported while touching him on and around his face, nose, and right ear.

"I have cancer?"

He was shocked.

"No, no—not cancer. Precancerous growths, if not treated in a timely manner they can become cancerous. So, we'll take care of them today."

"Surgery? Today?"

"No surgery, Joe. We use the puffer Rhonda's holding."

Smiling, Rhonda held a device not too dissimilar to a thermos bottle.

"The puffer contains some very cold nitrogen. I spray a little on each spot and the growth is done. You'll leave here cured."

"Doctor, the growth on Joe's ear may need a bit more than elsewhere," Rhonda offered.

"Let's take another look," the surgeon acknowledging the possibility. "Just a tad more, Joe. The ear may be a bit sore for a day or two."

"You don't want to put any pressure on it. Sleep on your other side so the pillow doesn't press on the wound," Rhonda advised.

"I'll have a wound? Will this hurt?" Joe was in a mild state of panic but working to something more than that.

"Joe, figuratively speaking, yes, it's a wound. Nothing that requires sutures or a bandage. Think of it as a small burn you might get from touching something too hot to handle."

"Can I bathe?"

"Yes."

"Should I apply an ointment? I have ointments."

"No, that shouldn't be necessary."

"Can I touch it?"

"Well, you should always wash your hands before doing any exploring. No sense in risking infection."

"It can become infected? Can I lose the ear?"

"Joe! Calm down. This is very routine. By tomorrow you won't remember any of this. You'll be well on the way to healing."

"The ear may bother you for a day or two," Rhonda chimed in to be helpful.

"Yeah," the surgeon dourly responded, "let's get going on this business so we can talk more to Joe about the other matter."

McRory was hit by the puffer in all four locations. The first three shots were minor with little or no discomfort. The fourth, directed at his ear, was another matter altogether.

"Christ, that really hurts!"

"All done!" Rhonda announced. "See, that wasn't too bad."

"It still hurts like hell. When does the pain stop?"

McRory started to raise his hand to the injured ear. The surgeon stopped it mid-flight.

"Leave it alone, Joe. It will burn for a while. Focus on something else. Take your mind off the pain. Now, let's talk about the other matter, shall we?"

McRory, still focused on his painful ear, started slowly, grimacing while he spoke.

"I want a nose with some character," he said.

"Joe, I gotta tell you," the surgeon chided, "you have a lovely nose. Most people who I see are in far more serious circumstances. The last thing they want is a nose with what you call 'character.' Character is what they came in with. They want to leave the character here in the office."

"It's what I want," he stubbornly replied.

"Tell you what," the surgeon was searching for middle ground. "How about I show you our picture book. Take a look at the people before and after surgery. Keep in mind, you're asking me to make you look like one of the before images." She paused. "Rhonda can you show Joe our book?"

"Sure, doctor. Joe, why don't you get dressed and I'll return with the book."

The "book," or the "befores and afters"' as Rhonda termed it, included some of the most disfigured faces McRory had ever seen. It also showed the removal of acne scarring, more aesthetically pleasing noses and chins, and more than a few removed "turkey necks."

It also included a set of photographs of Charles Lowandowski. Rhonda immediately took notice of McRory's interest.

"Do you know Mr. Lowandowski?" she asked.

"Who? No!" he stammered.

"I do like his 'before' nose."

"Oh, Joe, no," Rhonda was almost pleading. "See how wide and flat it was? See the curve right at the tip?" Her index finger drew a series of small imaginary circles around the tip of the "before" nose. "Your nose looks so much more attractive. Please don't ask the doctor to give you the 'before' nose?"

"You think?"

"Yes, I'm certain of it."

"Let me think about it for a while. Can you photocopy the photographs, so I can study the two? Maybe I'll change my mind, but I really like the 'before' nose."

"We're not supposed to do that," she admonished.

"It'd really help. Maybe it'd help me come around to your point of view."

McRory left with the photocopies.

His right ear hurt like hell.

CHAPTER 6

"JOE," EDDY O'CONNER greeted the familiar telephone voice. "I got the email and the two attachments. Bingo! Great work."

"Yeah, thanks," he replied.

"Is there something wrong? Your voice sounds funny."

"I'm in tremendous pain."

"Pain? From what? Did you sustain an injury?"

McRory filled O'Conner in on his visit to the plastic surgeon and his *cancerous* growths.

"I think you mean *pre*-cancerous, Joe," Eddy said in disbelief. "What you had was a preventative procedure. And it's a good thing, too. You don't want those things on your face to become cancer, do you?"

"No, no, of course not. But I'm telling you Eddy, my ear hurts like hell. It's been throbbing all day. I don't know how I'll get any sleep tonight."

O'Conner heard enough, "Do you want to tell this to Alice, Joe? The same Alice who's now recovered from real plastic surgery?"

There was silence at the other end.

"Joe?"

"No, Eddy," McRory retreated. "I'll survive. There's no need to get Alice involved in this. Agreed?"

"Absolutely," she concurred. *You are such a girl*, she thought.

* * *

A SHORT TIME later, Alice Linda joined O'Conner in the San Francisco penthouse living room.

"The DNI's office ran the photographs through ICE," Linda reported.

"Any hits?" O'Conner asked.

"Yes. ICE used their facial recognition algorithms. They got a match on an inbound passenger to Key West International Airport traveling on a passport from Vanuatu."

"Vanuatu? Inbound? From where?"

"Eleuthera. In the Caribbean."

"What do the passport authorities in Eleuthera report?"

"That's what I wanted to know," Linda responded. "So I asked the DNI's office to check."

"And?"

"That's the strange part. Eleuthera has no other inbound or outbound sightings. Just the one from Eleuthera to Key West."

O'Conner gave the matter some thought. She walked over to the large glass globe on one of her built-ins. She spun the sphere stopping at the Caribbean.

"What do you think, Eddy?"

"I think we don't want any more mistakes. I'm going to call Joe back and have him do some further checking."

"Joe called? How did he sound?"

"He was in pain. Really suffering."

"What happened to him?" Linda was visibly concerned. "Did he get stuffed in a trunk again?"

"Oh, Alice, you know Joe. Just more 'man problems.'"

"Eddy, you know about 'female problems,' right?" O'Conner's response was a stern glance right out of catholic school. "I'm asking, because every time you say Joe has 'male problems,' well, it's not the same thing. I thought, maybe you were confused. You know, about what might be a 'male' problem."

"Alice, I had a father. I still have four older brothers. I have more nephews than you can shake a stick at. Yes, I know what 'male' problems are?"

Linda was now thoroughly confused. She tried a different approach.

"Well, maybe it's me who's confused. Can you explain?"

"Alice, throughout the history of mankind it's women who give birth and experience the real pain life has to offer. Men, on the other hand, scratch their arm, and they're 'in pain.' Really!"

O'Conner was exasperated as much by Linda as she was by McRory.

"You don't have any children? Do you, Eddy?"

"Alice, I was in a religious order for most of my adult life. So, no, I don't have any children."

Against her own better judgment, Linda pursued the matter.

"One doesn't preclude the other, you know."

"Alice, I spent almost fifty years as a Nun. The only mothers in the order I ever met were all 'Mothers Superior.' Come to think of it, the same was true of the Vatican. Should we call Joe and put the question before him as well?" O'Conner challenged.

"No, Eddy," Linda retreated. "I'll survive. There's no need to get Joe involved in this. Agreed?"

"Absolutely," she concurred.

* * *

MCRORY RETIRED EARLY in the evening, exhausted as he was from his medical encounter.

Without giving the matter any thought, he brought his head into contact with the pillow. His damaged ear started to throb all over again.

"Joe," the owner of the house and his landlord lifted the window sash onto the sleeping porch, "there's a woman asking for you at the front door. I told her to go around back to see if you were still awake."

"Sorry about that. A woman, you say? Did she say who she was?"

Just as he asked he saw Rhonda from the surgeon's office make her way along the flagstone walkway leading to the steps and the sleeping porch.

The landlord closed the sash and the plantation shutters.

She knocked lightly at the door.

"Rhonda, this is an unexpected surprise."

"How's your ear?" she asked.

"It hurts like hell!"

Rhonda threw her arms around McRory's neck pushing up against his body forcing him to step back into the porch or risk falling."

The next morning, his landlord evicted him.

"We have young, impressionable children here," was all he would say.

McRory's ear still hurt like the devil.

CHAPTER 7

JOE MCRORY RETURNED TO San Francisco six days later. He took the BART subway system from the airport to Eddy O'Conner's downtown penthouse apartment. Exiting the station, the wind whipped down the street and caught his injured ear. If it didn't itch, it throbbed.

The front desk staff recognized McRory, handing him one of the elevator passes without which the cabs would not work. The high speed vertical climb deposited him at O'Conner's front door. The recently installed biometric reader automatically opened the door. The security system announced his arrival.

McRory made his way to the expanse of the main living area of the penthouse where he found O'Conner and Alice Linda. Each was deep in her own thoughts.

"Well, at least the security system welcomed me back," McRory huffed.

"Welcome back, Joe," O'Conner mumbled, her thoughts still dominating her actions.

"What's that in your ear?" Linda asked. She looked to O'Conner, "'Male' problem?"

"Yes," the only response O'Conner would offer.

"What? 'Male' problem?" McRory obviously out of the joke.

Both women waved the subject off preferring a change in topic.

* * *

AN HOUR LATER, McRory finished his verbal report.

"We know he passed through Immigration at Key West, they even had his new face and Vanuatu passport recorded, date, and time stamped. But that was a year ago—more or less. No one in Eleuthera could recall his passing through the island. The photo and passport images didn't help. The border folks in Eleuthera are very laid back. And here's a hint for the future: Never question their thoroughness. They tend to consider such observations as an insult to their nationhood."

Seeing no questions, he continued, "Day trips from the island are easily arranged by any hotel concierge in Key West. If you travel by boat, no one bothers to check your passport at the point of departure in Mallory Square. My concierge reminded me at least three times to carry my passport on my person. Maybe they check sometimes and not others."

At the mention of "concierge," O'Conner asked, "What concierge? We paid a full two month's rent for your stay with that family."

"Yeah, about that," he started. "The longer I was there, the more apparent it became the arrangement wasn't working."

"You pressed for a partial refund, I hope?" O'Conner wasn't going to let this go. "Under our contract with the DNI's Office we can't claim two sets of housing allowances, Joe. Did the hotel extend you the government rate?"

"Yeah, about that," and then realizing the futility of providing an explanation O'Conner would find acceptable, his voice trailed off.

"What, did you get caught bringing strange women to your sleeping porch?" Linda joked.

Ignoring Linda's comment, "Eddy, do you have any ointment for my ear?"

"You did!" Linda gasped. "You broke the rules. Loose women and all that."

"Rhonda came by to check on my surgical wounds and to talk me out of changing my nose. It was a thoughtful gesture."

"Sounds like a real Florence Nightingale," O'Conner sarcastically observed.

"More like the patron saint of lost causes," Linda countered.

"Saint Jude, Alice," Said O'Conner drawing on her own faith.

McRory realized his mistake too late. Linda was wrapping this excuse—and her sordid imaginings of Rhonda and her ministrations—until her version of the story wasn't suitable for adults under the age of sixty-five. He waited until her energy and interest waned.

All the while his ear throbbed.

* * *

AFTER LUNCH AND O'Conner's debrief on her meetings with the DNI, the three took a stab at their next moves. O'Conner let her two younger colleagues suggest strategies and tactics she knew to be ineffective. She patiently waited until they were done before she added her own.

"What we need is a classic Cold War strategy," O'Conner suggested.

Before her visit with the DNI, O'Conner was prone to believe her training, her game, was outdated in a world of iDevices and facial recognition algorithms. The visit and his comments caused her to re-evaluate those impressions.

"Which is?" Linda inquired.

"We're going to run a classic 'honey pot' operation," O'Conner declared, quite affirmatively, in fact. "Joe, you'll take the lead."

Both Linda and McRory learned their tradecraft at Camp Peary as CIA recruits. Of course, they knew what a honey pot was, although neither had any operational experience with this type of agency compromise.

O'Conner explained, "At one-time, sexual lures and blackmail were commonplace in countries behind the Iron Curtain. They did it. We did it. Why? Because it worked."

O'Conner could see McRory was so deep in thought he was no longer listening. A bright red flush worked its way up his neck, to his face, and finally, his ears.

"Joe?" O'Conner verbally poked at him. "You have any questions, any issues?"

"Yes," his answer tentative. "I don't know if I can pull something like that off. I'm not attracted to men—other men."

O'Conner suppressed a smile. She wasn't about to let him off the hook, however.

"Joe, you signed on to Triple Play. There are only three of us. You're the only male. If Lowandowski is gay, you're 'on deck.'" Her facial gesture changed to one of concern. "Tell you what. I'll get you a 'Gay for Dummies Book.'"

Linda looked like she'd explode if she didn't relieve the stress by breaking into raucous laughter.

"Does that mean if Lowandowski is straight you'll buy a 'Dummies' book for Alice?" he asked.

Linda's mood changed instantly. She punched his shoulder.

"Hey!" he yelled. "Not the same side as my ear!"

"What?!" Linda exclaimed. "You are such a girl."

CHAPTER 8

NOW THAT TRIPLE PLAY and the DNI had a photograph of Charles Lowandowski 2.0, arrangements were made for basic surveillance of Vanuatu and its port city, Port-Vila—Lowandowski's residence according to his passport.

Eddy O'Conner made all the many necessary arrangements. She also took the lead after a call to the Abbess of her former order. When she left her apartment the next morning, she wore the habit of her sisters.

Exiting the lobby elevator, she pulled her wheelie bag in the direction of the BART station. She was in character now. The sisters of her order did not use limousines. To be candid, the sisters spent most of their lives cloistered in the Abbey on a small, remote island in the San Juan's.

Her cover story arranged with the Abbess was true—at one time. Sister Evangeline, Eddy, was on contemplative leave from her order. Suffering a crisis of faith in her calling, the sister was visiting a remote island in the Coral Sea to paint and to think. Vanuatu offered the change in climate and scenery and it was hardly overrun by tourists. And most importantly, the cost of her food and housing fit within the modest budget provided by the Abbess.

Eddy was shocked at how easily she returned to her former calling. Peoples' reactions were both familiar and comfortable and markedly different from her more recent lifestyle. She patiently waited in the boarding area for her flight rather than in the executive club. She was seated in the middle seat in the middle aisle at the rear of the plane—not to be confused with her typical first-class accommodations.

Sister Evangeline spent two extended layovers on the Fijian island of Nadi, almost equaling one-half of her forty-seven-hour trip. During that time, she didn't have access to a spa or a bathroom meeting her newly exacting standards. She slept in two airports sprawled across chairs. Her diet consisted of airline meals, snacks, and drinks plus whatever she could afford in the air terminals.

There was a time in her life when these sacrifices were not unusual. Now they were extraordinary impositions.

She arrived in Port-Vila feeling much worse than her wheelie bag looked. Finding her guest house in Port-Vila, she removed her habit and collapsed into the sagging mattress of her double bed. She slept for the better part of two days.

✳ ✳ ✳

THE ABBESS HELD members of the order to a standard on the few occasions one of her minions traveled. However, Sister Evangeline was on leave to contemplate her commitment to her vocation, and she was permitted some slack. On finally emerging from her guest room, Sister Evangeline wore a pair of second-hand jeans appropriately tailored for a person of modesty, a plain white blouse, and floppy hat to protect her skin from the sun. She carried a canvas bag whose long straps fit comfortably over her shoulder. The bag contained a camera and an old-style flip phone both of which looked to have seen better days.

Courtesy of the DNI, the phone came to her possession by way of the technical wizards at Langley, Virginia. The camera housing reminiscent of a very old Kodak Brownie was refit with the latest in electronics, although it still contained room for a spool of Kodachrome film. The scratched flip phone featured a satellite antenna hidden in the strap of the canvas bag, although it could operate on the island's cellular telephone system. If one knew how to operate the keypad as Langley designed it, the phone could be made to do some very special things.

* * *

BY THE SEVENTH day away from home, Sister Evangeline had not yet sighted Mr. Lowandowski. Nor had she adapted to the time change. She was sleeping while everyone else was awake, and awake when normal people were sleeping. Much to her dismay, so very slowly, about one-to-two hours per day, her circadian rhythm came into synchrony with the diurnal cycle of the island.

At the end of her second week, she awoke just before the dawn. Taking a stroll along the beach not far from her guest house she encountered a jogger. It wasn't fully light yet and the hat he wore obscured his forehead. The young man was in outstanding physical conditioning and deeply tanned. They greeted one another as he passed by her, moving in the opposite direction.

An hour later, and one cup of coffee from an early opening, beach-side stand, the same jogger passed her again. Sister Evangeline followed in his wake.

The distance between them opened, but the terrain was flat and the beach otherwise empty. She was able to follow his progress. About a mile ahead, the jogger turned inland and away from the beach. She fixed the turn in her field of vision and made her way toward it. When she finally reached the pivot point, she turned her gaze. A small apartment complex was located across the road now filled with vehicles of every stripe and size, making their way to Port-Vila.

Rising before dawn on each of the next two days, Sister Evangeline made her way to the same spot. On each of those days, the same jogger appeared with the same hat dry at first but thoroughly wet at the end.

The stand where she purchased her morning coffee shifted to fruit smoothies after what passed for the island's morning rush hour. The clientele changed as well. In the morning, drivers of trucks, cabs, and cars parked along the beach to order their coffee and go. Afterward, walkers from the beach and the town center made their way to the stand in search of a smoothie. Sister Evangeline set up her easel one step off the concrete pad serving as the stand's patio and gathering point. Some days she painted seascapes. On others her paintings reflected the stand and its customers. She quickly attracted a following.

In short order, she was known to everyone. Most called her "Sister." To those who came to know her well, she was Evangeline. The latter included the old woman, Michaela, who owned the stand.

Michaela was the last of her immediate family remaining on Vanuatu. She never explained to Evangeline why her husband was no longer in the picture, only that he wasn't. Each of her three children moved further west initially for spouses and better jobs. They may have departed for Fiji where the tourist industry was more robust and a person willing to work hard could excel in the hospitality industry. Now, all three secure in their employment with large hoteliers, lived in Australia and New Zealand.

The visits from her children and grandchildren were few and dropping like a stone. There was no one to take over her business, if she wanted to retire, and no one she trusted to run the business in her absence. She was anchored to this spot for better or worse.

Evangeline's vocation was her instant cachet. People she met placed their trust in her without reservation. She took in their stories—always very personal, always confidential—only offering a suggestion, if asked.

Michaela asked.

Sister Evangeline answered.

* * *

JOE MCRORY ARRIVED a week later looking much better for the wear and tear of travel than did Evangeline. McRory's cover was a recovering alcoholic never far from his next meeting and a telephone call to his sponsor.

Evangeline vouched for McRory. Despite whatever misgivings Michaela might have had under different circumstances, she took McRory into her home and her business.

Initially, McRory and Michaela were tethered at the hip. They arrived to work together, worked within inches of one another throughout the day, and left each evening following the outbound rush hour.

* * *

THE DAYS GREW longer. The light of the day arriving earlier and remaining in the sky later each day. It was hotter, more humid as well.

Evangeline had since returned to her sisters and Michaela was on an extended visit to each of her children and their families. The only constant was McRory at the stand throughout the day.

Known to the customers as "M," he was a friendly face, a willing ear, and quick with a smile.

The morning jogger varied his course to stop at the stand for a smoothie at the end of his run. McRory didn't push their relationship. He didn't have to. He was one of the few U.S. ex-pats in the Port-Vila area. Lowandowski let the opportunity of a nearby American overcome his risk averse tendencies.

Initially, their conversations were limited to Lowandowski's orders. Over the days and weeks that followed, Lowandowski remained at the stand while he finished his beverage instead of moving on. Soon, he was there for an hour or more each morning, until "M" complained about his post-run hygiene. It became a joke between them. When "M" said, "Get outta here, get a shower," Lowandowski smiled and moved on. Always in the same direction. Always to the apartment circled in the photographs Eddy left behind for McRory.

CHAPTER 9

ALICE LINDA MADE HER first appearance at the stand two months later. Arriving in Vanuatu via a one-month stopover in Fiji, she was thinner than normal, darkly tanned, and her light brown hair colored in blonde streaks by the sun.

The plan called for Joe McRory to put the two of them together.

"I'm telling you, Joe, Lowandowski has the hots for me,"

"A bit over confident, aren't we?"

"No, you having the hots for me would be an example of over confidence. Also, grand delusions. Maybe even over mounting."

"What's 'over mounting'?"

"It's when a horse rider picks a mount he can never hope to successfully ride."

She smiled.

"What do they call a horse who's ready for the glue factory?"

"You."

He shot lightning bolts in her direction.

"Trust me to do the set-up," he declared.

"My better judgment tells me that's not a wise choice. But here's the thing. Eddy went to a lot of trouble to make these arrangements. If you screw this thing up between Lowandowski and me, it's Eddy you'll have to answer to."

"Trust me," he said. "I promise you'll be impressed."

* * *

THE NEXT MORNING, Lowandowski stopped by the stand for his usual following his morning run. On the other side of the patio, Linda spread her towel on the sand and performed her morning yoga routine.

"She's a looker," Lowandowski whispered.

"Who's that?" McRory asked.

"There are only three of us out here. I'm certainly not talking about you, M. I'd be ready for the loony bin if I was talking about myself. So, I must be talking about her."

McRory feigning disinterest, glanced in Linda's direction. She was doing one of those yoga moves where her fanny was high in the air aimed in their direction.

So much for subtlety, he thought. But if this is what she's giving me to work with, then I guess I have no other choice but to follow her lead.

"What do you think, M?"

"Her?" he shrugged and leaned in close to Lowandowski. "She's a pro."

"Pro what?" Lowandowski was impressed. "Volleyball? Tennis? Golf?"

"No," McRory laughed, "Not *that* kind of pro. The other kind."

"What *other* kind?"

Lowandowski was lost in this exchange.

McRory didn't respond verbally. Instead, he stared right back at Lowandowski.

"Oh," Lowandowski finally responded. "That kind, huh?"

"Welcome to the clue train. All aboard."

McRory could see the wheels turning.

"Don't get the wrong idea. She's really a nice person," McRory emphasized.

"She's a working girl, M. How nice can she be?"

"Look, dickhead, she doesn't stand on street corners soliciting the Johns who drive by." He paused, "She's different."

"Different? How different?"

"She only does the 'girlfriend experience' thing. You know, longer term relationships without the obligation of a real relationship."

"The 'girlfriend experience,'" Lowandowski repeated.

That evening, he went on-line and read everything he could find about "the girlfriend experience."

* * *

LINDA SAT ON the stool drinking the cup of coffee McRory just brewed. It was still too early for Lowandowski to appear.

"I think I'll make my move today," she said.

"Move?" McRory asked, "What move is that?"

"On Lowandowski," she responded in disbelief. "Who else could I be talking about?"

"I wouldn't do that," he advised.

"And why not?"

"I've got everything set up. Let him make the first move. If he isn't ready today, then tomorrow for certain."

"What did you do, Joe?"

"I gave you a damned good legend. A credible cover you'd kill to have."

"Which was?"

"You're a pro."

"Tennis? Golf?" she offered. "I am good at sports, Joe, but not good enough to pass for a professional."

McRory just looked at her.

"Son-of-a-bitch!" she spat at him. "He thinks I'm a hooker?"

"Hear me out," McRory responded.

She did.

Linda had to admit, if she was going to be the "honey pot," then it made perfect sense to do it this way. Joe had a point, although it didn't please her to make the admission.

They each laid out several strategies for going forward. For the first time ever they agreed on an approach.

McRory would broker the deal, seizing on what Linda described as his "inner pimp." They agreed on a price range McRory would share with Lowandowski. Linda would get in touch with Eddy to arrange for a bank account into which Lowandowski would deposit the payment.

"What name?" he asked.

Linda gave the matter some thought before responding.

"Tell him my name is Linda McRory. That's a good whore's name."

"McRory didn't find that funny at all. Linda was his mother's name.

"So, we're related?"

"Yeah. Distant cousins somewhere back in our mangled family tree. The recovering alcoholic and the working girl. What a family you have, Joe."

"It does give us a reason to see one another outside of this little joint," he said spreading his arms to embrace the small stand.

Both were quiet, but not for long.

"Alice, are you okay with this?" McRory asked with more tenderness than he intended.

She placed her hand on his.

"It could be worse," she said. "I could be sleeping with you."

* * *

THREE DAYS LATER, the deposit wire transferred to Linda McRory's account, Lowandowski was under the impression he had a girlfriend, or at least the girlfriend experience.

He wasn't the least prepared for what Linda had in mind.

CHAPTER 10

It WAS AS IF SOMEONE had lifted a heavy weight from his shoulders. Free of his virginity at long last.

"If I had a pack of cigarettes, I'd light one up," he smugly confessed.

"You smoke? If so, you failed to disclose that in our written agreement. Engaging in risky behavior, like smoking, increases the weekly fee by ten percent."

"You don't sound like a woman who just made love," he teased.

"Is that what you call it?"

"What would you call it?"

"A forty-yard dash. A wind sprint. Blink and you miss it. That's what I'd call it," she replied.

"Was I that bad?"

"'Bad' is something to which you could aspire. What you did was far worse than 'bad.' It was a waste of my time—and depressing."

"Why depressing?"

"This was an assessment of your performance. I was determined to see what you would do on your own, if left to your knowledge of female anatomy and your far less than prodigious talents and instincts," she sniffed. "Based on your performance, I have my work cut out for me. Had I known how backward you are, I would have charged substantially more."

"I think you charged enough," he retorted.

"What you think doesn't matter. I've agreed to take you on as a pupil in the "girlfriend experience." If I do well in transforming your piss poor performance into something that passes for an attentive lover, then the women who follow me will forever be in my debt."

"And based on my performance today?"

"We will have to look to a different species to find a 'female' foolish enough to climb into your bed or invite you into hers."

He sat up, the bed covers falling below his waist.

"Okay, I'm all in," he said.

"Good, I'll leave you this set of instructions."

She left a paper document on his dresser. He sprung from the mattress and flipped through each of the pages.

"If I'm reading this right, I won't get laid for another two weeks. That's simply unacceptable."

"If you don't read and master those exercises, you'll never get laid, again. And for the record, the objective isn't 'getting laid.' The objective is a mutually satisfying relationship of which sex is an important part. You perform well in that one regard, you'll have more sex than you can handle."

CHAPTER 11

JOE MCRORY WAS CURIOUS, but afraid to ask.

It had been a week since Eddy O'Conner confirmed the deposit of Lowandowski's deposit funding his purchase of the "girlfriend experience." Yet, every day since, Alice Linda was working her yoga on the beach and Charles Lowandowski all but disappeared—until today.

"Whoa, stranger!" McRory greeted the return of the prodigal son.

"Hey, M," came the subdued response from Lowandowski.

"Fresh from the 'boyfriend experience'?"

"Yeah, I've never been more miserable in my life."

"Yep, I'd say you're in deep. The blush is off that rose."

"The rose died."

Alice Linda—née Linda McRory—walked from her towel to join Lowandowski. Joe McRory took the opportunity to step away, providing the two lovers with some privacy.

"Did you follow the instructions?" she asked.

"Yes, room clean. Sheets clean. Bathroom clean. Kitchen clean. I'm clean."

She leaned in for a sniff. Lowandowski took offense.

"I said—" he started.

"I know what you said. Do you think I'm not going to check and double check?"

"It's like living with my mother." He was complaining now.

"Fat lot of good that did you. We'd be much further along in your training had you listened to your mother."

"I didn't sign up for the 'mom experience.'"

"Listen, we could be stuck in the 'mom experience' for a while, if you can't master the basics of hygiene. Have you been masturbating on schedule?"

"Geez," his shoulders dropped. "Do you think you could say that louder? Maybe 'M' over there didn't hear you."

"Oh, I heard," Joe McRory laughed. "No need to speak up on my behalf, although there may be a few folks in town who didn't hear."

Lowandowski's humiliation was complete.

"Tell you what," Linda McRory introduced an offer, "I'll meet you back at your place in ten minutes. If everything is set to rights as you claim, then we'll find an exercise you don't have to do alone."

He was gone.

"You're cruel, you know," Joe McRory said more as a statement than a question.

"He's like a big puppy, Joe. This is the only shot I'll get to train him the way I want him to be. Besides, if I do a good job, they'll name a holiday after me."

"They already did. It's a freak show called Halloween."

* * *

THIS TIME THERE was no wisecrack about lighting a cigarette.

"Was the second time any better? Than the first, I mean?" he politely inquired.

"If I had to rate you on a point scale, I'd probably give you a four or a five, for effort. A two, maybe a two plus, in style points. Right now, you're earning a zero."

"A zero?!" he exclaimed. "We're not even doing anything."

"True. But what do the instructions have to say on the matter?"

Lowandowski reached into the drawer of the nightstand on his side of the bed. He quickly rifled through the now dog-eared document.

"Shit," he muttered.

"'Shit'?" She was beyond belief. "How does your post-coital banter measure up? No, let me answer. First topic: Your performance. Wrong subject. You're to demonstrate an interest in *me*—not you. Asking me about *your* performance isn't about me, it's all about *you*. Second topic: And what does the 'rule book' say about profanity?"

He found the passage and read it aloud, "Wherever possible, profanity is to be avoided."

"So," she demanded, "just what part of 'shit' seems to be appropriate?"

"I thought—"

She interrupted.

"That's just the point, 'Big', you didn't think, you still aren't thinking. You're emoting thoughts you need to avoid giving voice. Perhaps—and I want to carefully stress, *perhaps*—you may think 'shit,' but you certainly can't say it."

Linda McRory was now fully dressed—her revealing two piece now back on her body. She started to leave his bedroom, but thought the better of doing so without making one last point.

"What does the 'rule book' say about post-coital bedroom hygiene?"

Lowandowski found the passage without having to search. She was at least impressed by that.

"It says: No woman wants to return to her lover's bedroom to find evidence of an earlier encounter—even if the encounter was with her."

"So, you know what to do next. The question remains, are you capable of following even the simplest of directions?"

She turned away before she could no longer hide her smile.

Damn, she thought. Why hadn't I thought about using this approach when I was younger? This may be the best damn assignment I've ever had!

⁂ ⁂ ⁂

AT THE END of the business day, Joe McRory returned to his room in Michaela's house. It was time for his daily check-in with Eddy O'Conner.

"Is Alice getting close to him, yet?" she asked.

"She's got him jumping through hoops. I don't think I've ever seen anyone more *un*happy," he reported.

"Let Alice know the DNI is pressing for information. Tell Alice that she needs to get Lowandowski to open up and start sharing."

"I'll pass along the message, Eddy, but you know Alice. She does things in her own time, and certainly in her own way."

CHAPTER 12

THEY WERE WALKING ALONG the water's edge. The night was still and the waves slapped lazily at the sand. Linda McRory suggested the walk following dinner.

"I don't know how to talk with—you know—a woman," Lowandowski confessed.

"Let's start with something simple," she suggested. "Were you good at school?"

"No."

"Did you play a high school sport?"

"No."

"Did you date in high school?"

He laughed, "No."

"See?" she said. "You're talking—to a woman no less. Let's try something else. Ready?"

He nodded.

"You have to say it, Charles."

"Yes."

"Yes, what?"

"Yes, I'm game, if you are."

"I'm definitely game," she smiled. She reached for his hand. "Here we go."

A brief pause before she started.

"Tell me about your mother?"

"I never met my real mom. I was placed into foster care by the county," he said.

"Do you know why?"

"I think it had something to do with drug abuse. The same thing with my dad."

"You lived in foster homes for how long?"

"Until I was in junior high school."

"In how many different foster homes did you live?"

"Five or six, maybe more. I'm uncertain."

"What happened in junior high school?"

"Against all odds, the county placed me in a decent home. They placed me with the Lowandowskis. They adopted me."

"Tell me about your *adopted* mom?"

"She was pretty, very nice. She was the athlete. She played field hockey and basketball in high school."

"Sounds like she was tall."

"Yeah, I guess she was. Tall and very determined."

"Her husband? Your adopted dad?"

"He was quiet. He spent a lot of time in his media room. Liked to play rock music from the 80s and 90s. Played with his computer some, but he wasn't a gamer."

"Nice home?"

"Very nice. Very expensive. They both drove high-end cars, SUVs."

"Where are they today?"

Lowandowski suddenly grew very quiet. He cast a small sea shell he'd been holding. It was too light to skip across the water and sank to the bottom.

"They died. Car accident. Really nasty."

"How did that make you feel?"

"Real shitty," he stopped and raised both hands in mock surrender. "Sorry. Change that. It made me feel real bad."

She smiled.

"Thank you for that," she said. "But, tell me, why did their accident make you so sad?"

"I didn't treat them well. I could—no, I should—have been a better son. I should have been a better *adopted* son. I had some real winners for foster parents. John and Mia were very good to me."

"Is that what you called them? You used their first names?"

"When I first came to their home, she—Mia Lowandowski—told me to call them 'mom' and 'dad' if I was okay with it. If not, then John and Mia. That's how it started," he shrugged his shoulders as if to apologize for a poor answer.

"And, after the adoption?"

"Didn't change. They were always John and Mia."

"You sound like you have some regrets."

"Yes, a truckload to be honest. I should have called them 'mom' and 'dad.' That wasn't too much for them to ask."

He started to cry.

It broke her heart.

* * *

LATER, THEY DRANK the white wine Linda McRory left in his clean refrigerator. His small balcony had just enough room for the two inexpensive lounges left by the last tenant.

"So, that's why sharing leads to better sex," his observation struck her as funny. True, but funny.

"It's a start," she spoke just above a whisper.

Just a simple statement created an awkward silence between them. As usual, Lowandowski didn't know what to say. So he chose what was for him the exceptional thing to do: He said nothing at all. No quip. As difficult as it was to veer so far from his usual habit, he nonetheless stayed the course—he remained quiet.

"After your parents died, did you go back into foster care?"

"No, I had just turned eighteen. The county folks didn't want me. The school didn't want me anymore. The judge in the probate court found a financial advisor to teach me how to live."

"Probate court? Your parents were well to do?"

"Yes and no. I inherited everything that was left. The estate paid off the mortgage and the car loans from the insurance money. There was the settlement for the accident. I almost had enough money to keep the house, pay the bills—all that stuff. But I needed a job for the health insurance and some extra money." He placed the wine glass on the wooden floor boards. "The financial advisor kept me on a short leash. I got a monthly allowance from the estate. He made sure the grass was cut, the shrubs trimmed—all that landscaping stuff. I guess he realized that wasn't my thing."

"Where is this house?" she asked.

"Gone. Sold it. Sold the cars. Furniture. Everything, gone now."

"You took the money and moved here?"

"No, I still have the financial advisor. He manages my money, my investments. I can go on-line and check stuff out. I do that less these days."

"How do you support yourself these days? You did pay a substantial fee for my services."

"I do some occasional day labor at the dock. Couple times a month I go on-line as an airline customer service rep. It pays the bills."

Linda McRory made a point of looking around.

"Not here it doesn't," she said. "This may be the end of the world, but it does cost a pretty penny for this apartment, utilities, food. Unless day labor and your work as an airline rep pay really, really well, then you're tapping into your financial reserves."

"I have another thing I do."

"A 'thing'? What kind of a thing pays that well?"

He didn't respond. She let it go, for now.

"I'd better shower. Change the sheets. You know, follow the rules."

She could hear him moving around the small bedroom followed by the sound his front door made when it closed. She knew the poor kid was lugging his sheets to the laundry on the ground floor. Must be the fifth or sixth time he'd laundered the linens that week alone.

When he returned, he made his way to the bathroom. She could hear the water in the shower.

Linda McRory carried the wine glasses into the kitchen and made her way to the bedroom. He was still showering. She opened his nightstand drawer. Beneath her instruction manual she found his passport from the Philippines and an English-German dictionary. She opened the passport to the identity page. It was issued in his real name, Charles Lowandowski.

* * *

THE NEXT MORNING, she was waiting for Joe McRory to open the stand. She stood among a small crowd of several others desperately in need of their morning jolt of caffeine.

"Sorry, folks. Running a bit late today," he said.

"I know the man," she said to her small group. "He's spent his whole life disappointing people. What can I say? He's good at it."

He pretended not to hear.

The morning rush traffic dwindled away another thirty minutes or so later. Seeing no one else was around or coming his way, Joe McRory turned to Alice Linda—addressing her by her adopted name.

"So, *Ms. McRory*, is that your idea of maintaining cover? Where did you learn your tradecraft? Walmart?"

"Whatever do you mean, Mr. McRory," she was playing coy—but doing so badly.

"*I know the man? He's spent his whole life?* Our covers don't *really* know one another. At best we're distant relatives because we share the same last name. Remember your cockamamie legend? *It's a good whore's name?*" he was sputtering.

"Someone's being overly sensitive?" she mocked.

"Linda McRory is my mom's name."

"Yeah," she said. "I do know that, I guess. Sorry, Joe—at least about the whore's reference. Your mom's a good woman, deserving a better son to be sure."

She mimed pulling a zipper across her lips. Joe McRory focused on the fruit he was preparing for the day's coming orders for smoothies.

"Different topic," she began. "Lowandowski confirmed his life story last evening. All of it. The foster homes, the adoptive parents, inheriting their estate—the whole nine yards."

"Great," he replied sarcastically. "The second coming of Mata Hari and the best you can offer is to confirm what we—and he—already know."

"What can I say," she teased. "I get a man in bed and he can't wait to spill his guts."

"You made him so ill he vomited?" McRory sneered. "Somehow I'm not surprised."

"Well, this will surprise you," she said as she put her iPhone in front of him.

McRory looked at the photograph.

"He has a passport from the Philippines?"

"Swipe to the left. Look at the next one."

"It's in his real name?"

She took back the phone, swiped up from the bottom, and selected the option to air drop the photograph of the identity page. McRory's phone beeped to signal it received the file transfer.

"I'll get this to Eddy this evening," he said. "What are you doing?"

Alice Linda was pantomiming a fisherman reeling in a fish.

"I'm reeling him in, Joe. Soon, all of his secrets will be ours."

"Not to mention his balls," McRory added.

"Done," she said.

CHAPTER 13

THE INTERNET SITE WAS ONE of many like it. Enter a person's name and you're rewarded with a series of teasers, screen images filled with possibilities. "Joseph McRory" was a common name. The site found hundreds of them across the country. Adding an estimated age reduced the number substantially, but still significant. Some with alleged criminal records.

The results for Linda McRory weren't any more encouraging.

A prolific family, Lowandowski thought.

He decided to stack the search in his favor by cheating.

Hacking into Vanuatu's immigration database was child's play. Here a search for Joseph McRory produced fewer hits. He arranged the retrieved record locators from most recent to oldest. Clicking again, he found links from the immigration entry record, but none with an exit date.

Clicking on the image link produced a photograph of the Joe McRory. Clicking on the entry stamp link showed an inspector's stamp dated forty-four days earlier.

He sat back in his chair contemplating his next move while drumming his fingers on the desktop.

He searched the immigration database for Linda McRory. Several records were returned. Each had a link to both entry and exit date stamps. The newest was over nine months old.

Here and already gone, he thought.

There were no records for a Linda McRory who was here now.

He returned to Joe McRory's passport identity page extracted from the database. He noted the address. And the date of birth.

Suddenly the people tracker application that proved worthless in his initial search zeroed in on the same Joseph McRory. This Joe McRory also had an entry in the public records database.

Another small fee paid, and he was looking at the public record. Mr. McRory was a principal in a recently formed LLC named Triple Play.

Searching Google and Bing for "Triple Play" returned the expected references to baseball. There were real-estate firms by the same name, rides at amusement parks, special bundling deals for internet access, cable, and telephone services, and assorted videos having something to do with the two words, however tenuous the connection.

On a whim, he tried "Triple Play" with the commercial database listing government contracts. There it was. "Unspecified services responding to an RFP published by Homeland Security.

Back to the listing for Triple Play in California's Secretary of State database showed the names of two other principals: Evangeline O'Conner and Alice Linda.

Well, hello, Alice Linda.

* * *

SHE WAS A fully-grown woman. She could do what she wanted. Only her opinion mattered. So why did she think of her morning walk from his apartment to the stand as a "walk of shame?"

Why am I carrying this baggage? she wondered.

Alice Linda resolved to evolve a bit more. She needed to be a lot more like the Linda McRory she pretended to be.

Two men in uniforms were already waiting for Joe to open the stand. He was late, again.

She spread out her towel and dropped into one of her usual yoga positions. Still a bit tender from last evening, she chose a different position instead.

The uniforms were impressed by both choices. She returned their smiles with one of her own.

I am such a slut, she thought. No, I'm not.

Still more evolutionary development in her near future.

She heard him before she saw him. By the time she transitioned to a move facing the stand, the uniforms were gone. That made no sense. Still no Joe, but she had heard his voice.

She stood.

There, back at the roadway, one of the two uniforms placed Joe McRory into the rear seat of an unmarked vehicle. Judging by his seated position, his hands were cuffed behind his back. McRory was under arrest!

"Hey!" she screamed toward the car.

The second uniform halted his entry into the driver's position. He waved back in her direction yelling, "Nice yoga!" He reinforced his favorable impression by flashing her a closed fist, one thumb up followed by a long flash of the whitest teeth she'd ever seen.

* * *

LOWANDOWSKI FLOATED the length of his walk to the dock in Port-Vila. He jumped aboard the older boat with several large cardboard boxes lashed to the deck. Known in the maritime trade as a "RoRo," roll-on, roll-off cargo ship, its days of ferrying passengers to the neighboring islands had long since passed.

Lowandowski jumped up on a wooden skid holding two small appliances for delivery. He leaned back pretending to smoke a cigarette. He held his backpack against his chest.

A flight between Port-Vila and Espiritu was only fifty minutes, but his passage easily traced. By this boat, the journey would last between four and five hours. The vessel wouldn't return for days. By then his tracks would be cold.

Lowandowski had lots of time to think.

* * *

IT WAS LATE. Very late, in fact.

"Where was he?" she muttered. "The rules are very clear, very specific about tardiness. Oh well, like training a puppy, I guess. One step forward, one step back."

When she awoke she realized Lowandowski had not returned home. A serious violation of the rules. That was two violations in as many days.

She should have been angry. Instead, she was worried.

The next morning, when Joe didn't make an appearance at the stand, she was the only one among the anxious who was worried. Mostly, they were angry at missing their morning jolt of caffeine.

She hailed a taxi to the Port-Vila airport.

Port-Vila Bauerfield International Airport was far more modest than its name. A building in three parts, the center portion towering over its components to the left and the right, featured a sign announcing its name that spanned the entire building. Alice Linda navigated her way to the Immigration Office. Through the office door she encountered a receptionist. Before she could ask after McRory she heard a familiar voice.

"Hey, Yoga!"

Looking up, she found the teeth first and the smiling face behind them second.

Adopting her most un-Linda-like demeanor, she flirted with her admirer as she slowly managed to extract the whereabouts of the missing Mr. McRory.

He was gone. Deported. Having overstayed his Visa by almost two weeks. They declared him PNG—*persona non grata.*

* * *

SHE WAITED TO call Eddy O'Conner until she returned to her hotel room. She hadn't accounted for the time difference.

"Hello?"

O'Conner sounded like she'd been rousted from a thick fog.

"Eddy, they took Joe," Linda reported.

She could hear O'Conner's yawn followed by, "Yes, I know. He's in Fiji now as a guest of their government. The DNI's office had to do some fancy footwork to avoid saying he was in Vanuatu on official business of the U.S. government. They pretended to believe the DNI's office, and the DNI's office pretended their counterparts in Vanuatu believed the story.

"So no one believed it," Linda replied.

"You got it. It doesn't appear Joe can ever return to Vanuatu. He was officially declared *persona non grata*."

"Is he okay?"

"I only spoke to him once. Couldn't get him to stop complaining about his wrist hematomas. You know, from the cuffs they used."

They both laughed.

"How is the Lowandowski project coming?" O'Conner asked. "Joe's been giving me status reports, but I prefer to hear from you directly."

"Until last night, I'd say things were going really well, Eddy."

"But today, you'd have a different summary?"

"He didn't come home last evening."

"You come home now!" O'Conner more commanded than suggested. "I'll have your arrangements waiting for you at the airport."

Linda didn't respond.

"Alice, did you hear me?" O'Conner's voice assumed a more commanding presence.

"Yeah. I'll just throw a few things into a bag and head on out."

* * *

SHE CONSIDERED HER word choice carefully. "She was heading out." She didn't preclude stopping at Lowandowski's apartment for one last reconnoiter. If he was still gone, she could give the place a good toss. Maybe even find something they could use.

Linda looked at her watch. She knew the airport had a limited number of outbound flights. She could spend two hours at the apartment, but not a minute more than that.

She checked out of her hotel.

Normally, she knocked before entering. This time, however, she unlocked the door and made her way in. If he was there, she'd go on the offense complaining about his rude behavior. How she didn't welcome being inconvenienced. The rules he violated and so on.

The place was spotless and put together well. The rules were working with the exception of last night.

She checked the nightstand. It was empty. The rules were missing. His Philippines passport gone.

She looked over at the small writing desk near the window. His laptop was gone. The power cord was missing.

Running to the kitchen she threw open the refrigerator door. Clean. Empty.

Trashcan empty.

All of his toiletry items in the bathroom, gone.

"Shit!" she didn't care who heard her.

Charles Lowandowski gave her the slip yet again.

CHAPTER 14

DESPITE THE FACT THEIR departures occurred on two different days, both Joe McRory and Alice Linda were on the same flight between Fiji and San Francisco. Neither was functioning particularly well. Each was unaware the other was aboard.

Linda was among the early boarders consigned to the cheap middle seats at the rear of the plane. She was seated next to a pregnant woman and her small child. The child was in the early stages of an intestinal malady. The immediate future was not hopeful.

The Fijian authorities assumed control over McRory from their Vanuatu counterparts and held him in detention at the airport until the boarding process was complete. Then he was unceremoniously marched through the concourse, down the jetway, and plunked into a business class seat.

For two days McRory existed on a steady diet of packaged, stale cheese crackers from a vending machine and bottles of warm water. Both wrists were thoroughly bruised from the use of handcuffs and his shoulders hurt from having spent hours with his arms bound behind his back. He was long overdue for a shower. He promised to throw away every article of clothing on his body just as soon as he possibly could. Until then, he was a very *unbusiness* presence among those in business class only because there were no seats available in coach.

* * *

IT TOOK EVERY bit of resolve for Linda to push her own misery out of her mind to notice the difficulties of her seat mate.

"Where is your husband?" she asked. She expected an answer that had the sick baby's father back in Fiji or awaiting their arrival in San Francisco.

"He's up there," she said.

"Here, on this plane?"

Linda was aghast, pissed—but primarily aghast.

"The airline cancelled yesterday's flight. We spent the night in the airport. Today, they didn't seem to worry about seating us together. They put us where they could."

"I'll fix that," Linda announced.

She crawled over the legs, torsos, and reclined seat backs from the next row to make her way to the aisle. She marched the length of the economy cabin to the forward bulkhead row—Premium Economy seating.

The woman's husband was sound asleep in the aisle seat.

She slapped the man's head with her open hand.

"Get your sorry ass back to your wife and your sick baby before I drag you to the restroom and stuff your body down the toilet!"

The man, startled by the head slap and what followed, pushed himself out of his seat and beat a hasty retreat to the back of the plane.

Linda took her time taking her seat, making herself comfortable.

* * *

MCRORY WAS STILL pissed that he'd been rounded up by Immigration for having overstayed his Visa time limit. Talk about a rookie mistake. He hadn't bothered researching the visitation limits beforehand. Neither had Eddy O'Conner on her trip to Vanuatu. They both were on the island for more than thirty days. Soon, Alice Linda would be as well.

Yet, only McRory was swept up by Vanuatu's immigration authorities. Inexplicably, they knew right where to find him.

There were only three possibilities. First, Charles Lowandowski was a lot smarter and more capable than anyone had reason to believe. Second, Linda was having fun at his expense. Third, Vanuatu had an immigration force second to none.

In reverse order: Unlikely, improbable, and holy shit!

* * *

THROUGHOUT THE LONG flight to San Francisco, the cabin attendants maintained the closed curtain separating economy and business class seating. No one in business class was guilty of trying to breach the line in a dash for economy. However, several economy class patrons did try.

It had not gone well for those bolting for the front. The cabin attendants might have been small, but they were fierce. It wasn't until the final approach to San Francisco that the curtains were opened and secured to comply with FAA rules.

That's when each saw the other.

Both shook their heads.

McRory smiled.

Linda did not.

* * *

THEY WERE ONLY separated by the curtain. Yet it took Linda a full ten minutes to follow McRory off the plane. The two didn't meet until she finally escaped the plane and the jetway to join him on the concourse.

"Son of a bitch," Linda muttered. "Geez, Joe, ever hear of a shower?"

He held out his wrists, "Look," he whimpered.

"Wow," Linda replied. She knew all about his heightened sense of body awareness. "Have you ever seen such hematomas?"

The sarcasm was hard to miss.

Eddy O'Conner waiting in her town car opposite the baggage claim area for international arrivals. O'Conner's usual driver opened the car's rear door for both Linda and McRory. McRory jostled her aside and entered first.

"Always the gentleman," Linda said to the driver.

"Indeed," he responded.

From inside the car, both Linda and the driver could hear the dismay in O'Conner's voice, "Oh no, Joe. Not more hematomas?"

"And ripe," the driver observed.

"Indeed," Linda acknowledged.

CHAPTER 15

"LET'S ADDRESS THE ELEPHANT in the room."

Eddy O'Conner served up the start of a tough conversation along with a choice of tea or coffee. The tall windows flooded the room with bright sunshine—a rarity for a San Francisco morning.

"Once again, Charles Lowandowski outsmarted us. Why do we continue to underestimate this young man?" O'Conner's frustration was evident.

Joe McRory offered his assessment first.

"Eddy, I've retraced my process step by step. I don't think Lowandowski smelled a rat in Key West. He was long gone by then. And, I didn't step onto the stage in Vanuatu until you set the scene."

"It's too early for mixed metaphors. They give me a headache at this time of day."

By that comment, Alice Linda set forth notice she awoke on the wrong side of the bed.

"What matters, Joe, is what you two had to say to one another during all of those hours at the beachfront stand."

O'Conner narrowed the discussion. The fact all three sat quietly following the comment reflected a general agreement.

"True," he started slowly. "And then I introduced him to you, Alice, as I recall. So, at the outset of your affair with Lowandowski, did you notice anything amiss? Did he, for instance, ask any questions of you about Eddy or myself? Had he offered any comment—perhaps innocent at the time—which in retrospect should have tipped you off?"

Yet another group silence. This time, remaining silent was tantamount to a "no" response to the questions asked by McRory.

O'Conner broke the quiet.

"Look, this isn't getting us anywhere. In a way, Michaela introduced me to Lowandowski. I introduced Lowandowski to Joe via that connection. Joe introduced you to Lowandowski, Alice. Yet none of us had sensed anything from Lowandowski—directly or indirectly—that he was on to us."

Looks of agreement were exchanged among the three.

She continued, "We know he did work his way from acceptance of our respective introductions to suspicion and then acted on those suspicions. Or, he may have sensed something was up, something was wrong, at some point along the chain of these introductions."

Linda didn't agree, "Eddy, we don't know that for certain. It's entirely possible one of us—maybe all of us—were made by a third party."

McRory took the bait, "You're saying *someone else* tipped off Lowandowski?"

"I don't know, Alice. Joe, what about you?"

"I share Eddy's reluctance to accept your point, Alice."

The lack of support from both her colleagues did little to improve Alice's demeanor.

"Like both of you," she began, "I've carefully reviewed everything I said to him and him to me, everything I did with—and to—him and him to me. Again, and again, until I've made myself crazy." She dug down deep for the finish. "I think we each played our parts, if not to perfection, then pretty damned close to it. I'm convinced Lowandowski was tipped off."

Linda's iPhone buzzed.

"You need to get that, Alice?" O'Conner asked.

Linda pulled the phone from her jean's pocket, fingers flying across the screen.

"It's from my mom," she said. "I can get back to her later."

McRory would look back on this moment and recall he didn't buy Linda's explanation about her mom's text message.

* * *

IN SAN FRANCISCO, COLONEL Katrina Saakadze followed her best GRU tradecraft in arranging the meet with Sam Littelwood. Now married with a small infant, Saakadze pushed the stroller out one storefront into the home goods store next door. Locksmith Sam Littelwood was on a business call to change the combination on the store's safe. The fact the two were in the same place at the same time wasn't an accident.

To an outsider it would look like pure coincidence.

The store owner arranged for Littelwood's services a week earlier. His evening manager was caught on nanny cam withdrawing small amounts of cash from the safe. The missing sums didn't originally suggest a pattern of theft, more like a series of accounting mistakes on the owner's part. The police strongly suggested the owner change the safe's combination. The arrangement with Littelwood was made in short order. And, in turn, Saakadze was notified accordingly using an agreed upon dead drop.

"Did you get any sun at all?" she asked.

"I wasn't there long enough," Littelwood replied quietly. "I spent most of my time in the air between here and that damned island."

"Did he take the bait?"

"Hook, line, and sinker."

"You Americans and your frustrating slang. I get enough of that at home with my new American husband. But I know this one," she congratulated herself. "It's a fishing metaphor, right? Like the fish who takes the bait and the hook."

"You got it." Littelwood didn't understand the mystery of the expression. "The kid split, McRory was deported, and Linda took off for—well, here."

"Good," was all that Saakadze said. "I love this tchotchke!" She grabbed the small item, and pivoting the stroller, she marched off to the cash register to pay for the purchase.

* * *

THE MORNING SUN was quickly replaced by cold fog and light rain more typical of the season. Saakadze stopped the stroller. She rearranged the infant's swaddling to protect against the change in weather.

Following General Kaledin's arrest, her orders from Moscow were clear, if not brilliant—or colossally stupid depending on one's point of view.

Saakadze expected to be recalled to Moscow and then moved on to another duty station. Surely, Kaledin would give her up to the Americans. If not immediately, then certainly over the period of his incarceration. She would do the same to him if their positions were reversed.

The logic of headquarters' decision was carefully explained: Kaledin hadn't rolled over on her, yet. By continuing to follow her tradecraft, she could remain in her current position. On the other hand, if the Americans did know about her, then sticking to good tradecraft became even more important. The answer was always "tradecraft." As her new superior explained, "The Americans know all about us. We know all about them." Extracting officers and moving them around wasted precious resources and introduced temporary network inefficiencies. Neither side liked tipping their hat unless it was necessary.

This was all above Saakadze's pay grade, and she was struggling with the additional operational information her superiors in Moscow now shared with her.

Kaledin was one of those unusual exceptions to the rules of engagement tacitly agreed upon by both sides. The Americans feared Kaledin was leaving the country for good. They did a quick cost-benefit analysis. If they let Kaledin out of the country and beyond their reach, they would never learn what he knew. Should they arrest him, it could take years and untold resources to extract and double check whatever he did tell them. Worse yet, after a point, his knowledge would be outdated whether he shared it or not.

So, they made a judgment call. Both sides knew Kaledin would control the pace at which he shared his secrets with his captors. The Russians knew they could adapt and maintain the status quo even if he did.

The next bit of guidance perplexed her. She had to marry and bear a child. The sooner the better. The imagery convinced the

Americans the Russians felt comfortable with Kaledin's arrest. Metaphorically thumbing their nose at America. In short, she was compelled to find a suitable man—quickly—become pregnant—again, quickly—to maintain a fiction that only she was to believe. Both sides knew the Americans wouldn't be fooled. Her marriage and motherhood served as an "in your face" dare to the U.S. intelligence agencies. "We know, you know. And we don't care."

What a crazy business this is, she thought. Her parents would never understand.

They only cared she was now married and a mother. They were coming for a visit. A necessary family act that was a scheduling inconvenience for her work. The husband, and now the baby, were distractions enough. Her job, already a challenge, was even more so given the changes in her life.

It was at times like these she wished she'd been born a man.

✳ ✳ ✳

LINDA WAITED UNTIL she made her way to her room at the YWCA.

The message text was brief and to the point. She sat on the unmade bed to think.

✳ ✳ ✳

LITTELWOOD CHOSE THE fog and rain to walk back to his shop. Visibility wasn't great, but after all those days on that damned airplane he took his fresh air where he could.

He texted while he walked. The distraction and the visibility contributed to the collision. A skateboarder clipped his right shoulder causing him to drop the phone.

"Son of a bitch!" he screamed. "Hey, asshole, what the hell?"

Littelwood stood over the sprawled grungy teen. His fists clenched. He was ready to engage but quickly reconsidered. Instead, he extended a hand to the youth pulling the kid to his feet. "Are you okay, son?"

"Sorry, man. Really."

Littelwood retrieved the phone from the sidewalk and sent the text message on its way. Giving the kid one last reproachful look, he walked away only to stop at a nearby trashcan.

Littelwood removed the sim card from the inexpensive phone and crushed the device under his heel—several times. The residual anger from his collision with the teen fueling the complete destruction of the phone. He picked up the pieces of what remained of the inexpensive device and tossed them into the can. Later, when he approached a crosswalk, he dropped the small sim card between the slats of a storm sewer grate. The rain water carried the card further into the sewer system.

The teen waited for Littelwood to become one with the fog and only then bent over the trashcan. Using the latex glove he pulled from his pocket, he reached into the receptacle, extracted the pieces of the phone and placed them into an evidence bag. He tapped the ear piece of his head phones.

"Got it," he said.

* * *

THE GLOOMY DAY served only to further depress McRory. He didn't mind the waste of his time, first in Key West and then in Vanuatu. He did, however, despair over disappointing Eddy O'Conner and Alice Linda and the thought it was him who might bear responsibility for the botched operation.

The flowers waiting by his apartment door pleasantly surprised him. No one had ever sent him flowers—ever. His gloomy disposition was instantly supplanted by the gesture.

"No wonder women like receiving flowers," he said to no one.

The arrangement included a card.

He opened the envelope and extracted the note within. Instantly, he returned to his previous disposition.

McRory leaned against the door jamb to gather his thoughts and make sense of it all.

* * *

O'CONNER KNEW SHE'D leaned heavily on both of her colleagues. Sitting alone in her expansive indoor living area, she thought it better to err on the side of caution. She picked up her phone and dialed.

"Yes, Eddy," the DNI answered after his PA patched through the call.

"Sir, I'd like to take you up on the offer of the other day," she said.

"Consider it done. We'll know immediately if either of them comes into range of the surveillance cameras.

"When will I know?"

"If they trip any of the alarms, you'll start receiving text messages on this phone."

CHAPTER 16

THE TEXT MESSAGE CAME from a telephone number Alice Linda didn't recognize. The message started simply with: *I'm sorry I left without telling you....* And, it finished with: *Be together?*

Her fingers flew across the virtual keypad.

Five minutes later a response text message: *48°41'05.0244", -116°17'35.5056", SFO, Delta.*

Linda mapped the coordinates, packed her empty go-bag, and took off for the airport.

Across town, Joe McRory followed the directions on the greeting card.

* * *

EDDY O'CONNER'S IPHONE buzzed with a text message: Expect telephone call from DNI in five minutes or less, Henley.

It was less.

"Please hold for the DNI."

O'Conner waited.

"Eddy, both your folks are on the move," the DNI reported. "I have to go to a meeting. Expect follow-up calls from Henley."

"Thank you, Director," O'Conner acknowledged. "I'll expect to hear from Henley."

The telephone link ended only to be followed by another incoming call.

"Henley, here," he said by way of introduction. Before O'Conner could return the greeting, Henley launched into what followed.

"Linda is on the BART. She's one stop from the airport—SFO, to be specific. Delta is holding a reservation for a pre-paid ticket in her name—Spokane, Washington, to be specific. Change of planes in Seattle—to be specific."

"O'Conner couldn't help herself, "How long is the entire flight—to be specific?"

Henley didn't miss a beat, "Two hours and eighteen minutes on the first segment—to be specific, followed by a layover in Seattle of 57 minutes—to be specific, and one hour and seven minutes—to be specific."

"What's Linda's destination?" O'Conner inquired.

Henley came right back, "Our information is limited to what's contained in the reservation record—to be specific. The destination beyond the final segment of her airline reservation is yet to be determined—to be specific."

"What is Joe McRory's status?"

Henley paused briefly before responding.

"Currently, McRory is traveling by vehicle, a late model Ford SUV—to be specific. We have verified his progress by surveillance camera at the Golden Gate Bridge eleven minutes and thirty-three seconds ago—to be specific. Recognition algorithms report a vehicle identification certainty of 97 percent—to be specific. Facial recognition algorithms report a facial similarity of 83 percent—to be specific."

"Henley," O'Conner started, "Can you project his destination?"

"With a high degree of probability, our algorithms project McRory's final destination in the Pacific northwest: Oregon, Washington, or Idaho states—to be specific. I can give you probabilities for specific cities in those states if you'd like. Simply name the city."

It was at this point O'Conner realized Henley wasn't a person. Instead, he was an artificial intelligence engine connected to an amazingly life-like speech and voice recognition system.

"I don't have any cities, right now."

"I will call to provide you with updates every hour—more frequently, if you'd prefer."

"No," she replied, "hourly will be fine."

"Okay," Henley said, "I will call you again—at this number—in one hour from now—to be specific."

O'Conner placed two calls. One to Linda and a second to McRory. Both calls went immediately into voice mail. Both voice mailboxes were filled and unable to accept an additional voice mail message.

So predictable, she thought. Thank heavens for that.

* * *

ONE HOUR LATER—to be specific—Henley sent a text message to O'Conner: *Expect telephone call from me in five minutes or less, Henley.*

Almost immediately, O'Conner's telephone brought forth Henley's voice.

"Hello, Eddy. As promised, I am calling to provide an update on the travel progress of two subjects, Alice Linda and Joe McRory. Do you want me to send these updates to your phone?"

"No," O'Conner replied. "Just provide them to me over the phone."

"Okay. Linda's original flight was canceled due to an equipment problem. Her rescheduled first segment is now Delta flight 4957 to Seattle departing ten thirty this morning—to be specific. Her second segment departs Seattle at three forty-five this afternoon. She arrives in Spokane at four fifty-two this afternoon—to be specific.

"McRory's vehicle is northbound on I-5. He was five miles north of the I-80 exit to Sacramento six minutes and 15 seconds ago—to be specific.

"My earlier projections concerning McRory's destination remain unchanged. However, are Linda and McRory traveling to the same destination?"

"Let's assume so," O'Conner offered.

"Working from that assumption, I project McRory will join Linda in Spokane two and one-half hours following Linda's arrival—to be specific.

"May I offer a conjecture?" Henley asked.

"Yes, please," O'Conner was surprised.

"A review of similar circumstances involving our colleagues makes Spokane an unlikely destination—to be specific. Are you interested in the likelihood of this assumption?"

"Yes, please."

"I project the likelihood of Spokane as the destination at less than forty percent. Do you wish to hear more?"

"Yes."

"I now project McRory's destination to be east of Spokane, based on the likelihood he is to join Linda enroute—to be specific."

"Why is that?" she asked.

"If McRory's destination was west of Spokane, and he is to be joined by Linda who is enroute to Spokane, then Seattle would have been a more likely destination for Linda, by 80 percent—to be specific. Remember, Linda is changing planes in Seattle."

"Do you have any suggestions to offer concerning their destination?" O'Conner was fascinated.

There was a pause.

"A review of our records shows there are areas of interest to our colleagues east of Spokane. I can rank order these locations by past trips. It's important to understand that historical data is not always an accurate basis for prediction. Nevertheless, there are two likely locations: Coeur d'Alene and Hayden Island—to be specific."

"What are the probabilities?" she asked.

"In both cases, keeping in mind my earlier warning, in excess of 95 percent—to be specific."

"How quickly can I travel to both?"

"The DNI has already authorized your use of agency aircraft in this matter. There is an aircraft in-bound to the Oakland Airport. It is expected to arrive in ten minutes and twenty seconds—to be specific. If you like, I can have the aircraft refueled, provisioned, and awaiting your arrival at the Executive Air Terminal. Is that your preference?"

"It is—to be specific," she said.

"That was hilarious, Eddy."

"Really?"

"No, but it is the appropriate response for a failed attempt at humor—to be specific."

* * *

FIFTEEN MINUTES LATER, O'Conner was in a town car heading for the Oakland Airport. The timing was perfect coming as it did mid-way between the morning and evening rush hours.

CHAPTER **17**

A MEMBER OF SAM LITTELWOOD'S team followed McRory's car—at a distance. The tracker placed on McRory's vehicle was designed to send a strong signal for a day before exhausting its battery. Signal reception was guaranteed by the manufacturer for up to five miles. The tracker played it safe. She was careful to maintain a two to two and one-half mile distance between them. McRory would never sense he had a tail.

At predetermined points, she sent a specific text message to the phone number provided by Littelwood. The tone of each message more forlorn and desperate than the last. The phone, using a special SIM provided by Littelwood, communicated by spoofing McRory's cell phone number.

Meanwhile, McRory's phone was turned off to avoid answering the emails, text messages, and telephone calls from Eddy O'Conner. Later he could claim his phone battery was run down or that he must have inadvertently turned the device off. Both excuses were lame but proven effective by millennials who dodged unwanted contact from friends and family members.

Alice Linda was doing likewise.

Sticking one's head in the sand was no longer the mark of a fool.

* * *

ABOARD THE CORPORATE jet, O'Conner received the now familiar text message, *Expect telephone call from me in five minutes or less, Henley.*

The next four plus minutes crawled by, or so it seemed, when her telephone finally rang.

"Hello, Eddy. As promised, I am calling to provide an update on the travel progress of two subjects, Alice Linda and Joe McRory. Do you want me to send these updates to your phone?"

"Yes," she replied.

O'Conner's concern for her two colleagues won out over her fascination of yet another conversation with Henley.

"A PDF file is attached to my next text message. Good-bye, Eddy."

Henley disconnected before O'Conner could complete a complimentary close as social etiquette of her day required. She was more troubled by Henley's abrupt disconnect then she was conversing with a non-human. But then, O'Conner was definitely not a fan of ducking communication either. She had her fill of this rude social habit with her own siblings and their children. Her recent attempt to congratulate her favorite niece on her college admission in Switzerland had been rebuffed.

Now she had to contend with both Alice and Joe adopting the practice. Were she not so concerned for their well-being, she might allow herself to feel angry. Instead, she was worried sick.

The text message and attachment arrived right on schedule. At least Henley didn't disappoint. The message was long winded, a trait of Henley's to which she was coming to expect. She had to scroll through the message several times to be certain she understood its detail and implications.

The message read just like Henley spoke.

Hello, Eddy. As promised, I am writing to provide an update on the travel progress of two subjects: Alice Linda and Joe McRory. You directed me to send these updates to your phone.

Linda's second flight segment, Delta flight 5760 to Spokane, arrived two minutes earlier than scheduled at four fifty this afternoon—to be specific. Fifteen minutes later, she purchased a one-way ticket on a ground transportation carrier, Greyhound Bus, from the Spokane airport to Hayden Island, Idaho. The bus is scheduled to depart in ten minutes and arrive at seven zero five minutes this evening—to be specific.

McRory's vehicle is eastbound on I-90. He was eighteen miles west of the Spokane airport two minutes and three seconds ago—to be specific.

My earlier projections concerning McRory's destination have been revised. I can no longer draw the inference supporting my earlier forecast that McRory and Linda would meet at the Spokane airport. I have revised my projection to reflect both parties will meet instead at Hayden Island, Idaho—to be specific.

An analysis of past travel by my colleagues indicates two possible conclusions. First, there is a matter of some significance taking place in Hayden Island, Idaho—where time is of the essence—requiring Linda to reach that destination before McRory rather than to meet and travel there together. Second, there is some significance to their separate travel other than time to destination. I project the likelihood of the first at 93 percent and the second at 86 percent, respectively—to be specific.

In light of Henley's analysis, O'Conner's concern only grew.

$$* \ * \ *$$

A SECOND MEMBER of Littelwood's team stood surveillance overlooking the cemetery. The graves and monuments were ground clutter that didn't obscure tracking people. Littelwood chose the cemetery and its geo coordinates to be certain no one followed Linda from the airport in Spokane. From the nearby hill, his minion had an unobstructed view of the grave sites.

Throughout the afternoon and into the evening, she watched for her teammate's text messages to Linda. Her phone's SIM spoofed Linda's device. Thus far, the two stalkers were exchanging soulful text messages between themselves. Linda and McRory were oblivious to the texting. Their phones were powered off.

Using an online vacation site, Littelwood rented a mountain cabin in Joe McRory's name and new credit card. Littelwood established the new line of credit on McRory's behalf while McRory was in Vanuatu, and he charged a number of small purchases in McRory's name while there.

The plan was right out of the GRU компромисс, or compromise, playbook.

CHAPTER 18

ALICE LINDA HAILED ONE of the few taxi cabs in Hayden Island from the bus stop. She looked around having stepped out of the cab at the cemetery. A family monument at the road's edge flew a small American flag with an envelope attached. She retrieved and opened the envelope.

"Do you know this address?" she asked the cab driver.

"Are you in some sort of game?" the cabbie asked. "Are there cameras recording this? Will this be on TV?"

"Not if we don't get to this address, quickly," Linda responded.

"Nothing like this ever happens in Hayden Island. This is cool. I'll have you at the address in a jiff." The cabbie was excited by the prospect of taking part in some sort of reality show.

* * *

SAM LITTELWOOD HID under the front porch stairwell. He could see through the thick log stair treads, but in the dim evening light, and dressed in dark colors, he was safe in the shadows.

The text message arrived. She's on the way.

He prepared the tranquilizer dart.

* * *

LINDA SENT THE disappointed cabbie on his way and walked down the chip gravel driveway to the impressive log cabin. The lights were on. Someone was listening to light jazz as the notes made their way through the open windows under the cover of the expansive front porch.

Linda was on the fourth stair tread when she felt the slight sting on her ankle. She lifted her foot to swat at the mosquito, rubbed the site of the bite, and then resumed ascending the stairs. Littelwood heard Linda collapse onto the floor boards above him.

* * *

EDDY O'CONNER WALKED down the jet's stairway onto the airport tarmac. A state police helicopter, arranged by Henley, was warmed up and ready to go nearby. The co-pilot, a corporal, escorted her to the passenger row of the bird as the blade spun up for flight.

The noise of the blades and the engine above her was deafening, the earphones notwithstanding. All she could think about was her last conversation with Henley.

"Eddy, I've checked the status of the cell phones registered to Linda and McRory. Both devices are either powered off or not accompanying either party. I've determined the likelihood both Linda and McRory traveling without their phones is so small that I do not believe it to be probable—to be specific. I conclude with more than 99 percent probability that both phones are inoperative—to be specific."

"I concur," O'Conner replied.

"Thank you, but your concurring opinion is unnecessary and is not a factor in the probabilities I just cited—to be specific.

"However, the local wireless networks show recent text messaging activity on the phone numbers assigned to Linda and McRory. I have a list of the cell towers, and their respective geo coordinates, where the messaging traffic originates and is received. I have sent those locations to you by email—to be specific.

"My analysis of the text messages does raise a question, Eddy. May I ask?"

"Yes," she replied.

"How long have Linda and McRory been involved in a romantic episode—to be specific?"

O'Conner started to laugh. The idea was too ridiculous to give any serious thought.

"They aren't," she responded with absolute certainty.

"Are you quite certain? You wouldn't be the first person in a multi-person relationship to be unaware of an ongoing romantic connection between two other people—to be specific."

"No, Henley, I am convinced that is impossible."

"To be clear, 'improbable' would be a better word choice as it allows the possibility, albeit remote—to be specific."

"Henley, can you send me the text messages?" O'Conner asked.

"I've already done so, Eddy," came the prompt response. "The email and its attachment have already been received by the appropriate app on your device—to be specific."

"Can you provide me with a short summary of what you believe to be the gist of the text message exchange?" O'Conner queried.

"Certainly. Linda has decided to end her life since she and McRory can no longer be together. It appears McRory has terminated their romantic relationship—to be specific."

"Henley, give me time to review the text messages. Can you call me back in five minutes?"

The connection ended.

O'Conner found the email and opened the attached PDF file. Henley annotated each text by person, although doing so was unnecessary.

Every fiber in her body told her the words she was reading could not possibly have come from Linda and McRory. However, there was no denying the overt characterizations in the texts. Henley was correct. If the texts were to be believed, McRory had behaved badly over Linda's honeypot assignment involving Lowandowski. He was unprepared to share her with anyone.

O'Conner simply couldn't believe what she was reading. *This could not possibly be true*, she thought.

Yet, here she was in some god forsaken corner of Idaho chasing down two of her associates, both of whom have shut her out of their lives with so simple a task as powering off their cell phones.

That's when it hit her.

The state police had already located the cabbie. They provided the helicopter pilot with the address. He set the bird down in the middle of the road after which O'Conner let herself out of the cabin.

"Wait, ma'am!" the corporal screamed over the prop wash. "Do you want me to accompany you?"

* * *

THE HOUSE WAS wide open. No doors locked, not even closed.

O'Conner went in first, followed by the corporal. Both were armed and followed standard practice in sweeping the premises.

After signaling the first floor was clear, O'Conner signaled her intent to walk the center staircase to the second floor. The corporal followed closely.

They found Linda sprawled in the tub. The water still very warm. Her wrists slit and a red ring forming around the tub surface.

"Oh my God, Alice?" O'Conner screamed. "What have they done to you?"

* * *

MCRORY PULLED INTO the drive way unprepared to find a helicopter, an ambulance, and several state and local police vehicles. Before exiting his truck, he powered on his cell phone and waited for it to complete the power on sequence.

A stream of text messages from Linda's phone flew across the front of his phone. He couldn't believe what he was reading.

"Joe!" O'Conner yelled from the front porch, "Get over here, now!"

CHAPTER 19

THE AMBULANCE DROVE UP the driveway and onto the state road, sirens blaring.

"Will she be okay?" Joe McRory's diminished voice made clear he was heartbroken over Alice Linda's injuries.

"The EMTs believe the blood loss wasn't catastrophic. Had I been a few moments later, she might well be gone, Joe. What the hell were you two planning?"

Eddy O'Conner was on a tear. McRory had never seen O'Conner angry. Angry, she was fearsome.

"Alice received a text message from Lowandowski," he explained. "At least she thought it was from Lowandowski."

McRory looked back at the cabin before continuing.

"Whoever texted her gave her a set of geo coordinates. She mapped them to a cemetery in town. I'm uncertain how she made her way from the cemetery to this place, but she needed to know if the text was genuine and we still had a shot at Lowandowski."

"Why keep this from me?" O'Conner demanded. "We're partners!"

"Eddy, we are *and* we're not. Look, you're the one with the big career and all that super spy stuff. You think Alice and I don't recognize who really pulls the weight here?"

McRory took a large halting breath before continuing.

"We know we let you down in Vanuatu. Hell, we don't even know how we blew the assignment, but it's clear we did. And we both knew—Eddy, we knew—we let you down. And that is the very last thing either of us wanted. This was our way of making it right, making amends."

"Why the secrecy, Joe? Why turn off your phones?"

"We wanted to surprise you—no matter how this thing worked out. We wanted to show you we aren't screw-ups."

"And, how did that work?"

* * *

THE NEXT MORNING, O'Conner and McRory sat around Linda's hospital bed. Each reconstructing the events of the last twenty-four hours.

"I was walking up the front stairs and I felt a sting on my ankle. I thought it was a mosquito—some sort of insect. I didn't pay attention to it. The next thing I know, two male EMTs are pulling my naked body out of an oversized clawfoot bath tub and I have tourniquets on both wrists."

"The ER Doc who got a look at you when you arrived said you looked like you'd been tranquilized or poisoned. He found the mark on your ankle and quickly ruled out anything with enough venom to bring you down. There was no swelling or bruising typical of a snake bite or spider bite. They don't get a lot of murder and mayhem here. So they start with the most obvious things, like snakes and spiders."

O'Conner's assessment followed.

"Whoever did this wasn't Lowandowski. This was a major effort by a team."

Both Linda and McRory reacted with quizzical looks on their faces.

"Have you seen the text messages you allegedly sent to one another?" she asked.

Linda had no idea what O'Conner was referencing. She held her bandaged arms in front of her—a wordless WTF.

"I've had a chance to look them over," McRory said. "Actually, Alice, I had no idea you had such strong feelings for me."

"What?" she asked. "You and me? Me and you? Do you have a death wish?"

O'Conner shook her head, "You two," she said dismissively. "Henley sent me a list of texts that allegedly originated from each of your phone's and were sent to the other. This, while your phones were turned off, so you could avoid me.

"Joe, the messages allegedly sent from your phone matched your progress north of San Francisco, along I-5 north, and finally onto I-90 east.

"Alice, the messages allegedly sent from your phone didn't start until you took a taxi to the cemetery.

"Henley determined both of your phones were spoofed. That means there was one person following Joe. Another who picked you up at the cemetery. And a third who was waiting for you here."

McRory was just a tad indignant.

"Eddy, no one followed me. I checked throughout the trip."

"Joe, there's no arguing with the facts. Henley traced each text message to its closest wireless tower. You string those towers together and they match your trip and the times of day you passed into and out of tower range.

"Alice, this whole 'burg is served by a single tower. All of your messages were sent starting at the time the cabbie's log book shows he stopped at the cemetery."

Both Linda and McRory asked the same question, "Who's Henley?"

"Henley works in the DNI's office," O'Conner responded. "The DNI put traces on both of you before you left San Francisco. Henley personally supervised tracking both of you," she smiled. "I have his reports. You can read them, if you'd like."

"Eddy," Linda asked, "How did you get here so quickly—I'm very glad you did, but—"

"Again, Henley," she answered. "He tracked down your flight to Spokane. He even deduced you went on ahead to this place by bus and from there by taxi. Although, he had to get the state police involved to track down the cabbie to learn the address of the cabin.

"Henley even arranged for my private transportation to Spokane and the helicopter flight from there to the cabin complete with a state police escort.

"Alice, you owe your life to Henley—not me. Henley put me here and he did so just in time."

"Is he cute?"

"McRory's face told the tale, "I think she's fine, now."

CHAPTER 20

BACK IN SAN FRANCISCO, Eddy O'Conner awaited the inevitable call from the DNI. She wasn't disappointed. Henley served up his usual warning: *Expect telephone call from DNI in five minutes or less, Henley*.

"Eddy, how are your two young people?"

"Fine, sir. Me? I'm a bit less certain," she replied.

"That's why I called—one old Cold Warrior to another."

The DNI's voice turned serious.

"They broke the rules, Eddy. You don't go after the other side's people without expecting some form of retribution."

"What did you have in mind, sir?"

"Me? I don't have anything in mind. We old Cold Warriors live with a new set of rules. Even in the name of 'national security' I can't even muss a hair on someone's head without fearing an inquiry from the Inspector General, Congress, or even DoJ. People in my position are no longer above the law.

"Am I clear, Eddy?"

"Yes, sir, you are."

"Oh," he said, "I almost forgot. Henley tracked one of our persons of interest on westbound I-80, not far from Hayden Island. Vehicle and license plate recognition algorithms are coming along nicely I'd say.

"In any event, we rolled him up this morning. He's a lower level GRU asset out of San Francisco, but he was also in Washington, DC, Miami, and Key West the same time our friend Lowandowski decided to end his burgeoning federal career."

91

"Who's his controller?" Eddy asked.

"I thought you might be interested."

They spent several more minutes on the phone. The DNI did most of the talking. O'Conner was doing most of the planning.

"Let me end on this note, Eddy."

The DNI's voice, always serious in tone, became even more so.

"We still don't know what young Lowandowski stumbled into with his access at the FBI. Add to the 'list of things we don't know,' is what he shared with the Russians. Their recent attempt on Ms. Linda's life suggests the Russians must know something, and they're prepared to do whatever it takes to keep that secret."

At the end of the conversation, she received another text from Henley: The DNI has authorized the installation of my app on your telephone. If at any point you wish to contact me, just say, "Hey, Henley"—to be specific.

* * *

WHEN THEY RAIDED his shop, he went along nicely without resistance. Thus far, no one laid a glove on him. Then again, they didn't need to. The flying machines did that.

Sam Littelwood lost count of the number of hours he sat in the unusual room. The space held five concrete beds bolted onto the wall. There was a combination, stainless steel communal toilet, wash basin, and drinking fountain in one of the corners. And he wasn't alone. There were four others in the same space.

There were also fifteen small flying drones, each the size of his thumb.

There were three drones per detainee. Each set of the airborne devices hovered silently below the ceiling and above their assigned detainee. The drones didn't appear to have a means of propulsion, but the room was filled with the sound of rushing air like an HVAC system produces.

One of the detainees moved from his bed in the direction of the toilet. The three drones, obviously in communication with one another, shadowed his progress to the toilet. At all times, the drones formed a three-point halo just beyond an arm's reach above his head.

As the detainee lowered his pants and sat on the toilet, each of the three drones maintained their distance from his head. It was a choreographed movement.

Just then the door opened, and a woman entered.

"Jesus Christ!" toilet man screamed. "Can't I have some privacy to take a shit?"

"Nothing I haven't seen before," she replied not missing a beat. "Just go about your business."

One of the other detainees, located at the far end of the room, bolted from his bed charging in the woman's direction.

She didn't react.

She didn't have to.

Each of three drones emitted a high-pitched sound—not pleasant, but not unpleasant either to Littelwood's ear. Whatever produced the sounds also rendered the charging detainee limp, but his mental faculties and speech were unimpaired. The detainee remained otherwise incapacitated on the floor.

"Mr. Littelwood, I'm an attorney with the Department of Homeland Security," she said by way of introduction.

"And your name is?" Littelwood pleasantly inquired.

"My name isn't important."

For some reason, her voice reminded Littelwood of the jaws of a bear trap snapping shut and breaking bone.

"How am I to address you, if I don't know your name?"

She just looked at him.

"I get it. I'm not supposed to talk—just listen, right?"

She never stopped staring at him. She didn't make any attempt to acknowledge and respond to his two queries.

The room was now quiet. She remained stone silent. And now Littelwood stopped talking as well.

"I have in my hands two items which concern you," she said. "The first is a signed Presidential Directive all about you and what we may do to you, for however long we choose to 'do it' to you, and wherever we choose to stick you."

Quiet again.

"The second item is a copy of the FISA Court order authorizing us to take you into our custody."

"When may I speak to my lawyer," Littelwood asked.

Without directly responding to his query, the woman resumed her canned speech.

"Under the original Patriot Act and its various amendments since its passage into law, detainees taken into custody for matters involving a breach of national security forgo the rights traditionally afforded to citizens and legal residents.

"Not to put too fine a point on it, you are unlikely to speak to anyone you knew before this morning. Further, no one knows you are here. We aren't about to tell anyone you are our guest. And you cannot have access to a telephone, the services of the U.S. Postal Service, or any other form of communication."

Littelwood didn't scare easily. He was scared shitless now.

The woman turned back in the direction from which she came, closing the door behind her. There was no sound of a lock or other similar device. As a locksmith, Littelwood noticed these things.

The previously incapacitated detainee slowly stood shaking his limbs and rotating his head to verify all systems were in good repair and still functioning. He started toward the doorway, when the drones emitted that sound, once again. The man abruptly stopped. The sounds ceased, but the drones continued their personal three-point surveillance, out of reach, directly above his head.

What happened next made a lasting impression on Littelwood.

Suddenly, the man jumped, extending his right arm and hand in an attempt to swat at one of the drones. In perfect synchrony, the targeted drone moved up and away by a like distance while the two remaining drones closed in on his head. In a fraction of a second, the sounds reappeared, and the man dropped to the floor for a second time.

By early evening, all five occupants of the room understood why the doorway was unlocked, no guards were present, and no single detainee could pose a danger to the others, let alone anyone who entered their confinement space.

The arrival of the dinner trays for their evening meal served yet another test.

A pushcart with five dinner trays was wheeled into the space prior to 6:00 p.m. Each of the five detainees looked at the other to determine who would go first. Littelwood claimed the dominant role and stood before the others. Cautiously, he moved in the direction of the cart. One of the other detainees made movements to suggest he would stand as well, but his drones moved into position and the sound reappeared. He reconsidered his move and fell back onto his bed.

Littelwood grabbed the tray with his name and carefully made his way back to his bunk. The detainee whose earlier attempt was aborted tried again. His drones faithfully shadowed his progress toward the cart.

Then the man did something stupid.

Looking at one of the other detainees, he said, "I like what's on your tray better."

He reached for the tray and the moment his fingers made contact, the drones rendered him incapacitated. This time, however, the man was unconscious—an autonomous version of three strikes and you're out.

Shortly thereafter, the door opened, and two unarmed attendants entered the space, hoisted the man's upper body off the floor, and dragged him across the linoleum to the base of his bunk. Then they exited the space.

Future meals were more civilized affairs.

* * *

LINDA AND JOE McRory claimed the Fedex parcel from the front desk and delivered it to O'Conner in her penthouse. The box contained a solid piece of high density foam. There were three thumb-like indentations, each exactly fitting a bean-like device.

She opened and read the accompanying folded card.

Eddy, these are the three devices of which the DNI spoke. There is nothing similar commercially. If they are lost or misplaced, please let me know at your earliest convenience.

I downloaded and installed a device controller app on your iPhone. The controls are self-explanatory, but if you need assistance, please feel free to call upon me, Henley.

McRory pulled one of the devices from its encapsulating foam subjecting it to his scrutiny.

"What the devil is this?" he asked.

"Toss it here," Linda suggested.

O'Conner silently watched, prepared to be amused.

McRory provided his best underhand toss and the device flew out of his hand destined for Linda who now had both hands positioned to catch it. Then the damnedest thing happened: The small black device sharply veered from the trajectory McRory established, and under its own power, took up a stationary position in the center of the room one foot lower than the room's high ceiling.

Almost immediately, the two companion devices took flight from their respective foam cushions. All three devices were now in a three-point formation high above O'Conner, Linda, and McRory.

"What the hell?" McRory muttered.

"What are these thingies?" Linda asked O'Conner.

"Alice, that question would take too long to answer. Here's my phone. The 'device controller app,'—that's what Henley called it—allows you to operate the 'thingies.' Here."

She handed the phone to Linda.

The app presented three virtual buttons: *Subject*, *Shadow*, and *Control*.

Within the next several minutes, Linda instructed the drones to focus solely on McRory, shadow his every move, and subdue him if he made any movements toward herself or O'Conner. The third time McRory was disabled for approaching Linda, O'Conner seized the phone and issued a "park" command. All three drones returned to the foam container.

CHAPTER 21

"**W**HAT'S THE STORY ON these little bastards?" Joe McRory demanded to know.

"After the disastrous events at the Abu Ghraib Prison in Iraq, the president ordered DoD to work with DoJ to implement better detention facilities for alleged prisoners of war.

The Defense Advanced Research Projects Agency, DARPA, had just completed a project where they successfully demonstrated that a swarm of drones could both operate independently but in a coordinated manner with the balance of the swarm."

Eddy O'Conner could tell by Alice Linda's facial gestures she was already losing her attention. She decided to shorten the story.

"The Army Research Labs worked with some university scientists. They shrunk the size of the drones and increased their lethality using ultra low frequency sound waves."

"Sounds like a huge success," McRory sarcastically observed.

"It wasn't, Joe. It was a spectacular failure."

O'Conner ignored the sarcasm and looked to Linda for her approval to continue the story. Linda reluctantly provided it.

"They established an open-air prison yard at some location in Iraq. Deployed swarms of these devices. For a short time, it all looked good."

"What were the benefits?"

Linda was finally engaged.

"No guards were required to watch the prisoners. Lower manpower costs, more resources for force projection. One person sat in front of a monitor and controlled the whole shooting match."

McRory dropped the sarcasm. He was genuinely confused.

"Just how, then, was this project a failure?"

"Each swarm of three—Henley says three is the optimal number—kept each prisoner away from the others it also kept them away from the fences and gates. On that count, the technology was a hit.

"The problem: It freaked out the prisoners.

"After they gave up trying to outfox their own swarm, the prisoners began to believe they couldn't speak with one another because the devices were listening. Of course, they were. But the conversations from a hundred plus prisoners would be a challenge to process in a timely manner, let alone in real time.

The prisoners stopped communicating among themselves. The prison guards and commanders no longer needed to speak to the prisoners. The swarms did all the heavy lifting. The prison facility became deadly silent.

"The stress among the prisoners grew by the hour with no outlet possible. The swarms kept them too far apart to play board games, trade war fighter stories, and even establish their own governance system. It effectively ended tribal rule among the prisoners. For a tribal society that's serious business.

"Slowly, at first, and then more rapidly, the prisoners suffered mental breakdowns requiring treatment the Army was unprepared to provide. Sending the prisoners home meant reintroducing crazy people—literally mentally unwell—back into the Iraqi population.

The Federal Bureau of Prisons has the same problem with the supermax prison in Colorado. With one important difference: The only expected way out of a supermax prison is feet first. You either die while incarcerated, or you're executed by order of a federal court."

"Christ," Linda swore, "that just made Abu Ghraib look like a child's game."

"It certainly created a serious problem. So the DoD ordered the experiment dropped and the technology shelved.

"The Department of National Intelligence watched this whole scenario from afar. They took over the technology and program, gave it a hush-hush security classification, and made it the center piece of their psyops program. As psychological warfare, these little things are unstoppable.

"Sam Littelwood who's one tough customer according to the DNI, cracked like a walnut after seven days. Not one member of the DNI's team spent even a minute interrogating him. At the end of seven days, Littelwood was screaming the names of his team, his controller, the jobs he's done, and of course, what he *almost* did to Alice."

"What's the plan, Eddy?"

At the mention of Littelwood's name and his now diminished mental state, Linda was eager for the next step.

"We're going after Littelwood's controller. A woman. GRU Colonel Katrina Saakadze. She operates out of Oakland."

O'Conner pointed in the direction of the Bay Bridge crossing from San Francisco to Oakland across the bay.

"Here's the background information on Saakadze, courtesy of Henley.

"Remember the goal here. This is only partly about revenge. We need to know what the Russians learned from Lowandowski. If he's their operative, then we can learn from Saakadze where they're keeping him now."

McRory chimed in, "Eddy, the Russians might have been duped as badly by Lowandowski. They might not know anything."

"Joe, if that's the case, then we need to know. The DNI wants even a whiff of uncertainty in the Lowandowski case chased down and eliminated. When the congressional oversight committees catch wind of what happened at the FBI Field Office, they'll want real, verifiable answers."

CHAPTER 22

KATRINA SAAKADZE'S PARENTS WERE besotted with their only grandchild. Her mother, in particular, all but pushed everyone else out of the way to minister to the child's every need and wish during his wakeful hours. Always the pragmatist, Saakadze knew her parents would be in the U.S. for several more weeks. She used the found time to resume running to lose the last of her baby weight.

Henley's background on Saakadze was nothing, if not exhaustive. Her usual running path started at the parking lot at Pine Hills Drive too deep in the hillsides to see any of the bay. The trail was a moderate challenge for an experienced hiker or runner with unleashed dogs and talkative owners as the only hazards.

Eddy O'Conner was more of a hiker—walker actually—than a runner. Since moving to San Francisco, much of her walking took place along the Embarcadero. She looked forward to the change of pace and scenery offered along the heavily forested loop.

O'Conner looked like any other hiker taking a break. Her backpack was on the ground between her legs as she leaned against the fallen tree trunk. The trail was an eight-mile loop. Sooner or later, Saakadze would have to pass her.

Normally, O'Conner would have Joe McRory and Alice Linda set up as watchers along the loop to keep her apprised of Saakadze's approach. This time she couldn't take the risk. Littelwood found both Linda and McRory in Vanuatu. He probably had his own intelligence packet on the two complete with photographs. He might even have photographs of her.

O'Conner did her best to look *unlike* her normal self.

It took several hours of waiting, but Katrina Saakadze did not disappoint. She was slightly heavier than the photo surveillance suggested. She was clearly struggling. Her shirt was soaked, her hair plastered to her scalp.

O'Conner threw all three drones into the air. Had anyone been watching, it would have appeared to be an empty gesture.

Pulling out her phone, she quickly navigated to the app. Instantly, she received streamed video. There was some pixelating due to the weak cell signal and the photo was standard definition— not high or ultra-high definition quality—but the overhead shot was clearly Saakadze.

The devices locked on to their target.

From O'Conner's vantage point, she could watch Saakadze's back grow smaller as she continued running, until she suddenly dropped entirely from view. The drones reported their status, streamed video of Saakadze lying flat on the trail, and then returned to their box at O'Conner's feet. O'Conner placed the box in her backpack and pushed off in the opposite direction.

Saakadze suffered several more disabling events throughout the week. The last, in the nearby Whole Foods Market, proved embarrassing as she took down an elderly woman who had the misfortune of standing nearby. Afterward, a shaken Saakadze stopped at the Urgent Care storefront not far from her home in Oakland.

O'Conner received the message from Henley the next day.

Urgent Care filing for health insurance reimbursement by subject received by insurer last evening. DRG-related encoding reports fainting, cause(s) unknown. Requests referral to a neurologist—to be specific, Henley.

Saakadze was no longer driving or running or walking. She relied exclusively on Uber to get around the city. No doubt fearing another episode.

Henley notified O'Conner when Saakadze's HMO issued the referral as well as the name of the neurologist and her practice's location. On the scheduled day, the Uber dropped Saakadze at the Alta Bates Medical Center. Six hours later, Saakadze emerged exhausted from the rigors of a complete neurological study.

CHAPTER 23

THE LAST CIA OPERATION OF WHICH Joe McRory was a part took place in Italy. A joint operation with the Israeli Mossad, McRory was a bit player responsible for extracting one of the Mossad team members following the execution of a middle eastern diplomat.

The murder was investigated by Interpol and the Italian security service, SISDE. The slain high-ranking diplomat was a guest in a hotel with excellent CCTV coverage. Investigators readily identified the Mossad agents including several CIA operatives, plus McRory.

For weeks, McRory's photograph, among others, was splashed across the television sets and the print media. The citizenry was outraged by the killing of a foreign diplomat on Italian soil.

McRory's exit from Italy was hastily arranged and he found himself in Langley, Virginia, at a temporary desk performing grunt work until he was summoned to the directorate to whom he reported. The press coverage was so extensive that he and several colleagues could no longer work in the field. They were offered unappealing desk jobs throughout the agency doing work no self-respecting field operative would ever accept.

The alternative was a retirement whose financial reality consigned him to an otherwise bleak future. It was better than being terminated without financial support—but just barely.

McRory wasn't the first field operative to be compromised and consigned to the CIA diaspora. Those preceding McRory welcomed him into the fold and suggested he contact Elsemere Assessments.

At Elsemere, McRory supplemented the tradecraft he acquired at the CIA. One of his new skill sets involved hacking into health care and hospital management systems. These systems were a goldmine of information—all he illegally obtained—as part of the background investigations Elsemere was commissioned to perform.

McRory sat in a waiting room designated for family members awaiting patients in surgery. While there he was able to spoof the credentials of one of the critical care nurses who went off duty as McRory arrived. Once inside the hospital system, McRory substituted a complete neurological radiology study for a patient with a glioblastoma for outpatient Katrina Saakadze. Saakadze's patient file now included a genuine set of skull x-rays complete with an end-stage glioblastoma.

She had terminal brain cancer—except she didn't.

Saakadze's neurologist rendered a bleak diagnosis based on those x-rays.

Two days later she was scheduled for a follow-up visit with the neurologist.

Using her Uber app, Saakadze summoned a ride.

* * *

ALICE LINDA WAS now a registered Uber driver using an upscale rental car. She had been parked around the corner from Saakadze's townhome since the early morning hours.

The box holding the drones sat next to her. After Saakadze pulled the passenger door shut, the drones took flight. Using the earlier acquired photographic data for Saakadze, they immediately took up position around her head.

The cramped confines of the vehicle didn't provide the drones with much room in which to work. Saakadze reacted like anyone might finding themselves in a swarm of flying insects. After unsuccessfully trying to bat the devices away, she tried to open the passenger door while the vehicle was underway. Unfortunately, Linda had already locked the doors and enabled the child-proof safety system.

Saakadze was hopelessly confined in the car.

Sensing the futility of a traditional escape, Saakadze tried to launch herself into the front passenger seat where she could bring the battle directly to Linda. The drones reacted immediately. Saakadze was rendered unconscious.

* * *

GRU COLONEL SAAKADZE wasn't an idiot. She awoke in a private hospital room without windows. She also knew she was being detained by one of the U.S. security services or the FBI. The arm and leg restraints binding her to the hospital bed were a good hint.

The drones hovered above her.

The x-ray reader across from her bed held a series of three skull x-rays. The glioblastoma was impossible to miss—even to the untrained. The large white mass on the left side of her brain destroyed the balanced symmetry typical of a normal scan.

Suddenly, being detained was the least of her problems.

* * *

EDDY O'CONNER, LINDA, and McRory entered Saakadze's room. Each was cloaked in the standard green scrubs of a hospital. All three wore a visitor's badge around their necks.

"I know you two," she gestured to Linda and McRory. "From Vanuatu."

Turning her attention to O'Conner, she added, "And you must be the person in charge of these two idiots."

"O'Conner replied, "I am. They may be idiots, but they are all mine."

"Hey!" both Linda and McRory offered in unison.

Everyone in the room laughed, and then it got very quiet until O'Conner commandeered the conversation.

"Colonel, you are very sick. You have what's called a fourth stage glioblastoma—or so the medical staff tell me.

"Had you made it to your appointment this morning, your neurologist, Dr. Khan, would have advised you to put your business and family affairs in order, and select a hospice care facility."

"How much time do I have?" she asked.

"Well, on that point there is some difference of expert opinion. Dr. Khan's notes suggest you have from four to six months. Our medical experts insist, if your current quality of life is considered, the number is closer to one to two months."

"Quality of life issues?" she mumbled.

"After two months, if not sooner, you lose all motor control, blindness, suffer non-stop headaches, and worse. The list of symptoms is bad, very bad."

"When can I see my family?" she asked.

"Well, that's entirely up to you," O'Conner held out false hope.

"If it's up to me, then I want to see them now!" she angrily responded.

"I'm afraid you don't understand. So, let me give you the facts: You are under arrest for numerous breaches of the Patriot Act among other laws in this country that prohibit acts of espionage. Under the law, we are permitted to hold you indefinitely, and we choose whether or not you will see any of your family ever again."

Saakadze gave a knowing chuckle.

"I get it. I cooperate, *then* I can see my family."

"I think that's the general position," O'Conner replied.

"We have an old expression in my country: Go fuck yourselves!"

"Isn't it amazing how well certain idiomatic expressions cross cultural divides?" McRory dryly observed.

"Come, boys and girls. At the Colonel's suggestion, we are all going to leave in order to go fuck ourselves." O'Conner looked back at Saakadze. "Enjoy your solitude, Colonel. Every minute you waste in this charade is one less minute you'll share with your new husband, that cute little baby, and your parents who have come to visit."

'Wait!" she yelled, but the three were already out of her room.

* * *

THE DNI BROUGHT Alexi Kaledin to visit with Saakadze, his former direct report.

"Katrina, hello," Kaledin began. Gesturing to the x-rays he adopted a more somber tone. "I'm told you do not have much longer to live."

"General," she returned the greeting with appropriate deference. "It's good to see you are alive and well. Are you receiving adequate treatment?"

"Katrina, we can dispense with the formalities, please. Yes, I'm being treated very well. Remarkably so under the circumstances."

"And those circumstances are?" her question lingered in the air between them.

"Come, Katrina. The laws are the same in both countries. Either I cooperated, or I would live the rest of my life in a shoe box, or if the saints are still with me, a quick death."

"What of the *Rodina*?" she asked.

"Katrina, the *motherland* died with the USSR. Are you the last to know the *New Russia* is open for capitalist business? A place where everything is for sale? Where everything has its price?"

"I cannot believe you, *General*."

"Believe me, Katrina. I had already received word that my many good years of faithful service were for naught. In words attributed to my old school-mate, Vladimir Putin, I was now considered to be a useful idiot.

"And, you, Katrina? Do you not know that people speak of you as the *Georgian*? Surely you are aware the term is used to draw a connection between you and Stalin? The same Stalin whose statues and commemoratives are now in junkyards and trash heaps all across Russia."

"I will not sell out my country, General," she spat.

"Katrina, don't be an idiot.

"This conversation—all of your conversations—are recorded or will be. What might the FBI and the CIA choose to share with our superiors in Russia? A little edit here or there a snippet of this or that video, and our former colleagues will not know what to believe.

"Actually, that is incorrect. They will know *exactly* what to think," he concluded.

"So, General, according to you I am already screwed. I can never go back. I must live here—or wherever they stick me—for the rest of my life. Is that it?"

"From what I've been told, Katrina, you signed your own death warrant when you authorized Littelwood to take his little trip into bumfuck Idaho.

"Listen carefully to the next advice I offer you: You may want to consider doing more than 'just cooperating.' You need to be the best traitor they've ever encountered—better than me, even. If not, then they'll put you and your family into some God forsaken shit hole, in the middle of nowhere, with a bare subsistence lifestyle. No more expensive homes, cars, clothing, shoes—and a very unhappy mother and father looking over your shoulder every miserable hour of every God forsaken day."

"Littelwood? Where is he?"

"Touching, Katrina. Now you care, huh?

"For your information, Littelwood is considered legally insane. These little drones swimming above you drove him crazy. He can't even speak without drooling now.

"Our captors are likely to smuggle him into the Ukraine—near the border—and set him free. Can you imagine the warm reception he'll receive?"

Saakadze and Kaledin spoke for another hour, after which he departed. When the door closed behind him, the drones came to a rest inches from her head.

She was unconscious, again.

* * *

THE MEDIC REVIEWED the instructions one last time.

"You insert the needle into the port on the IV bag. Inject the contents of the syringe into the bag. She'll regain wakefulness in less than a minute. Got it?" he asked.

"Got it," Linda replied.

The medic exited the room as the stenographer finished arranging her temporary work space.

"Ready, Gloria?" O'Conner asked.

"Ready," the stenographer replied.

O'Conner gave Linda a nod. Linda inserted the syringe and emptied its contents into the IV bag as earlier instructed. She carefully replaced the safety cap on the needle and deposited the used syringe in the collection box mounted on the wall.

Saakadze slowly emerged from her sleep state.

"How long have I been here?" she asked.

"Three days," O'Conner replied.

"I've been out for three days?"

"Yes, given your medical prognosis, we want to keep you as comfortable as we can. It will improve your willingness to cooperate."

For the next three hours, O'Conner asked a seemingly unending set of questions for which each of Saakadze's answers were faithfully recorded by the stenographer and the room's CCTV system. The questions checked, cross checked, and triple checked the same set of topics to ensure Saakadze's answers were consistent.

At the end of the session, the stenographer collected her equipment and departed leaving O'Conner and Linda alone with Saakadze—if the drones weren't counted.

"What's next?" Saakadze asked. "Will I be given the opportunity to finalize my personal affairs?"

"That depends on whether the answers you just provided are shown to be truthful."

"I've told you everything. The whole truth. Once word gets out, I'm a dead person," she lamented.

"You're already a dead person walking," Linda retorted, a broad smile on her face. "Of course, that's what this 'idiot' thinks."

Both O'Conner and Linda left the room. Only then did Saakadze realize the restraints were gone.

She unsteadily sat up in bed only to have the drones descend upon her.

* * *

IN THE DREAM, she was floating. She knew she was airborne because there were times when her feet were higher than her head, while at other times her head was above her feet.

At first, she heard the voice in the distance. She couldn't make out the words, but someone was yelling at her.

So very slowly, her mind began to operate before her limbs would respond to commands. After many attempts to open her eyes, she finally succeeded. Standing before her was a short man wearing a hard hat. Fresh air and light came streaming in through the door behind him.

"Ma'am, you can't be in here. We were told the unit was empty. You'll have to leave. Now!" he barked.

Saakadze made her way from the bed by holding on to the walls as she walked toward the open door. *No drones*, she thought to herself.

What she saw simply didn't register.

She wasn't in a hospital at all. She was in a shipping container. Half was outfitted as a hospital room complete with white drywall walls, ceiling tiles, and hospital linoleum floors. The other half of the shipping container was bare.

The container had been lifted by a crane and was now sitting on the back of a truck ready to be hauled away.

"What is this thing?" she asked the worker.

"This is a portable emergency room container. We use them at hospitals for disaster planning exercises and other health emergencies." He made the sign of the cross. "Thank God, we haven't had one of those for a while! They say we're overdue for the next 'big one.'"

"Where are we?" she asked.

"In the storage yard. You know. Where we keep these units stored and under power so they're ready to go when needed."

Saakadze did the math.

"Lady, you've got to go. This unit needs to be at San Francisco General in an hour. They're having a flu pandemic exercise in two days. Chop, chop," he said, hurrying her along. "Time is money."

Her phone buzzed in her jacket pocket. The text was from her neurologist's office: *Call immediately! Wrong patient x-rays. Sorry. Dr. Khan's office.*

CHAPTER 24

"**H**AVE YOUR STAFF HAD THE time to analyze the video and written record of Saakadze's interrogation?" Eddy O'Conner asked the DNI.

"Indeed, they have. They're thrilled—no ecstatic would be a better description—with her statements.

"They've also analyzed the audio to determine if she was truthful."

"And?" she queried.

"Again, she passed with flying colors."

"Can we close this chapter and move on?"

"Eddy, this isn't the end of anything. This is only the beginning—and a very promising start."

The DNI's voice took on a tone of retribution.

"We now know the Russians gained nothing in the way of actionable intelligence from young Mr. Lowandowski. We can breathe a sigh of relief on that point. What we don't yet know is whether Lowandowski took anything with him?

"Even if he didn't walk away with paper records, photographic materials, or other source documents, there's still something locked away inside his head. And the GRU would be more than satisfied to have access just to what he knows."

"Is this a scorched earth program? Do we take prejudicial action against Lowandowski?" she asked.

"Eddy, that's a term, 'prejudicial action' that takes me back to the Cold War days. The balance of our efforts is so skewed toward electronic intelligence and warfare these days that we have little invested in human intelligence. With the former, you just move from one operation to the next. The latter always involved some sort of wet work."

He sounded almost wistful.

"The congressional oversight committees used to have representatives and senators who understood the need for extreme measures. Today, there's less appetite for that sort of thing. And the folks at the White House don't really care whether we use extreme measures or not. All they worry about is micromanaging each operation.

"Give me the old Cold War days anytime. Things were a lot clearer then. We were clearer eyed back then."

"Sir, you didn't answer my question?" she noted.

"You noticed, did you?

"Eddy, we let you and your team run this operation the way you wanted. Sure, we arranged for the toys and that portable hospital room you put to such good use. But you made the calls."

"Plausible deniability?" she quizzed.

O'Conner could almost see the DNI wince when she used the term.

"There's an excellent example of one powerful person ruining a valuable concept. You can't even use the term without someone throwing Richard Nixon at you. I'm telling you, that man's legacy is like tar. You can never get rid of it once you step into it.

"Keep me posted."

He rung off.

It wasn't lost on O'Conner that she didn't receive a clear-cut answer to her last question.

* * *

THERE'S NOTHING LIKE a successful operation to lighten the mood in a room. The success of the Saakadze operation had both Alice Linda and Joe McRory in a state of euphoria.

O'Conner wasn't quite so thrilled.

"The DNI has asked me to run Colonel Saakadze," she announced.

Both Linda and McRory sensed her ambivalence.

"Has the CIA run out of controllers?" McRory asked.

"There is a jurisdictional issue," O'Conner replied. "By law, the FBI counter-intelligence folks would run the show."

"The same local FBI field office?"

Even McRory saw the questionable nature of the assignment.

"Yes, they do some of that now with the foreign embassies in DC, but it's not really their specialty. And, whenever the CIA is mentioned, the FBI folks go ballistic. Some rivalries will never end.

"The DNI wants a Cold War approach to handling the Colonel. Unfortunately, even that sort of experience is in short supply at the CIA, and because of jurisdictional constraints, the CIA would have to bring someone back from a European post to do the job. It's the only task this person would have. So there are inefficiencies—yada, yada, yada."

"What should we be doing to help?" Linda queried.

"Unfortunately, you can't. Plus, there's some additional bad news to report."

Both Linda and McRory were all ears.

"The DNI wants us to locate Lowandowski."

Linda took the lead.

"It's a big Pacific Ocean. He could have gone anywhere. And we don't have any cover to use. He knows us both."

McRory couldn't let the opportunity pass.

"Yeah, and he knows you a lot better than me."

Linda looked like she was ready to pounce.

"Geez, guys. Saakadze was right. You both *are* idiots."

CHAPTER 25

CHARLES LOWANDOWSKI BOUNCED FROM one small island in Vanuatu to another, all the while trying to reconstruct recent events. He felt foolish for having failed to recognize Alice Linda and Joe McRory were operatives for the federal government—especially Linda. He also feared for his safety. How had Sam Littelwood returned? Had everything he endured thus far, all his moves and counter moves against both groups been for naught?

Worst of all, Lowandowski was disappointed in himself. He wasn't the same person he'd once been, yet he acted as he always had: Fearful.

Lowandowski once believed if he fell far enough off the map— and Vanuatu was that—he would be safe from pursuit. Clearly, he was wrong.

He had traveled too far under his real name on a single fraudulent passport issued by Vanuatu. He realized too late that his reserve passport issued by the Philippines was unusable. Even the cover he developed as the child of bohemian parents living off the grid on a remote island in the Philippines was worthless.

He needed to exercise greater care to cover his tracks.

* * *

LOWANDOWSKI CAUGHT ONE ride after another, from one island to another, within Vanuatu. Immigration officers and controls were weak to non-existent, especially among the smaller, more remote islands. Vanuatu immigration authorities didn't fear being overrun by terrorists. Passengers disembarking from the small freighters and ferries hopping from one island to the next were expected to check in with the island's port authority. It was a quintessentially laid-back approach few nations could afford in today's world.

Lowandowski spent the daylight hours hanging around each island's harbor port. He watched the freighters and ferries arrive, drop-off their passengers and cargo, and depart. He read the travel itinerary and shipping schedule of each vessel. While most of the traffic originated and ended within the island nation, there was the occasional freighter from points west somewhere in Asia.

Lowandowski's new plan was based on the arrival of new cars to each island he frequented. These old beaters weren't new in a traditional sense, just new to Vanuatu. He started catching rides on the ships carrying the cars, which provided the opportunity to give each a closer look.

Other than their antiquity, the cars shared a common trait: Almost no residual value. If you were in Manila, you could buy any of these cars for less than fifty U.S. dollars. Here, in Vanuatu, the cars retailed for ten times that amount, and no one complained. Why? The true cost of the car was its transportation from some place in the real world to no place in Vanuatu.

* * *

IT TOOK ANTHONY Charles' parents the better part of a month to meet, settle down, and start a family. It took another month for Charles to be born, finish his public schooling, emerge two years younger, and acquire a new passport from the Philippines.

This time around, his parents weren't Americans who married and established a life on some remote island in the Philippines. That fiction maintained a tenuous connection to the U.S. In this iteration, Lowandowski—née Anthony Charles—wanted no connection whatsoever to the U.S. Instead, both of Charles' parents were Filipino mestizos. His new grandparents were couples of mixed races. His paternal grandfather was a Spaniard. His maternal grandmother was from France. At his heart, the new Anthony Charles, whose private school nickname was "Charlie," was European.

This time around, he wasn't home schooled. In fact, he was the product of a second-tier private international school with ambitions in Manila. He didn't just complete a public-school education, he had completed the more demanding International Baccalaureate program. And because he regretted not taking his real high school education seriously, he decided his reborn persona was every bit the scholar he wished he had once been.

* * *

CHARLIE READ EVERYTHING he could find about IB programs. He studied their curricula and downloaded copies of the suggested textbooks and reading assignments. Most of all, he read—actually devoured—and resolved to enjoy the experience. The "real" Charlie loved to read and his thirst for knowledge knew no limit.

During his brief gig with the airline, his supervisor encouraged him to learn conversational German. German speaking customer service representatives were in high demand and low supply mirroring the rapid growth in the German ex-pat community across the Philippines.

IB graduates were expected to be fluent in at least one foreign language. So he took the path of least resistance. German would be his new second language. Next, he needed to immerse himself in German culture. Other than Germany, Austria, or Switzerland, that left the ex-pat communities.

It was too soon to travel beyond the remote locales of the southern Pacific rim. Anthony Charles needed some additional work before he could venture forth under his new identity. For days he considered ex-pat communities in Australia, New Zealand, and the Philippines. In the end, his home country, the Philippines, won out.

There were ex-pat communities throughout the smaller Philippine islands. Getting there was the challenge.

The path of least resistance involved entering through Manila and picking a connecting flight to the island of his choice. The new

Charlie recognized choosing 'paths of least resistance" was both an avatar of his earlier life and usually carried an abundance of risk. The new Charlie gave thoughtful consideration to the alternatives before him. The new Charlie had a bias favoring experiences that widened his horizons and made him a better person.

The used cars were the answer.

Charlie became a student of the shipping schedules of the freighters carrying cars on their cargo manifests. It was a challenge Anthony Charles relished. He didn't search for the shortest journey. He looked for the one that broadened his knowledge.

In the end, he backpacked his way across the southern rim, visiting noted, and lesser known, archeological sites. The freighters became an inexpensive means toward that end.

He even started a diary to chart his course, made drawings, maps, and all of the things a well-educated traveler might do— especially a graduate of an IB program from a school with ambitions and high expectations for its graduates.

CHAPTER 26

MALAYBALAY CITY IS HOME to Bukidnon University on the island of Bukidnon. The island lies southeast of Manila with year around weather much better than what can be found in Zurich, Switzerland—according to Dorli Schmid. Most notable to Schmid is the complete absence of snow and ice. She could live with the rain and humidity, but she had her fill of the snow and ice she had known all of her life.

Schmid retired from the Business Faculty at the University of Zurich and moved to the Philippines when she discovered an active German ex-pat community on Bukidnon. Her pension and savings provided her with a comfortable standard of living on the island. Nevertheless, she easily secured a part-time position at the university where her new colleagues were overjoyed to have found a resident with Schmid's outstanding curriculum vitae and publication record.

Schmid combined several lots in a new subdivision and built a townhome much larger, and more modern than the family home she sold before leaving Zurich. She rented two of the bedrooms in her new home to further supplement her income as much as for the companionship of young people.

Her first tenant wasn't a native-born Filipino. His parents were clearly from some other place, but he had an interest in conversational German. He was working in one of the town's new international restaurants as the eatery's maître d' due, no doubt, to his warm personality and outgoing nature.

To Schmid, Anthony Charles was a most pleasant young man. As a bonus, he was quite fastidious, had a fascination with German language and culture, and his presence helped her ease the transition from Zurich to her new home in the Philippines. Best of all, Charles, or Charlie as he wished to be addressed, was a scholar, like herself. His current literary endeavor, the Greek classics, was a joy to her.

Schmid was impressed with Charlie's ability to master conversational German. The young man was clearly a polyglot, and a proven avid reader. He breezed through the popular magazines and newspapers she had delivered to her new home. In return, Charlie tutored Schmid in the use of a web browser where she could get her news from home on a timelier basis and at a great savings in cost. Charlie's presence presented an additional bonus: He spoke English exceptionally well for a Filipino. Schmid had the opportunity to work on her own mastery of English.

The two easily shifted the roles of teacher and student between them as the subject matter required.

Charlie was also a gifted mimic. He not only improved his facility with German, he acquired Schmid's accent as well.

* * *

SCHMID AND CHARLIE reserved the daily breakfast for a discussion of the day's events. She spoke in her improving English. He spoke in his near flawless German.

"You know, Charlie, at the university I always asked my students, 'What do you want to be?' It occurs to me that while we have had many conversations, I still have no understanding of your plans for your future."

"I've come to regret not continuing my education after high school," was his response. "I wasn't the best student. I've been traveling this past year using the opportunity to re-read the classics and visit some of the places about which I'd only read."

"Really, I've seen your school transcript. You did very well. Your schooling followed the International Baccalaureate model. That alone is noteworthy.

"You are being modest. No?" Schmid chided. "You cannot afford to hide your light under a bushel basket. At this point in your young life you have much more potential than demonstrated experience. You should be proud of your high school education. *Mein Gott im Himmel*, an IB graduate? And in the Philippines, no less!" She puffed out her chest in an exaggerated manner. "Be proud of what you've done here."

Charlie raised his hands in mock surrender.

"You win, Dorli," he laughed. "I don't want people to think I'm a braggart."

Schmid walked over to the coffee maker to pour a fresh cup.

"So, where do you want to study?"

Sticking to his falsified history, "I've spent my entire life in the Philippines. I love my home, but I want to go where the terrain is different, the people are different—and the weather is different!"

Schmid chuckled.

"Believe me, I understand your sentiment, especially the part about the weather. What would you think about my university—I mean my *former* university?"

"Is that a possibility?" he wondered aloud.

"Charlie, I sat in many meetings of the admissions committee over my career. I can tell you for a fact that we invited far less qualified young men and women to join us. If you like, I can contact my former colleagues on your behalf. Would you agree to my doing so?"

He sat there stunned. Is it possible I've finally caught a break, he thought?

"I don't know, Dorli. That would be an imposition, wouldn't it?" he asked.

"No, not at all, Charlie. It would be my pleasure." She paused. "There is one possible sticking point, however."

"Which is?"

"If you go to Zurich, the government will want to know if you can support yourself during your studies. I know it is impolite to discuss certain personal financial affairs. I certainly don't wish to intrude into your private matters. Can you provide such assurances?"

Charlie couldn't let Schmid know he was independently wealthy. Any revelations about his true financial picture would prompt a longer, more embarrassing discussion of his past. He chose to improvise instead.

"I have some money saved. Not much really. Could I work while I went to school?"

Schmid frowned. *Ah ha!* she thought to herself. *The fly in the ointment.*

"As a foreign student without a post-graduate degree, you would have to wait six months before you could look for work. Even then, you could only work fifteen hours a week." She paused. "Can you—as you say—swing that?"

Charlie knew the next stop in his travels was Switzerland.

This time, he would be ready.

CHAPTER 27

"**H**ello, Astrid. It's me, Dorli."

"Dorli Schmid, I know it's you. I can see your face on the Face Time window. *Mein Gott im Himmel!* Dorli Schmid using a computer—video conferencing no less. None of the other faculty will believe me."

Both women shared a laugh typical of those whose friendship spans many years.

"*Und so*, how did my young protégé do before the committee? You know he's very modest, that Charlie."

"Not to worry Dorli. He acquitted himself quite well indeed. He even answered my question about the Greek classics."

"Ach, Astrid, you and your damned fascination with your beloved Greek Classics. Which one did you quiz him?"

"Plato's The Republic."

"Ah, yes, one of your favorites."

"Dorli, nothing here changes. I ask the same set of questions. Those *dummkofen* on the admissions committee, sit there not knowing anything. And they are all university graduates. Not one of them could answer my questions."

"Charlie did?"

"He was magnificent, Dorli. We had to cut him short on the answer because of time limits."

"Will the committee recommend his admission?"

"*Mein Gott in Himmel*, of course, Dorli. We are talking about the baccalaureate program after all. He'll be at the top of his class. You watch."

"Good," Schmid was very pleased.

"And, Dorli, it doesn't hurt that he is so handsome. The women staff in our faculty are all—what is it the Americans say?—giving him the eye. Including Frau Meier—her especially."

"Meier?" Schmid was beyond belief. "She's old enough to be his mother!"

"True, Dorli, and she has a room to rent. You know, she always rents a room to one of our *male* students."

"The rumor was Frau Meier is in charge of the Continuing Education Program."

Both women chortled.

* * *

CHARLIE WAS IMPRESSED with Switzerland and especially Zurich. The town was expensive. It's shops and restaurants skewed toward the rich rather than struggling students.

Thank heavens I don't have to find a place to live, he mused as he walked along the Bahnhofstrasse. His new landlord, Frau Meier, owned a large flat and his room was very private, already furnished, and with its own ensuite. Better yet, the rent was a steal.

Frau Meier seemed disappointed Charlie would not be moving in immediately, even though he paid for the first three months in advance. With the student visa stamp in his passport, Charlie was going to take some time and see the sights before classes started for the fall term.

He leisurely made his way to the train station.

* * *

CHARLIE STOOD IN the only open line to purchase his student euro rail ticket. Two beautiful young women were ahead of him.

"I can hardly wait to see Venice," the dark haired, taller woman said to her friend.

"Yeah, Venice," the blonde friend was clearly less thrilled. "Been there, done that—with my parents." Her facial gesture at the word "parents" conveyed that they more than Venice were responsible for her less than effusive travel summary. "I'm really looking forward to Florence. After all my high school literary classes and art history courses, I can't believe I'm going to see things about which I've only read." Now she was enthused.

"Remember our pledge: no men."

"'Men?' What are they? I don't recall studying 'Men' in high school."

Both women laughed.

Charlie finally arrived at the front of the line.

"One student euro rail ticket, please?" he said.

"Passport and student Visa," the no nonsense rail clerk demanded—politely, but a demand nonetheless.

More than once the rail clerk compared the photo in the passport with Charlie's face. Charlie started to feel uncomfortable. The passport was the best money could buy. He feared the whole ruse could fall apart and his future ruined.

"How long?" the clerk broke through his worried state of mind which already had him being duck marched off to a Swiss jail.

"Sorry?" Charlie replied.

"How long?" the clerk repeated.

Charlie, still concerned his fraudulent passport didn't pass muster was too slow to respond. The young blonde overhearing the conversation and wanting to help stepped in.

"He wants to know how long you wish to travel by train."

Charlie was just climbing out of the deep hole his fear managed to dig. He wasn't prepared for the helpful intrusion. He was still lagging a second or two too long behind each of these conversations.

The blonde offered him a lifeline. Directing her attention to the clerk, she said, "He's traveling with us. He'll need to buy a two-month pass."

The clerk, eager to have this group on their way, looked to Charlie. "Is that correct, sir?"

Charlie looked at the young woman and nodded in the affirmative.

"What's wrong?" the blonde teased. "Cat got your tongue?"

While Charlie completed the financial transaction, the young woman returned to her disbelieving friend.

"I thought you said, 'no men'?"

They both laughed as they walked out of the station.

Charlie stuffed the paper currency left over from the purchase into his wallet. He apologized to the clerk for his behavior. The clerk smiled and whispered conspiratorially, "I wouldn't let that one get away."

Charlie smiled and ran to catch up to the girls. They were standing outside.

"Hey," he started. "Thank you for the assist." He jerked his thumb back in the direction of the rail clerk. "So, when do we leave?"

"The dark haired one leaned in "*We* aren't traveling together," she informed him.

"Oh, but I thought we were." He looked at the blonde putting on his best imitation of a confused facial expression.

"Tell you what," the blonde offered, "we'll let you buy us lunch. Then, my good friend and I will decide what, if anything, follows that."

"So this is what you mean by 'no men,'" her friend teased. "Ten minutes at the train station and you've already picked up this stray mutt."

"Hey!" both Charlie and the blonde admonished.

"Let me apologize for my friend's impolite behavior," the blonde continued the friendly tease. "She lacks any experience with men."

"That's why we're traveling together," the friend replied. "Lisa, has more experience with men than all of my other girlfriends put together."

Lisa wore that assessment as a badge of honor. She smiled to graciously accept the dubious accolade.

Turning to Charlie, "Beth just left the convent for the first time in her life. Men were only discussed in the books the library kept under lock and key. And Beth didn't read much," Lisa's tease was starting to wear a bit thin.

"Oh," Beth retorted. "I read a *lot*." Looking at Charlie, "I read a *whole* lot."

After the words left her beautiful mouth, she instantly realized how that must have sounded and what it implied.

Charlie, ever the gentleman, looped an arm around each of the two women and gently escorted them in the direction of a nearby eatery.

"Well, since we're all telling the truth," he said, "I have absolutely no experience with women—especially beautiful women."

Both women rolled their eyes casting doubt on his claim of inexperience.

All three laughed their way to lunch.

CHAPTER 28

JUDGING BY HER BRISK pace, Katrina Saakadze had fully recovered from her bout of drone-*itis* and the usually terminal glioblastoma. She pushed the stroller into the coffee shop. Like the other mothers, she parked the stroller at an empty table and made her way to the Baristas to place her order. The whole time she kept one eye on the child.

Eddy O'Conner claimed one of the two empty seats. She looked into the stroller fussing over the infant.

By now, Saakadze was no longer shocked whenever she ran into O'Conner. The coffee shop, grocery store, the gym, and even her OB-GYN's office—no establishment seemed out of bounds. She doubled her usual order.

Walking back to her table, she glanced inside the stroller to ensure nothing untoward took place in her absence.

"Here, I got one for you too," she said as she lowered the plastic tray to the table.

"Which one is mine?" O'Conner asked.

"The one with the extra dose of strychnine," she responded. Her attitude as straightforward and absent any emotion, like having stated, "two sugars."

Not one to take a chance, O'Conner swapped the two cups.

"Here's to your continued good health," O'Conner toasted just loudly enough for Saakadze to hear.

"Well, you know how it is," Saakadze dryly observed, "One day you're a terminal patient, the next you're the picture of health."

O'Conner teased, "I wonder when the 'Stockholm Syndrome' kicks in for you?"

"For you?" Saakadze was flabbergasted. "Never!"

O'Conner smiled sweetly, "You're just too good to me. I don't deserve it."

"You're right about that," Saakadze countered. "If you like, I can give you a list of the things you do deserve."

"My list for you would be much, much longer. And here's the kicker. On my list there's a toss-up between two different outcomes: The first, life in prison here. The second, a firing squad for you back in the Rodina."

"The *Rodina*?" Saakadze projected mild shock. "Haven't you heard? The Rodina died with the fall of the Berlin Wall, thanks to Comrade Gorbachov. The New Russia, the Russia of Vladimir Putin, is open for the business of capitalism, comrade."

"Almost word for word what Alexi Kaledin told you back in the hospital. You remember? When you were convinced you were dying from brain cancer?" O'Conner threw a reproachful look in Saakadze's direction.

"What do you want, comrade?" Saakadze relented. "What is it now?" She blew over the top of her coffee cup to cool the liquid and then took a tentative sip. "Do you want to know if Vladimir wears boxers or briefs?"

"If I did," O'Conner replied, "You would be the first—the only, actually—person I'd ask. Surely you would know." O'Conner pushed the coffee cup aside. "Too much strychnine. It leaves an after taste."

This skirmish was over. The war? That was doubtful.

O'Conner got down to the real business of her drop-by visit.

"How did your people know where to find Charles Lowandowski?"

"How am I supposed to know?" Saakadze responded.

"Sam Littelwood made the trek to Vanuatu. Surely, he didn't stick a pin in the map, like pin the tail on the donkey, and just happened to land on a small island in the south Pacific. And, oh yes, he used to work for you. He reported directly to you."

"Why would anyone try to pin a tail on a donkey?" Saakadze inquired. "I may still be learning about your country, but even I know donkeys have a mean temperament. In my country, we would ask: Why poke the bear? Both sound stupid."

"Bears, yes," O'Conner thoughtfully responded. "Slow, ponderous, hibernates a fair amount of the year. You would seem to know a lot about bears—and let's not forget, Vladimir's personal preference in undergarments." She briefly paused. "Easy to trick a bear. Easy to trick you."

Saakadze had enough of this interplay.

"If I'm supposedly so slow and ponderous, then how did I know you were the one to fly to Vanuatu?" She arched her eyebrows to mock O'Conner. "You lead us directly to him. It was so easy I could send someone like Littelwood rather than waste the time and effort of a better qualified operative."

At that point, O'Conner slipped her hand into her bag.

"Oh please," Saakadze objected. "Don't tell me that I've wounded you so badly that you're going to pull out your big American gun and shoot me?"

"Why would I ever waste the ammunition," O'Conner countered. "After all, you have a gun. You have ammunition. And you've proven quite adept at shooting your own feet."

There are some expressions that traverse the cultural divide without requiring further explanation. This was one of those cases.

Instead of a gun, O'Conner withdrew five surveillance photographs and laid them out on the table before Saakadze.

"This is the entirety of your—what should I call it?—*day* labor force. Each a fine example of tradecraft. Five of this country's dregs that are so poor at what they do that they stand on the corner outside of the local lumber yard on the lookout for work opportunities."

Saakadze said nothing. She drank her coffee. Her face giving away nothing.

"Just give me the word. I can have all five picked up. You'll never see them again. How would you explain the loss of your entire 'inventory' of 'studs'?"

Saakadze laughed exactly once. "Even I got that one. Standing outside a *lumber* store." She poked O'Conner in the elbow. "*Studs* are wooden 2 by 4's. Aren't you the clever one?"

"Alexi was right about you, right about Georgians," O'Conner was twisting the knife. She knew that Kaledin did not consider Saakadze his best operative. And she also knew how Stalin was consigned to the trash heap of history within the New Russia, and with him the less than glowing regard true Russians had for their Georgian cousins.

The mention of Kaledin and her ancestry gave O'Conner the upper hand.

The end of the second skirmish. Proof the war was not yet at an end.

"Again, Eddy, what do you want?"

"The name is '*Ms. O'Conner*' to you, comrade."

"Stop referring to me as 'comrade.' When spoken aloud, the term attracts attention in your country—with its unhealthy obsession with communism and communists. The use of the word is hardly subtle. It is nasty and brutish. Much like you, I suppose. You're all cowboys here. I know. I married one."

O'Conner smiled, yet again. Enough was enough.

"Speaking of whom," O'Conner began, "imagine his shock and horror if he was to learn he married a *Georgian*, a spy, and not a very good one at that?"

"Men," she clucked. "There are always other fish in the sea."

"True, that," O'Conner acknowledged. "But in this country, the courts would take away your child. He will raise your son. Neither you nor your parents would ever see the baby again."

The last statement brought an end to the third skirmish of the day and all other possible atrocities that might have otherwise followed.

"Again, I ask, what do you want, *Ms. O'Conner*?"

O'Conner flashed a cruel smile. "That's better, much better, in fact. Here's what *we* want you to do."

Their meeting lasted only a few more minutes. When she was done, O'Conner left the shop, but not before reaching into the stroller to rub the infant's stomach.

* * *

ALICE LINDA AND Joe McRory sat across the street from the coffee shop. The interior of the unmarked panel van held the latest in audio and video technology along with two technicians who could put the electronic surveillance packages through the necessary paces.

All four individuals had a front row seat on the cage match that ended when O'Conner took her leave.

"Remind me to never piss off Eddy," Linda said under her breath.

"It's a bit late for that, isn't it," McRory countered.

The panel van had a roof vent which was opened just enough to keep the van and the electronics from overheating. McRory opened the box and three of the drones spiraled their way toward the ceiling and out into the open air of the street.

Saakadze pushed the stroller out of the shop and back in the direction of the nearby BART station and her townhome in Oakland. The drones took up surveillance but at a height where it was unlikely they'd be noticed.

Saakadze reached into her stylish Burberry raincoat to withdraw her cellular phone. The drones were too high to capture the audio, but they continued to stream the video of her walking in the direction of the BART station.

"Yes, the damned O'Conner woman barged in on me, again. This time at the coffee shop."

The entire conversation was captured and streamed back to the panel van. The wafer-thin device lay on the stomach of her child but hidden under the baby's shirt. O'Conner knew Saakadze would discover the transmitter, too late of course.

Game, set, match.

CHAPTER 29

Eddy O'Conner WAS IN A foul mood. It didn't escape notice by Alice Linda and Joe McRory.

"Eddy, why let Colonel Saakadze get under your skin like this?" Linda asked. "Your *bona fides* are well established in this business. You have the full support of the DNI. Who cares if she fails to show any respect?"

O'Conner hadn't realized she was openly wearing her discontent. She smiled at both Linda and McRory.

"I'm sorry," she said. "It's a family thing that has me distraught. Trust me, it's not the good Colonel."

"Anything you wish to discuss?" McRory was being solicitous. "We'd understand if you didn't. After all, everyone has 'family issues.'"

O'Conner thought before she spoke and then chose her words carefully.

"I've been particularly close to one of my nieces. When she was younger, we corresponded all the time." O'Conner paused to drink her coffee. "I was away during that period. So we had not met. I was an abstraction to her—the whole family now that I think about it. Yet, this sweet child wrote to me faithfully. As she grew older and came to understand her siblings, parents, aunts and uncles better, she was my only connection to my own family. I kept in touch with everyone through her eyes, her thoughts, and her words.

"Now, she's fallen off the grid. I know she's getting my text messages—I hate communicating with her by texting. During the last year or so, we spoke often. We even spent time together. And now I don't know whether to be concerned by her quietude.

"I know my sister is worried, too. Although, she has two other children, a bit older, who screen her calls. But now that my niece is away in Europe, this lack of basic communication cannot last much longer before I take action."

"Let us know if we can help," McRory added. Linda nodded her agreement.

There was an awkward pause in the conversation that served as segue to more pressing local matters.

"What did you think about Saakadze's cooperation?" O'Conner asked the two.

Linda jumped in, "She's showing a ton of attitude to someone who has life or death power over her."

"Back in the day," O'Conner responded, "we ran operatives. Some came to us willingly because they found the East German regime corrupt and they had enough. The Stasi had everyone in the GDR spying on their own families, neighbors, and fellow workers. It truly was horrible.

"We also had some of their highly placed party members in compromising positions. The sort of circumstances where their disappearance and death were guaranteed if we let our information become known."

"Did that ever happen?" Linda queried.

"Only in exceptional cases.

"One that comes to mind involved a highly placed Stasi executive. We had him dead to rights. We made our expectations clear to him—things we wanted him to do, but more importantly, people on our side we wanted him not to harm."

"What happened?" Linda was fully engaged.

"We didn't mind if he dragged in for questioning one of the folks we wanted to protect. We were prepared to overlook some rough treatment, because it was what the Stasi did."

O'Conner could tell Linda and McRory wanted to hear more details.

"If you had the misfortune of being picked up on the street, or dragged from your home and family, everyone knew you might not return. That's the way it was in the GDR. People learned to look the other way, but deep in their own thoughts you knew they were saying, 'There but for the grace of God, goes I.'

"Almost no one walked out of Stasi headquarters unscathed. They were locked away for days—sometimes weeks. The torture and questioning, complete deprivation, spies in the jails reporting anything you said, even in your sleep, if you managed to get any sleep. It was horrible.

"The few let free returned to their homes filthy, bedraggled, and scarred for life—mentally and physically.

"Worse yet, it wasn't unusual for Stasi patrol activity and surveillance activity to increase after your release. That made everyone in the neighborhood fearful. The reports about anyone's activities, even the most mundane, were possible acts against the state. It wasn't unknown for spouses to take the children and move in with a relative. So many suicides.

"The Stasi could make your life a living hell."

"This Stasi executive crossed the line," McRory suggested.

"My superiors thought his behavior was on the borderline, and they instructed me to tell him so. But I knew this gentleman very well. Our periodic chats made the one I had with the colonel look tame.

"I took matters into my own hands."

"Didn't your superiors have a problem with your—" McRory had some trouble before finding the right word, "initiative?"

"I was in the GDR. They were either across the border in the FRG or here in the U.S. They may have had their suspicions. But I took the 'initiative' I believed appropriate and *just*. Sometimes, life puts you in those circumstances."

Looking at both, she ended the story by stating, "I sleep very well, Alice, Joe. Very well indeed."

CHAPTER 30

ONCE AGAIN, ANOTHER WARNING message from Henley: Expect a call from the DNI within the next five minutes, Henley.

"Hello, Sir," Eddy greeted her expected caller.

"Hello back at you, Eddy," he responded.

O'Conner could hear talking in the background. She could also hear the DNI making an effort to mute his end of the call by placing his hand over the microphone. This went on for several more seconds, although it felt much longer to her.

"Sorry about that, Eddy. We've had a number of developments on our end.

"Placing the dummy wafer transmitter under the child's shirt worked as planned. Saakadze smuggled the device to the GRU's technical branch folks. They got it out of the country via the diplomatic pouch."

"What did they find?" O'Conner asked.

"Unfortunately, we don't yet have anyone inside their technical group. We were only able to track the device's receipt at the consulate and from there into the diplomatic pouch and on to Russia.

"We do know the folks in their technical branch aren't stupid. If they haven't discovered by now that you planted an intentionally damaged piece of silicon on the baby, they will very soon."

"It was certainly a good decoy," O'Conner stated. "I wonder how long it will take the Colonel to discover the real transmitter that's still embedded in the stroller?"

"Our technical folks tell me that depends on how well you inserted the device into the fabric."

"They had me practice insertions for the better part of an hour. Toward the end, I managed to push it under the stitching and into a seam in the material. I'm willing to wager it will take her a while."

"God help me," the DNI confessed, "I do so love this part of the game. Let's talk about the directives you gave her."

"As we agreed, I made it clear they needed to find Lowandowski—but not why," Eddy reminded the DNI.

"Walk the timeline," he suggested. "At the point you gave the order, she didn't know we were listening. Good tradecraft would suggest she assumed as much, however."

"Then she left the shop to return home," Eddy continued on the time line. "She felt comfortable enough to call someone in her command, report my unexpected intervention into her morning schedule, and the substance of our conversation. We have to assume that she didn't discover the fake bug until after her conversation ended. Possibly as late as arriving at her home with the baby."

"Our friends at the NSA picked up her telephone call. The usual tradecraft practices. She used a burner phone and replaced the SIM card after the call. Nevertheless, we got the conversation."

The DNI was pleased.

"To whom did she speak?" Eddy wanted to know.

"Her new supervisor works out of Vancouver. We think the assignment is temporary until they can transition someone with impeccable credentials into the U.S. That could take a while," the DNI reported.

"This person works out of the Russian Consulate there? The main building on Granville?" Eddy asked.

"No. The temporary controller works out of their satellite visa processing office on West Broadway," he replied.

"Good cover," she said. "Lots of calls coming into the Visa office, probably foot traffic as well."

"'True that,' as my youngest grandson is fond of saying. Unfortunately, we must work through our contacts in Canada. Doing so slows us down a bit. And we always have to worry about what they're *not* telling us." He paused. "We're waiting on the Canadians to share the identity of Saakadze's contact there. Perhaps we'll know a bit more over the next several days."

"It would help to know now."

"Yes, I agree, but we can't change the facts on the ground. So, let's review, shall we?

"We all prefer to make decisions under absolute certainty of the ground truth. There are fewer contingencies to anticipate, tactics we don't have to simulate and plan, and Lord knows fewer assets to deploy."

"Some things never change," Eddy agreed. "But we're making decisions with a fair amount of *uncertainty*."

"True. Our objective remains simple, however. We want to put our hands on Charles Lowandowski. We need to know what he knows. What he has locked up inside his head."

Eddy knew what was coming next.

The DNI continued, "Failing that, we want Lowandowski terminated with extreme prejudice. We want him gone. The congressional oversight committees are getting closer to a discussion about what happened in that local FBI office. It's only a matter of time before they start playing the waltz and I'm called to dance over to the Hill and brief them."

"They'll want answers to questions you don't *yet* have," Eddy cautioned.

"Either we get our hands on Lowandowski, fully debrief him, and verify what we can, or I report he's no longer a problem. The committee staff will recommend to their members there's nothing to be gained with their involvement if we prevail on the former."

"What of the *latter* option?" Eddy persisted.

"Termination with extreme prejudice?" he replied.

"Yes, that," she responded.

"The members will want to poke around in the details. They'll peel me like an onion. It's not the discomfort to which I object," he laughed. "I'm a very old onion. I've been peeled many times in the past. I suspect I'll be peeled a few more times before I retire, or the president sends me home with my pension.

"I don't welcome the prospect of our duly elected senators and representatives walking around with that kind of knowledge. Sooner or later—but always at the most inopportune moment—those details will come tumbling forth. After that, everything turns into a real shit storm, pardon my French.

"They'll hold meetings, formulate legislation, and discuss what they can in public—which is always too much. In the end, we'll have even more laws restricting what we can and cannot do. Worse yet, the FBI's reputation in counterintelligence will suffer a public loss of confidence.

"That's why I am reluctant to authorize termination."

"What if there's no other viable option?"

"Just to be clear, Eddy, what are you suggesting?"

"Sir, I've already mounted a substantial effort at corralling Lowandowski. It took us two months to find him. It took another month to complete our preliminary surveillance. Finally, we spent a full fourth month in the honey pot. And we have nothing to show for the effort.

"He's given us the slip twice now. Once in Washington, DC, and another in Vanuatu. At each stage of our pursuit, he's demonstrated a growing mastery of tradecraft.

"If we do manage to locate him, who's to say we'll have any more success, let alone whether we can do all of that in a timely manner?"

"You're recommending termination?"

"Yes," she insisted. "I am."

"You still have to find him? How long will that take?"

The DNI already knew the answer.

"Too long, sir. I have another suggestion."

"Which is?"

"We've already chummed the water, so to speak, with the Colonel. We've told her of our continuing interest in Lowandowski—"

"True," the DNI interrupted. "Go on."

"But *not* why we're still interested. We need to tell the Russians that Lowandowski started doing his own research in addition to what the FBI succeeded at doing. We need to plant the belief in the Colonel's mind that Lowandowski has a complete map of their North American network."

"So you want to outsource the termination of Lowandowski to the Russians."

"I do. And if we succeed at raising the stakes, they'll stop at nothing to get the job done."

* * *

WHILE O'CONNER WAS on the phone with the DNI her phone accepted a text message. She was not a digital native capable of multi-tasking on her phone. She made a mental note to check the text at the end of her conversation. Before she could do that, Alice Linda and Joe McRory entered her apartment.

"We have new tasking on Lowandowski," O'Conner's opening statement was a bit of a surprise.

"Not another honey pot, I hope," Linda replied.

"I didn't mind the time in Key West and Vanuatu," McRory observed. "Where's the next stop on the Lowandowski tour?"

"There isn't," she said to Linda, and turning to McRory, "We aren't going anywhere."

Both looked flummoxed.

"We're going to let the Russians do the work for us."

CHAPTER 31

THE VISIT BY KATRINA SAAKADZE'S PARENTS—the adoring grandparents—was extended several times. Recently, all talk of returning to their home came to an end. They applied for a green card and permanent residency. They also assumed full-time child care duties leaving their daughter and son-in-law with more time to spend on their careers and leisure time together. As a result, the new parents were often out of their house.

Over the next week, Alice Linda and Joe McRory stuck to Saakadze like glue. Their surveillance didn't follow the best tradecraft, far from it, in fact. They made it a point to be obvious in shadowing Saakadze. In fact, they were often within several feet of her no matter where she went, and she was out of her townhome a lot.

One of them stood next to her in line at the coffee shop. They shopped for produce at Whole Foods at the same time. They boarded the same BART subway cars. Linda even followed her into the restroom. Their conduct went well beyond harassment, but under the circumstances Saakadze couldn't get the police involved.

Saakadze's patience fell just shy of the breaking point when Linda and McRory asked to sit at the café table occupied by Saakadze and her husband.

"Katrina, hello!" Linda gushed. "We seem to run into you all the time now."

Saakadze's husband looked surprised that his wife knew the couple but never made mention of them. He made the requisite social greeting.

"Hi," he said. "I'm Katrina's husband, Guy. It's nice to meet you."

McRory extended his hand in friendship.

"I'm Joe," he said.

"I'm Alice," she added.

Everyone smiled, although Katrina's smile was a bit forced.

"How do you know Katrina?" her husband asked.

Linda turned to McRory.

"You know, Joe, I was trying to recall how we met. It seems we've known each other forever, but I can't recall when we first got together."

McRory followed up.

"Alice, you make it sound like we work together." Looking at Katrina's husband, "We both work from home. We're out in the neighborhood more than most of our neighbors. So we found ourselves in the same places, at the same times as Katrina."

"And don't forget that beautiful baby," Alice gushed, again. "Speaking of that handsome devil, where are you hiding him?"

The husband, eager to make up for his lost time in this supposed relationship, plowed ahead.

"The little monster is at home with Kat's parents. They're visiting from Europe and totally in love with the little guy. So we scored some 'alone time,' if you know what I mean?"

His arm bumped against McRory's in a non-verbal point of emphasis. McRory was quick to pick up on the message.

"I know *exactly* what you mean, Guy. When our little ones entered the picture, 'us' sort of disappeared. It became all about them. It's taken us years to get something of our private relationship back. Otherwise, we're mom and dad twenty-four by seven."

"That's what you have to look forward to," Alice whispered conspiratorially. "Not so much 'Guy and Kat' any more. Instead, it's always mom and dad." She paused to dab at her eyes. "But I love the little bastards. What can I say?"

The meal and bonhomie extended for over an hour. Toward the end, "Kat's" face was hard as stone.

"Listen," her husband started, "what do you say we all take in a movie tonight? I'm dying to see the latest Star Wars flick."

Katrina started to object, "Sweetheart, I think my parents planned an evening out together."

"What? Those two? You've got to be kidding me?" Turning to Linda and McRory, "One of them is always holding our kid. They're totally dedicated to him." Turning back to his wife, "Hon, we need the night out. What do you say?"

* * *

SAAKADZE WAS PROVOKED. She didn't mind being tailed by the two dolts. They provided her with the definitive lessons on what not to do in tradecraft. Having to socialize with them, however, was another matter altogether. This especially after the cruel hoax of the glioblastoma and her humiliation when she finally discovered her medical emergency was a cruel joke.

Her professional pride would not let these transgressions go without some tit-for-tat.

That evening before leaving for the theater, she placed a switch blade in her pocketbook.

* * *

GUY AND KAT walked arm in arm to the theater lobby where they met up with Alice and Joe.

McRory broke the ice.

"I purchased the tickets while we waited for you to arrive."

Guy was embarrassed.

"Dude, that's a nice gesture, but really, let me pay you back?"

"No, it's our treat."

"Well, how about you let us buy you both a cup of coffee after the show?"

No one said "no."

As they turned to enter, Kat saw the metal detector.

"What's this about?" she asked.

"It's becoming a standard precaution," Alice responded and then adopting a more somber tone. "After the shootings in Colorado, the theaters started doing this—" she pointed to the detector "—to ease tensions. Notice the police are on duty here as well."

Kat moved to withdraw her phone from her purse.

"It's my mom," she announced to them all. "I'll be but a moment. Let me take the call outside."

The three stood by and watched Saakadze make her way to the sidewalk outside the theater where she appeared to be conversing with her mother.

"That's odd," her husband remarked.

"New grandparents? First grandchild?" Linda asked.

"Yeah. But they already act as if they've been around infants forever. I can't recall Kat's mother ever calling after we've left the house."

"It's probably nothing, Guy," McRory tried to assuage the husband's concern.

* * *

SAAKADZE WALKED OUT of their view and around the corner to the large parking lot while holding up her end of the non-existent telephone call. Looking around, but seeing no one nearby, she pulled the knife from her purse and set it atop of the front tire of one of the parked cars.

It wasn't obvious unless you stooped to deliberately examine the car's wheel well.

One more scan of the area to ensure no one saw her deed, she made her way back to the theater lobby to join the waiting threesome.

* * *

ONE HUNDRED AND fifty minutes later, the two couples stood outside the theater.

"Sweetie, we do need to get back to mom and dad. This is the longest we've left them alone with the baby."

"Sure we can't lure you away to a cozy café for a nightcap?" Alice teased.

Guy might have been a new husband, but he'd learned to read his wife's mood. She wanted to return home.

"Kat's probably right. We should check in on the grandparents. Make sure everything's okay on the home front. What would you say about getting together during the week. Early dinner? Nothing fancy. Pizza, Chinese, whatever?"

Kat's reluctance to spend time with Linda and McRory suddenly melted away.

"That's a great idea," she blurted out.

Both Linda and McRory didn't have to feign surprise. They were shocked!

Kat moved in on Linda giving her a big hug and a kiss on both cheeks.

"This was great. We had a good time. See you for dinner? I'll call and we can set the day."

As they walked away, McRory leaned in and whispered, "She doesn't have your telephone number—does she?"

Linda leaned away giving him an idiot's appraisal.

"Are you fucking crazy?" she asked.

Then, she pointed to her jacket pocket. Pulling the flap out permitted him to see the listening device Saakadze planted a few moments earlier.

McRory indicated he understood.

As the turned to walk away, Linda started a conversation for Saakadze's benefit.

"How much longer do we keep this up?" she asked.

"Until we know she's done what Eddy tasked her to do," he replied.

"We know she hasn't done that yet. What makes you think she'll call in a three-alarm fire to find Lowandowski?" Linda challenged.

"I asked Eddy the same question. I don't know why we can't tell her the truth?" McRory was a convincing idiot.

"Geez, are you dense? What are we going to say, 'Hey, Kat, Lowandowski has a complete list of the GRU's operations in North America?" Linda's taunting of McRory wasn't acting. Her belittlement of him was well honed through practice.

"Why not?" McRory responded. "Do we care if Lowandowski lives or dies?"

"Kat was right about you. You *are* an idiot. Of course, we want him alive. We need the information he has."

They silently high fived one another.

* * *

SAAKADZE'S JOG TOOK her past the now empty parking lot early the next morning. She found her knife, somewhat worse for the wear, and thought about the recorded conversation from last evening.

The old Saakadze wouldn't have given the matter a second thought.

Who knows what Alexi Kaledin has told the U.S intelligence agencies? She reminded herself. So what if the U.S. knew the structure and placement of the GRU network. Worse come to worst, she'd be placed in another post somewhere else. She might even make her way back to Moscow.

The new Saakadze had a husband, a new infant, and her parents were prepared to emigrate and live with her. This wasn't solely about her any longer. Truth be told, living in the Bay Area spoiled her. Moscow no longer held the appeal it once did.

She gave the proposition additional thought for the balance of her morning run. Later that day she made a telephone call to Vancouver.

"Hello, thank you for calling the Russian Consulate. How may I assist you?"

"Hi, I'm calling to check on the status of my visa application," Saakadze replied.

"Your name, please?"

A few moments later, her call was forwarded to a consular official.

"Hello, this is Pyotr Grishna speaking. To whom do I have the pleasure of speaking?" he politely inquired.

"I'm Katrina Saakadze, cousin to Yuri Gagarin," she replied.

"Hello, Kat. What's new?"

"Our cousin has become a problem."

"Yes, we discussed his behavior during our last conversation. Our family elders do not see any reason to do what you've been asked to do. Has anything changed?"

"You could say that," she responded. "He's purchased a subscription to one of those genealogy services. The idiot has managed to recreate our entire family tree."

"Everyone?" Grishna prompted.

"Everyone," she replied.

"It's not a problem if all of our relatives already know," Grishna counseled. "It's only a problem if some of our more remote relations received an unexpected visit from a long-lost family member."

"Oh, I think many of our distant relatives will be very surprised. There are likely to be many unexpected visits."

* * *

IN AN EARLY morning staff meeting in GRU headquarters, the discussion had been brief and to the point. The working assumption thus far held that Alexi Kaledin had yet to spill his guts. It was a tenuous assumption among the group. Some held the belief more ardently than others.

Those distrustful of Kaledin would think the worst of him no matter what. The most recent news from America via Vancouver did much to buoy Kaledin's detractors.

He still had his supporters, however. They believed no matter how long the Americans held him captive, Kaledin would never give up state secrets.

The decision: Play it safe. Find and terminate Lowandowski.

CHAPTER 32

EDDY O'CONNER WAS JOINED on her apartment terrace by Alice Linda and Joe McRory for a light lunch.

"The DNI tells me nothing's changed," O'Conner reported. "Whatever you said to her last night failed to push her over the edge."

"I guess we'll continue to socialize with our new best friends," Linda's disappointment was obvious.

McRory didn't look any happier.

O'Conner sensed the need to change topics.

"Let's discuss the new opportunities the DNI has asked Triple Play to undertake, *after* Colonel Saakadze sounds the alarm." O'Conner was using the promise of future assignments throughout Europe as an inducement to complete the current task.

"There are assignments in three different sets of city pairs: London and Paris, Vienna and Zurich, and Rome and Florence."

"Why 'pairs,' Eddy?" McRory inquired.

"Budgets are getting tighter—even in national security. The three pairs are where the CIA, FBI, and Homeland Security have combined staff" she explained.

"That sounds stupid," McRory interjected. "What dumb ass bean counter decided to combine those six cities into three pairs?"

"Joe, the DNI assures me it wasn't a decision made lightly. They've run into budget ceilings. As people retired, resigned—or worse—replacements haven't been available. Camp Peary has been running smaller than usual classes. Last year, they didn't have an entering class at all. So the pipeline of replacements is out of kilter."

"We're going to fill in the gaps?" he asked.

"You got it," she answered. "The work won't always be challenging. We'll be filling in here and there. Most often we'll join operations already underway. But it's work we've all done in our past.

"So, who wants London and Paris?"

"Me," Linda responded.

"Joe, can you take Italy? I'd like to go to Vienna and Zurich," O'Conner stated.

"Can't," he replied.

"Why not?" both Linda and O'Conner asked.

"I was PNG'd in Italy. I set foot in Italy, and you'll never see or hear from me again," Joe reminded them of his past experience.

O'Conner was clearly disappointed. She looked to Linda.

"Eddy, two points. First, I've done a lot of work in Italy. While I don't have Joe's notoriety, I do know a lot of people there. Not all of them think kindly of me. I'm reluctant to press my luck. Second, I was the honey pot in Vanuatu. That has to count for something."

"It's settled then," O'Conner unhappily summarized.

They spent the remainder of the afternoon reviewing the ongoing operations in each geographic locale.

At the day's end, O'Conner received a text from Henley. Five minutes later, the DNI was calling.

"Eddy, good news. NSA picked up a telephone call to the Vancouver visa office in the Russian Consulate. The Colonel took the bait. She sounded the alarm."

O'Conner was perplexed. "When did she make the call?"

"About 90 minutes ago," the DNI reported. "Why is that of concern?"

O'Conner explained.

"Eddy, you may be over thinking matters. I'm sure there's a reasonable explanation for the delay. She has a new baby. Her parents are in residence." He laughed. "I can tell you that a visit from my in-laws—especially when the kids were small—turned my household upside down. Maybe she couldn't break loose to make the call until later in the day.

"Listen, I'll share your concerns with the folks here. Maybe some of our experts can come up with a reasonable explanation.

"Have you reviewed the new assignments with your colleagues," he asked—clearly a deliberate change in topic.

"I have. Linda is going to London and Paris. McRory is going to Vienna and Zurich—"

"—and you're going to Italy. Good call. McRory wouldn't be welcomed in Italy given his high profile last time around. See if he can't stay out of trouble while he's in Vienna and Zurich.

"Anything else," he asked.

"No, sir. I think we've covered it all."

"Good. Each of you are to check in with the head of station right after you land. No one will be at the airport to do a 'meet and greet.' We want your entry to be low key.

"Oh, before I forget. Each of you will be staying at the embassy compounds. All embassies are providing meals and groceries as well.

"Talk soon."

And he was gone.

O'Conner shared the information on logistics. No one was pleased—including O'Conner.

CHAPTER 33

ALICE LINDA WAS INTO HER third day in the new embassy compound. Her "quarters" was a throwback to contemporary university dorm rooms with communal areas designed for group activities—even meal preparation.

She hated it.

An hour later she was walking around Victoria Station. She drafted behind a group of rowdy soccer fans into a sports grill and pub located inside the cavernous station.

The noise was at its peak.

"What time does our train leave for Bath?" The voice came from the group she'd followed, but it was too noisy to determine which of the group had asked the question.

The answer was an over ripe mélange of gutter language, idiom, a reference to balls and someone's mother. Linda was comfortably certain the "balls" had nothing to do with sports equipment.

If only the British pub owners adopted the practice of chilling their beer.

This was her kind of place.

* * *

JOE MCRORY'S EXPERIENCE differed. The embassy staff placed him in a nicely furnished two bedroom flat with all of the conveniences he'd come to expect.

He arrived too late to join in the formal dinner hour the embassy staff embraced. As he walked past the dining room, he overheard several spirited conversations. The topic was the president and one of his recent tweets.

No one was defending the president's behavior.

This wasn't his first stay in Zurich. Far from it.

McRory still harbored fond memories of going to the opera and the activities afterward. Nothing could top the coffee and pastries served in Zurich's cafes—except of course, those in Vienna.

And then there was the skiing.

* * *

EDDY O'CONNER HAD the sense she was being followed.

She took the Leonardo da Vinci express train from the airport to the train station in downtown Rome. Instead of making her way to the embassy, she found the track for the departing train to Milano. Once aboard, she made her way forward from one car to the next. She kept an eye on her tail as she did so.

The woman tailing O'Conner didn't expect her to remain in the station let alone board a train for Milano. She turned from the platform and made her way to the ticket agent windows where she purchased passage for one.

The final call for the Milan departure was announced on the overhead speakers. The woman sped up her pace as she searched for her assigned car.

O'Conner used those last moments and the ensuing confusion on the platform to step off the train. Once safely away from the platform she turned to watch the train slowly depart. When the train was out of the shed, and now absent her tail, O'Conner made her way to the taxi rank.

* * *

LINDA HAD THE presence of mind to hold her drinking to a minimum. She was still a bit jet lagged, and her sleeping schedule was not yet reflecting her new time zone. So, she concentrated on the games in the pub. Tonight was television trivia night.

Linda knew nothing about British television. Still, she had a damn good time.

Around 11 p.m., Linda said her good-byes and made her way to the tube station. As she descended into the Underground, she saw the platforms were under construction. Workers had erected temporary passage ways which made an ordinarily simple transit from the tube to Victoria station above far more complex. Given the late weekday hour, the number of inconvenienced passengers was at a minimum.

Linda had to weave in and out of the construction barriers as she navigated to the location where passengers for the Victoria Line were instructed to wait. She could feel the head winds begin to build as her train approached the station. The next thing Linda knew, she received a strong push from behind and she found her body unwillingly flying to the tracks below.

She had nursed a single draft all evening. Linda's judgment wasn't impaired even if her self-respect just suffered a blow.

Linda tucked and rolled onto the train bed. As she rotated toward the oncoming train, she had the presence of mind to follow through until she was standing erect. Immediately, she gingerly stepped over the electrified outer rail and flattened her body against the ornate tile facing the platform. She became one with the wall.

The train came to a stop several inches from her face.

* * *

MCRORY'S ROUTINE TO overcome the effects of jet lag involved exercise—and lots of it. Early the next morning, he stepped out onto the street to begin his five-mile run. Earlier, while dressing, he took notice of the poor state of his one shoelace. It looked like it would fail at any moment. He hoped the lace would survive the run.

There's hope, and then there's reality.

No more than twenty paces into his run, the lace failed, and he almost stepped out of his shoe. He dropped to his knee to see what repair might be possible.

McRory heard the sound before he noticed the shattered glass on the sidewalk beside him. He quickly scuttled under the adjacent car and crawled to the other side where he slowly—and carefully—looked in the direction from which the bullet was fired.

He saw no one. Nothing obvious.

In the distance he heard the sound of the approaching police siren.

CHAPTER 34

Eddy O'Conner, Alice Linda, and Joe McRory each received warning text messages announcing the teleconference from Henley. At the appointed time, the DNI joined the call.

"Eddy, rumor has it you picked up a tail in Rome. We had a team waiting for her at the Milan train station. We now have a very cooperative GRU asset singing like a bird. Unfortunately, she's so low in the food chain that there's not much of value in what she can tell us."

"Sir," Eddy began, "we've encountered problems with both Alice and Joe as well. Someone pushed Alice in front of an oncoming tube train. Another someone else took a shot at Joe at the outset of his morning run. Three problems in as many cities."

"Yes," the DNI responded, "Henley provided me with the embassy staff reports on both incidents before this call. I don't need to remind any of you of the importance of situational awareness. Eddy, good SA on your part took you out of harm's way. Your tail was armed to the teeth, so her intent was obvious.

"Alice and Joe, you can take a lesson on tradecraft from your colleague, Eddy. To be safe, I want both of you to remain in your respective embassy compounds. Try not to go out. Everything you need is available on site. What isn't will be cheerfully brought to you."

Eddy asked before either Linda or McRory had the opportunity to whine.

"Sir, it sounds like you have something underway."

The DNI chuckled.

"I shouldn't make light of this experience. After all, we could have lost all three of you. However, I've put a number of operations and directives out in the field. We haven't seen this much of a reaction from the Russians in quite some time. Let's just say that Colonel Saakadze will cease to be an issue. And, I believe, there are enough of the old Russian Cold Warriors still alive in Moscow who can help their current generation of leaders understand that either they stand down on this type of retribution or we'll show them what a true escalation of hostilities looks and feels like."

O'Conner asked, "Is Saakadze still alive?"

"Oh, yes," the DNI responded. "Very much so. But I'd venture to guess that she's not been this unhappy, this miserable, in quite some time—if ever. And the next two weeks won't be much of a picnic for our good colonel."

✳ ✳ ✳

THE DNI KNEW of what he spoke. Katrina Saakadze was mired in a bottomless well of anger and misery.

She never remembered her childhood bed and bedroom in the compact family home in Gora, Georgia as so small. Nor for that matter did she recall the coarse sheets, thin blankets, and lumpy bedding. And the small house harbored a damp cold that wouldn't quit.

Gone forever were her custom mattress and pillows. Gone were her Egyptian cotton sheets with the obscenely high thread count. And the luxurious bed covers to which she and her new husband retreated following a memorable evening—they were gone as well.

But the greatest luxury of all was her parents taking charge of the infant. Out of sight. Out of hearing range. Saakadze and her new husband were sleeping in without a care in the world. Sleep was so under appreciated by those without children, especially when a new born was in residence.

It had all come crashing down. Literally crashing down.

The FBI Agents leading the raid used a battering ram to knock the heavy front door off of its hinges and onto the newly refinished hard wood floors.

"FBI!" the lead agent repeatedly screamed. "We're looking for Oleg and Drina Saakadze, and Katrina Saakadze. If you're in this house, identify yourselves immediately!"

Katrina Saakadze heard one team of federal officials marching up the stairs like a herd of elephants to the bedroom level of the townhome. Next, she heard the small voices of her parents in their native tongue insisting they'd done nothing wrong.

Then she heard her infant start to wail.

The wailing of her child compelled the mother to spring from her bed, abandoning her husband as she rushed to her closet where she kept a weapon hidden in the safe.

"Kat, what are you doing?" her husband screamed.

He followed her into the closet unaware of her true intent.

They were both nude.

Their antique bedroom door with its leaded stained glass insert shattered into pieces large and small creating an immense debris field of splinters and glass shards that scattered across the lush oriental area rug.

Saakadze's husband responded to his own inner voice following the invasion of the bedroom sanctum. He emerged from the closet in full rage where he encountered four federal agents prepared for the worst. They wore protective body armor, protective eyewear, and helmets. Each was equipped with a spray that immediately disabled the charging nude form. He collapsed into the middle of the debris field and rolled over onto his stomach.

They didn't lay a hand on him. They didn't have to. He was down and no longer a threat.

Three of the agents formed an arc facing into the closet as Saakadze managed to open the safe. As she reached into its confines to withdraw her loaded weapon, the order rang out.

"Gun! Gun! Gun! Take her out!" screamed the squad leader.

Three taser shots rang out. The thin metal wires followed the dart-shaped electrodes as they embedded into her naked back and buttocks.

They pulled Saakadze's form out of the closet by her legs, her arms extended beyond her head dragging along the high-gloss wood floor.

"All clear!" rang out throughout the three-story home. All that remained was to secure the two adults who lay prone in the master bedroom.

* * *

THE EMTS SPENT the better part of an hour removing the splinters and shards from the back and front of Saakadze's stunned husband. Katrina Saakadze's ankles were bound with plastic restraining cuffs. Her upper body was shrouded in a heavy-duty straitjacket partially shielding her nudity from everyone in the townhome.

The jacket did nothing to provide for her modesty below the waist. And it did absolutely nothing to disguise Saakadze's preference for vaginal jewelry. The bling, as it were, captured everyone's attention and fascination until even the federal agents started going out of their way to direct their attention elsewhere. Unfortunately, the jewelry was a siren's song summoning their attention, yet again.

Looking away, looking back, the jewelry exercised its powerful effect.

Having recovered from the taser delivered shock, Saakadze became increasingly irritable at remaining on public display and the fact that the invading group was waiting on the arrival of a person or persons yet unknown.

The wait finally ended.

"Are you Colonel Katrina Saakadze of the Russian GRU?" came from the voice of a woman entering the room.

"Who wants to know?" Saakadze defiantly responded.

"I do," came the response—more of an order than an answer. "I'm Elizabeth Fournier, Deputy U.S. Attorney representing the United States Government."

They both maintained their uncompromising attitudes.

"Well, are you? If you fail to cooperate, Colonel, I will amend the charges here today to include resisting arrest and failing to comply with a federal officer's directives resulting from the execution of a detainer warrant issued under Title V of the USA Patriot Act."

"Kat, what is this about?" her husband screamed. "Why is she calling you *Colonel*? A Colonel in what?"

Saakadze never broke her defiant gaze at DUSA Fournier to look at her husband. She ignored his questions. Instead, she finally responded to Fournier's query.

"I am Colonel Katrina Saakadze of the Main Intelligence Directorate of the Russian Federation. I demand to speak to my attorney," she spat—literally, at the DUSA.

Fournier chuckled at the absurdity of the request.

"You certainly don't look the part, Colonel. Tell me, is your pussy jewelry standard issue to GRU officers these days? She paused, "Or is the bling something you've fashioned for the benefit of your poor husband here?"

"Hey! Watch your fucking mouth!" Saakadze's husband roared.

He launched out of the ongoing ministrations of the EMTs headed in Fournier's direction. One of the agents used an armored elbow sleeve to slam the husband's face halting his forward progress.

"Mr. Saakadze!" she yelled in his direction. "If you pull another asshole stunt like that I'll add your name to this warrant and declare you to be a co-conspirator under Title V of the USA Patriot Act."

"His name isn't Saakadze," the colonel stated. His name is Guy Miller. You'll kindly address him as such and with the dignity he deserves as a U.S. citizen."

Fournier was enjoying this *tête-à-tête*.

"Colonel, from where I'm standing, it looks like you wear the pants in this little family drama. We know his name. However, I refuse to speak the name of any U.S. citizen who unknowingly or not harbors a terrorist."

Her voice took a nasty turn. Addressing the federal agents in the room, "Will *someone* put *something* over her body? I'm appalled at the bling staring at me."

Throughout the ordeal, the colonel's parents sat quietly on the floor nearby. They were no strangers to an overwhelming display of force by government authorities. They recognized the virtue in maintaining their silence. And once his daughter's nude form was fully cloaked by the throw blanket appropriated from a nearby sofa, her father stopped gazing at the ceiling and trained his eyes on his daughter. They reflected his deep disappointment.

The old man had no idea at that point in time just how disappointed he would become that day.

The awkward silence was pierced by the infant's shrill scream coming from the adjoining room. The initial response from both grandparents was to attend to the child. Fournier, however, used her hand to signal they were to stay put.

* * *

DUSA FOURNIER WAITED for the search of the home to be completed. Throughout the search the child continued to wail. He was clearly unaccustomed to not being the center of attention. The longer he was ignored, the louder, shriller his wail.

Saakadze's mother, nodding in Fournier's direction, spoke to her daughter in Russian, "Doesn't this daughter of a whore care about a screaming infant?"

"She's only worried about the next big dick she's going to suck," the colonel responded—again, in Russian.

Fournier's response was delayed, but unsettling. She cackled—not laughed—like one of the wicked witches in a childhood story.

She spoke to both women, in Russian.

"Old lady, who are you calling the daughter of a whore? Your own daughter sits there with more jewelry on her sacred parts than the Czarina owned before the peasants shot her and threw her body down a well. Maybe we should pull up your skirt to see what family jewels you have to offer."

The old woman turned a brilliant shade of crimson and pursed her lips. She despised Fournier, but she was beyond furious with her own daughter.

The old man's body sagged as if the weight of it all was too much to bear.

* * *

ALMOST AN HOUR after the search was completed, the social worker arrived with a court order in hand. The social worker presented the paperwork to the colonel's husband.

"Mr. Miller, the Alameda County Department of Social Services has sought and received an order from the juvenile and family court to take custody of your son, Gregory. He will be placed with an approved foster family."

"No!" The husband and both grandparents screamed simultaneously. The colonel sat stone faced.

The social worker continued her prepared speech.

"A hearing has been scheduled in this matter two days from today. You are advised to seek competent legal counsel. You may contact me at the number shown on my card."

As the social worker left the townhome with the infant, the grandparents started to sob. Guy Miller sat in stunned disbelief, unconcerned about his injuries and his partial nudity.

DUSA Fournier explained what was to happen next.

"Mr. and Mrs. Saakadze, your petition for a residency permit is hereby denied. Your visitor's visa is canceled forthwith. These agents from Immigration and Customs Enforcement will escort you to the airport. There you will be placed on a flight to Moscow where the Russian Federation can decide your fate."

She paused for dramatic effect before continuing.

"You may not enter the United States ever again. You are barred from future visits. If you attempt to enter the U.S., you will be arrested and imprisoned.

"Do you understand?" she asked in Russian.

Both of the elder Saakadzes nodded in the affirmative. It was unlikely they would ever again see their beloved grandson.

Fournier turned her attention to the colonel.

"Colonel Katrina Saakadze, you are hereby declared to be an enemy of the U.S.A. However, in your case, we are prepared to offer you one of two choices: First, if you agree to assist the federal government, you may remain in this country only as long as your cooperation is genuine and of value to my office. Second, you will accompany your parents on their return to Moscow, and like your parents, you may never enter this country ever again."

The colonel snarled and spat in Russian, "Go fuck yourself!"

Fournier addressed the ICE agents.

"Take them away, now. Leave the blanket here. Let her return to Moscow flashing her bling for everyone to see."

The senior ICE agent addressed the DUSA, "Fournier, are you serious?"

"Deadly serious, agent. If the reflection of the sun on her bling doesn't blind all of the neighbors patiently waiting outside to watch the perp walk, I'll have your badge."

At the airport, one of the ICE agents fashioned a cloak for the colonel out of two large black trash bags. She sat in the hot plastic, tethered to her seat by plastic restraints, for the duration of the flight.

* * *

KATRINA SAAKADZE ONLY left her bed to toilet. Otherwise, she hid under the covers and on top of the scratchy sheets to preserve what little warmth existed in the small bedroom.

It wasn't until her third day in self-imposed exile she saw the wire cutters on her night stand.

Saakadze's personal tastes developed to reflect American attitudes and preferences. That's what her training taught her to do. "Become one of them. Disappear into their ranks. Adopt their manner of dress and their conduct."

And so she had.

Now she was back in Gori in her parents' home, hiding in her old room, with the expectation she conform to a very different lifestyle.

Her marriage was over. Her child lost to her and her parents.

The wire cutters haunted her.

She knew what her parents expected her to do. The less said about it the better.

Katrina Saakadze wasn't at all sure what her life would become.

But she certainly knew who was responsible. With every piece of jewelry she removed, she vowed vengeance.

CHAPTER 35

EDDY O'CONNER CONTACTED HER two colleagues daily for the next several weeks, before she finally received another summons from Henley and the phone call from the DNI that followed.

"What's the status, Sir?" O'Conner asked.

"Good news," he replied. "Saakadze is back in the town of her birth along with her parents—a very unhappy trio, or so I am told.

"Our station head in Moscow had one of those off-the-record conversations with a known member of the GRU at a recent embassy function. It was a non-official conversation, never to be confirmed by the Russian Federation, on the topic of Colonel Saakadze and the recent misadventures you three experienced. Long story short, they agreed there was merit in the cessation of further hostilities."

"I gather Joe and Alice can resume their station support?"

"Yes," he responded. "That's a reasonable inference. Tell Alice, Joe, their 'house arrest' is over."

"I may take a day or two to meet with my niece. She's going to be in Rome for a week or so."

"How old is she?"

"Eighteen."

"Oh my," he chuckled. "That's an interesting age. I have a niece who's a bit older now, but she was a handful when she was eighteen."

"This one's a bit different," O'Conner boasted. "She's eighteen going on forty. One of the few teens I know who acts much older than her age."

* * *

O'CONNER SAT ACROSS the small café table from her niece. The girl—young woman, O'Conner was forced to reluctantly accept—was aglow.

"I'm so pleased you are so happy to see me here," O'Conner whispered. "I was afraid you'd be unhappy when I insisted on lunch today." She paused while she assessed the stylish young woman. "I can't get over how mature you look."

"I am glad to see you Aunt Eddy. Honest, I am," the young woman started.

"Do I hear a 'but' coming down the pike?" O'Conner said.

"I just have to share a secret with you. You can't tell anyone. Not mom, dad—no one from the family."

And there it was.

The glow had nothing to do with their reunion over lunch.

"I'm going to explode, if I don't tell someone!"

The niece made one of those teenaged facial expressions. The kind where the neck compresses, the shoulders rise, and eyes grow wide.

"I have a man," she whispered.

O'Conner's first instinct was to recoil in horror, to call the police, to tear every limb, poke out both eyes, and do other unspeakable things to whatever leech robbed this cradle and sank his hooks into her precious niece.

She thought the better of it.

Instead, O'Conner fashioned a more acceptable response. But first she was forced to consign to the trash heap all the images floating in her head of the cute, impish child who was her faithful correspondent those many years when Eddy was too busy to attend to her own family.

She leaned across the table. Their faces only inches apart. "Dish!"

Her niece knew at that moment her decision to trust her beloved aunt was the right thing to do. *Eddy will understand*, she'd told herself.

One woman sharing the table was comfortable in her own body, knew she'd made the right choice, and welcomed the opportunity to share a treasure trove of intimacies.

And then there was Aunt Eddy.

No longer hungry, unsettled as she watched a cherished childhood disappear in the rear-view mirror and a new, unsettling future coming at her.

* * *

IT WAS THE longest two-hour meal O'Conner had ever experienced. Her face hurt from smiling throughout lunch. She was exhausted from playing an unfamiliar role in a live theater production for which she was unprepared. The non-stop improvisation left her exhausted. Her head hurt, more from the dump truck load of facts her niece unloaded than the tension caused by finding herself in unfamiliar territory.

Unlike her sister, O'Conner had no children. She didn't have the luxury of watching a child grow, mature, and leave the nest. O'Conner's entire experience with her niece was now partitioned into two parts—all around a single event announced by the words, "I have a man."

My sister! Oh my God, what do I say to her? O'Conner panicked.

She sat in the park to take stock of what she could recall from the avalanche of information.

What's his name?

"Anthony Charles," she said followed by, "He's so handsome."

Where did you meet?

"In the Zurich train station. He's a student at the university, like me," she smiled.

Where's he from?

"The Philippines, where he attended a private school," she gushed. "He actually studied the Greek Classics, Eddy. He's not some dumb jock or gross guy."

School starts in the fall. Have you been traveling together?

"Yes. Lisa and I have been touring Switzerland, Austria, and Italy by train. Initially, Anthony tagged along. I thought he had the hots for Lisa. I treated him badly at the outset."

What changed?

"He wasn't interested in Lisa after all. We were hardly out of Switzerland when Lisa made her play. Anthony wasn't interested. We thought he might be gay—which would have been okay."

Nothing wrong with being gay. I guess he isn't. Gay, I mean.

Laughter. "No, far from it. He's not bi-sexual or cis-gendered, if you know what I mean? He's a red-blooded American—I mean Filipino—guy."

Well, how did you two become involved? You are involved, right?

"If you mean physically, then *yes*. We didn't start sleeping together until we crossed into Italy."

I don't want to pry. Are you taking precautions?

"Oh my God, Eddy, you sound like my mother. Of course, I am. I visited a gynecologist in my senior year."

Speaking of your mother, does she know?

"About Anthony?"

Well, yes, him too.

"Eddy, don't tell me you are such a prude. Who do you think took me to the gynecologist? So, yes, in general, she knows I'm 'exercising caution,' and no, she doesn't know about Anthony." Her niece paused to sip her tea. "We don't share everything."

You're keeping him under wraps?

"For now. If I tell Mom about Anthony, she'll want to know all the details—and I do mean *all*. I'm not prepared to discuss everything. There are parts of my life that are mine and mine alone. You understand, don't you?"

When do I get to meet this special young man?

"He made an appointment for a private tour of the papal crypt. His Bishop from the Philippines is in residence at the Vatican and made the arrangements. I was supposed to go with him."

I hope your missing out on the tour isn't my fault.

"I don't mind. Really, I don't. I'd never miss a chance to share lunch with my favorite aunt to dish about my guy."

* * *

O'CONNER DIDN'T WANT to be like one of those parents—the ones that check the social media sites trolling for the child's paramour. First, she wasn't Beth's parent although while her niece was in Europe she did feel as if she was *loco parentis*. Eddy had a strong sense of loyalty to both her sister and her sister's daughter. Right now, she felt she was in the middle of a tug of war between these two competing interests. She felt duty bound to spill the beans to her sister. But her niece was more an adult than a child, and O'Conner's bond with Beth rivaled any of her own sibling relationships.

Second, and more importantly, O'Conner had far better tools than Google, Facebook, and Instagram. If she wanted the dirt on Anthony Charles, she could summon it out of the ether with all of the force the U.S. intelligence community could muster.

Her first reaction was to request some basic background information on Mr. Charles. She justified this course of action as a precaution—to ensure he was whom he alleged to be.

Her second thought was of profound embarrassment. The kid was only eighteen. Who else could he be? O'Conner took herself to task. It's not like he was a criminal or master spy. He was a recent high school graduate. From a private school, no less. And he studied the Greek Classics while growing up in the Philippines. Get a grip!

She settled on a more benign course of action: Do nothing. Be happy for her niece. Beth is eighteen and starting out on her own. What could possibly go wrong?

CHAPTER 36

AT THE END OF HER TRANSITIONAL leave, Colonel Katrina Saakadze was summoned to the headquarters of the GRU just outside of Moscow near the Khodynka Airfield. The chauffeured limo drove along the Khoroshevskiy Highway as it approached the GRU campus. Saakadze noticed the substantial change in the compound since her last visit almost five years earlier. The new buildings were a proxy for increased military and intelligence funding within the Russian Federation.

Irina Rybolovlev's personal assistant was dispatched to greet Saakadze and escort her to the upper floor of the glass tower. Following Alexi Kaledin's arrest in the U.S., Rybolovlev was now the GRU executive providing oversight from Moscow.

Saakadze had never seen Rybolovlev in uniform before. In her visits to the San Francisco bay area, Rybolovlev looked like she'd stepped out of the couture magazines into a much less stylish reality. She was a strikingly handsome woman, and the military dress did nothing to change that.

"General," Saakadze saluted her superior.

"Colonel," Rybolovlev responded. "Let's take a seat." She gestured to the small living room-like corner of the spacious office. A file with Saakadze's name on the filing tab was the sole item on the otherwise empty sofa table.

The personal assistant returned to the office and placed a modern Scandinavian styled tea set alongside the folder.

"Thank you, Sasha," was Rybolovlev's perfunctory dismissal. The general poured two cups of hot, dark Russian tea. "I trust your visit to Gori was pleasant. How are your parents adjusting to their new—reality?"

"I think they wish they'd had a son instead of a daughter, especially this daughter," Saakadze said with a mixture of sadness and anger.

"You know, Katrina, right up to my own mother's death she considered me her most profound failure. No husband. No children. Not even one domestic bone in my entire body. On the other hand, her son, my only sibling, could do no wrong. He was in her eyes a gifted academic—the truth was a bit less flattering. He married a wonderful woman—who was unfaithful even during their honeymoon. And their children were like sunlight to her—they despised the old woman, no doubt the influence of their mother.

"I cannot speak for you, but I will say this about me: From my perspective, there are worse conditions than to be a disappointment to one's parents. I say this knowing full well had I married and presented her with a bounty of grandchildren, those beautiful children I never had would have despised her as well.

"She was a miserable bitch. There was no mistaking the importance of her preferences, her choices over mine.

"If you're open to some personal advice?" Rybolovlev awaited Saakadze's response, her teacup suspended in mid-air between the table and her mouth.

"Absolutely, General, please," Saakadze's response demonstrated she wasn't an idiot.

Rybolovlev wasn't under any false impressions where her subordinates were concerned. Whether the colonel actually agreed or not wasn't important. Saakadze's willingness to appear cooperative was, however.

"Good."

Rybolovlev emptied her cup before returning it to the tea set on the table.

"Forget what your parents want, what they may think, and how they judge what you've become. You must live your life for you and you alone. Let them come along for the ride, if you will. Should they choose to do so, fine. If not, there is an old Russian epithet that fits the bill."

"Which is, General?"

"Fuck them."

* * *

THE TWO SPENT the next hours reviewing each of Saakadze's ongoing operations she left behind in the U.S. That exercise included a review of the subordinates and assets that were under her purview. At the end, Rybolovlev switched to topics of a more personal nature.

"The GRU has tasked our Consulate in San Francisco to represent the division of the marital estate between you and your former husband, Mr. Miller."

"He's still my husband, General. To be quite honest, I haven't decided how to deal with my husband or our assets."

Rybolovlev sat passively examining the face before her.

"Colonel, *you* may not have decided what to do. Your husband, however, with some assistance from the U.S. authorities, has already received a separation order and an entirely unnecessary court order barring you from having any contact with him or your child. I am informed a divorce decree will automatically be issued at the end of the six-month separation period.

"It appears your former husband harbors a vitriolic animus toward you. He has fully cooperated with the U.S. Attorney's office that issued the deportation orders for yourself and your parents. The family court judge has declared you to be unstable and a public menace. She has awarded sole custody of your son to his father. There is no provision for you to have visitation rights.

"If we don't look after your interests in this matter, then who will? You certainly cannot. So, let's face the reality of the situation and move on."

Saakadze sat before her superior in a state of shock. She hadn't envisioned Guy's eagerness to dissolve all that remained of their life together and the anger he must feel for her. The shock rapidly gave way to an impromptu analysis of the situation.

Her former husband's prompt actions before the American courts augured well for her career where the GRU was concerned.

She convinced Guy she was a travel consultant who worked with European travel agencies to arrange trips for citizens of eastern Europe eager to visit the U.S. In particular, women in the last trimester of their pregnancies wanting to deliver in a U.S. hospital. Another child would on birth automatically become a U.S. citizen.

It was the perfect cover.

Guy wasn't surprised by the number of men who visited their home, especially those who spoke English with eastern European accents.

It also explained the periodic trips she took—some with little or no advance notice.

It also paid well, handsomely, in fact.

In the end, he never knew who she was or what she really did. The GRU must have found that comforting. There are not many couples where one involved in treason could keep suspicious activities hidden from a spouse. They say, "the spouse always knows."

Clearly, they had never met her husband.

"How will the Consulate represent my legal interest in these matters?" she asked.

Rybolovlev smiled. "They've engaged an American law firm specializing in what the Americans call 'matrimonial law.' Strange term for lawyers who specialize in destroying marriages. It should be called 'divorce law,' but what do I know of such things?"

Rybolovlev shrugged her shoulders. A sign she really didn't comprehend.

"Moving on," the general continued. "The word from on high is that the vendetta—*your* vendetta—with the O'Conner woman, the ex-nun and her stupid firm, Triple Play, comes to an end. You will take no further action where this person and her firm are concerned. Are we clear?"

"Yes, General," Saakadze's smile was an outward show of fealty. Inwardly, she had a different opinion: *This will be over when I say so.*

"However, there is still the issue of Mr. Lowandowski. We know he is important to the Americans. They need to know what he knows from his employment with the FBI. And, they have yet to discover his financial misdeeds which is nothing short of amazing to me, if I may be permitted an unofficial opinion. Those crimes were what brought him to our attention.

"I still find it hard to believe they won the Cold War with such shoddy tradecraft. The truth is easier to believe. Our old system was corrupt and financially bankrupt. Like true Americans, they simply managed to outspend us. In the end, they had more dollars than we had rubles.

"Vladimir will make them pay, however. Don't you agree, Colonel?"

Another test.

"Yes, absolutely, General," she responded with as much alacrity as she could muster.

"Good. Why don't you take in the ballet or the symphony while you are here? Do some shopping. Yes?

"Oh, before I forget, here." Rybolovlev placed the folder in Saakadze's hands.

"What is this, General?"

"The deed to your new dacha. It's just down the road. Not far from my own. We'll be neighbors."

Saakadze dug to depths she didn't know she possessed to bring forth her best smile.

"We take care of our own, Colonel."

Rybolovlev looked at her Hermes watch.

"Let's have lunch in the dining room. I want to bring you up to date on what we've managed to learn about Mr. Lowandowski.

CHAPTER 37

SEVERAL WEEKS LATER, KATRINA SAAKADZE stepped into the jet way leading to the terminal. The oppressive heat and humidity overwhelmed the air conditioning in the long metal rectangle.

She cursed.

In all her preparations, she overlooked the need to buy sun screen to protect her fair skin. It was the first purchase she made while in the airport.

The GRU trackers and cyber sleuths determined Charles Lowandowski had purchased a fraudulent passport under a new identity. They'd been unable to determine his new name and legend. But they knew the forger who produced the document. He lived in Manila. So, Saakadze flew to the Philippines to expedite the balance of her research agenda.

She booked a room at the Pan Pacific Hotel in Manila's Malate district. The area was one of two serving as the city's destination for tourism and commerce. Her room was adequate for a four-star establishment featuring all of the comforts she might require.

There was a knock.

"Yes?" she safely asked on her side of the door.

"You have a delivery from the Embassy," was the response.

Saakadze took the delivery and tipped the young woman. The "parcel" was a secured pouch used by the foreign ministry to shuttle important documents and contraband between Moscow and the foreign capitals where the Russian Federation maintained a formal presence.

Using her secure cell phone, she sent a text message containing the code embroidered on the outside of the pouch. She received a return text with the combination to release the locking mechanism. Now open, Saakadze removed the weapon, a silencer, and several clips of ammunition from the bag along with a vial of powder.

The hotel car rental desk produced a serviceable, late model sedan with excellent air conditioning. She drove the short distance to the travel agency.

The shop was located on the border separating the safe area, which included her hotel, from a more transitional district the guide books suggested avoiding. The agency was clearly a one-person operation. Saakadze stepped through the door, turned, and secured the lock.

The owner was engaged in a telephone conversation. He paid little attention to her arrival, and he certainly didn't notice when she locked the door.

Saakadze stood before the man who continued to ignore her presence. She withdrew the pistol, attached the silencer, and inserted a clip of ammunition. Still he ignored her.

She placed the business end of the gun on the man's left knee cap. Now she had his attention. He terminated the call and lowered the cell phone to the desk.

"What do you want?" he asked in flawless English, no accent.

Saakadze dropped a photograph of Charles Lowandowski into his lap. The picture was taken in Vanuatu.

"Have you done business with this man?" she asked.

He studied the photograph carefully. "No," he responded.

Saakadze released the gun's safety. "Look at it again. More carefully this time."

"I've already told you. I've never seen this person."

Saakadze pressed the muzzle firmly into the man's flesh.

"That's an interesting answer," she replied. "It's designed to avoid the question I asked yet permit you to respond to a question I didn't ask. So, let me repeat *my* question. Have you done business with this man?"

"No, I have never done any business with this person."

"See? That wasn't difficult."

Then she shot him through his knee cap.

The man screamed, bent at his waist, and with both hands grasped the injured leg. While he suffered through the initial agony of the gunshot, Saakadze removed the vial of powder from her purse. Placing the gun muzzle against the man's forehead she ordered him to, "Sit back."

She sprinkled the powder into the wound. The bleeding immediately ceased. The opioid compound provided near instantaneous relief from the searing pain.

"This was developed for use by injured war fighters on the battlefield. It stops the bleeding and provides an immediate reduction in pain levels. It almost makes you forget you've been wounded. However, if I were you I wouldn't try to walk on that knee."

She pointed the muzzle at the man's other knee. She held the vial in front of his face.

"There's not much of this miracle powder remaining. I'm going to continue shooting you until you give me the information I want. You can pour some of it into each new wound. Sooner or later, however, there won't be any more left. I'll keep shooting. Do you understand?"

"Yes," he said.

"The choice is yours. How many of your joints do you want me to destroy? I can shoot the other knee. Then your left elbow. Then your right elbow. Then your left ankle. Then your right ankle. Do you understand?"

"Yes," he said again.

"You'll be crippled for life. And that's after you spend weeks— maybe months—in the hospital. And then there's the oh so painful physical therapy. So, when you think about it, wouldn't it be simpler to give me the information I'm seeking?"

"Yes," he replied.

And then he gave her what she wanted.

She shot him, twice. Both times in the forehead.

* * *

SAAKADZE SPENT THE night in her hotel room ordering from room service a late dinner and a bottle of wine. The next morning, she checked out of the hotel and took a taxi to the Russian Embassy.

The Embassy occupied two adjoining buildings on Acacia Road not far from the swanky and exclusive Manila Polo Club. One building provided consular functions. The other housed the embassy's corporate offices. Saakadze's arrival was announced at the latter. She waited in the lobby until her escort collected her.

Later she was seated alone in the office of the GRU attaché. The secure telephone line permitted her to place a call to the GRU campus on Khoroshevskiy Highway outside Moscow.

She made her report to her colleagues in Moscow. She was told to expect a full response in several hours. Following the call, she accepted an offer to join her GRU colleague for lunch at the polo club.

True to their promise, the information she required was awaiting her return to the embassy compound.

* * *

THE NATIONAL SECURITY Agency's headquarters is located at Fort George Meade outside Washington, DC, where its electronic eavesdropping activities are managed. The actual data collection activities take place worldwide and are communicated through a combination of truly secure satellite and fiber cables to a primary processing and storage facility in Saratoga Springs, Utah.

The NSA maintains an extensive database of voice recordings belonging to persons of interest identified by the nation's intelligence community. These recordings are matched to incoming telephone conversations intercepted by the agency.

Through its surveillance operations in San Francisco, the agency first identified then Major Katrina Saakadze during her meetings with her then superior, General Alexi Kaledin. Those recordings were supplemented by the audio component on the video Eddy O'Conner provided when Saakadze received "treatment" for her alleged glioblastoma.

The overwhelming quantity of Saakadze's voice conversations on file with the NSA provided the agency an unassailable level of certainty when identifying intercepted telephone conversations.

Both telephone conversations between Saakadze and the GRU campus were collected and sent to Saratoga Springs. Her voice was promptly identified, and a notice sent throughout the intelligence community where the activities of Saakadze were thought to be of interest.

Henley sent a text to O'Conner.

O'Conner listened to the voice recordings which were translated on the fly from Russian to English.

She was thrilled.

First, they now knew what had become of Charles Lowandowski. Second, she'd get another shot at the colonel. Third, she had the perfect excuse to visit her niece.

CHAPTER 38

BETH MCFARLAND AND ANTHONY CHARLES met for lunch following their morning classes. The fall day was sunny but cool. The trees in the city center were in their full color. The colder weather was just around the corner. So they chose to sit at the nearly deserted outdoor tables to enjoy what little remained of the season.

They both wore heavy sweaters and woolen scarves to ward off the cooler breezes typical of Zurich at this time of year. McFarland was a committed chocaholic. She cradled a steaming mug of Swiss hot chocolate to warm both hands. Charles drank a mug of hot mulled cider. Their love was in full bloom and intoxicating.

"Here, let's take a selfie like the Asian tourists we saw in Rome," Charles suggested.

McFarland leaned in, her head next to his. Charles did his best imitation of a Japanese tourist saying "smile."

They both giggled uncontrollably and segued into a long kiss while Charles lowered his phone to the table. He was distracted by the beautiful young woman he held. His phone carelessly tapped against hers as it softly landed on the table.

The phone software automatically transferred the photograph from his phone to hers. Her phone automatically posted the picture to her Instagram account.

A moment captured for the ages.

* * *

EDDY O'CONNER'S SISTER placed her call without regard to the five-hour time difference separating her home from her sister's rental flat in London.

Susan McFarland taught art history at the community college. Her daily schedule started early and ran non-stop until she returned home in the late afternoon. Once home, she prepared a dinner for two in a house that once held seven. Now that her youngest was off to Europe for her own undergraduate education, she had the luxury of time to do what she wanted, when she wanted. But she was a creature of habit. Her husband joked Beth chose Switzerland for her studies because it was one of the few places on earth where an entire country operated with the same clockwork precision of his wife's home and hearth.

At 7 p.m. sharp, Susan opened her laptop and navigated to her collection of social media sites. Her children documented their lives on these sites. Watching their postings, cross postings, and photographs was her way of silently stalking.

Her youngest, once a prolific poster, had largely gone silent once school was underway.

"She's busy with her classes," her husband told her. "Leave the poor kid alone."

Likely story, she thought. I hope there's a boy in the mix somewhere.

When she opened Instagram, she found that was exactly the case.

"Hello, Eddy, did I wake you?"

"Susan, you know you did. It's after midnight here." She paused to yawn. "Is everything okay?"

"Better than okay," she said. "Beth *finally* has a beau."

"'Beau.' Who even uses that term these days?"

"An art history professor for starters," her sister smartly replied—as if the answer was self-evident.

"How do you know this, Susan?"

"She posted a very hot picture of them kissing on her Instagram."

"Really?" Eddy was wide awake now. "That doesn't sound like Beth."

"Love will do that to you, Eddy. I once shared a hot kiss just like that with Edward and look what it got me. I'm sitting in an empty house with my five children scattered to the winds."

"Susan, you always had a flare for understatement," she responded with a sarcasm she reserved for her sister. "Three of your children live within ten miles of your home. If they were scattered, it was more likely by a gentle breeze than the wind."

"Eddy, the kid looks hot. I can't get over it. Beth hardly dated in high school. She didn't even go to prom. Now she's sitting at a café table somewhere in Zurich playing tonsil hockey with the cutest boy I've ever seen."

Eddy didn't want to point out the obvious. At this hour in Zurich she wasn't sitting at any outdoor café. But she didn't want to start down that road. Not with the mother who marched her daughter off to the gyno for birth control pills in her senior year of high school.

Boy, she thought, it's a good thing their mother was no longer among the living.

"Did Beth mention a boy—especially a hot boy—when you two met for lunch in Rome?"

Eddy instantly regretted telling her sister about the lunch.

"She may have mentioned she was traveling with friends. I recall her talking about a Lisa person, but nothing about an Anthony."

Shit! She kicked herself.

"*Anthony*, Eddy? There's an *Anthony* and you conveniently neglected to tell me that."

"Did I say 'Anthony'?" she lied. "Look you woke me in the middle of the night. My mind is really unfocused now. I work with a man by that name. That must be why I said 'Anthony.'"

Her sister laughed.

"You were always such a bad liar. Every time mom put the screws to you, you cracked like a raw egg. You're lying now. You know damn well there's an Anthony."

"Susan, now you're mixing your metaphors. Have you been drinking? Speaking about Edward, how is your darling husband?"

"Good try, little sister. We're talking Anthony here and now. So, dish!"

"Susan, we met for a short lunch—"

"You said lunch lasted two hours!"

"—we ate alone. If there was someone else, she didn't bring him along. I've never set eyes on this man"

"He's a full-grown man, Eddy? Not a boy? Not someone her own age?"

"I don't know that, Susan. Like I said, Beth came to lunch alone."

"Were there any pictures? Did she dish anything you can share? Come on, Eddy. This is my youngest daughter we're talking about."

"Only that you made sure she was on the pill!"

Eddy couldn't keep her own foot out of her mouth. By the end of this conversation she'd never need to wash her feet again. Apparently, the wrong O'Conner went to work for the CIA.

"The pill? She's sexually active with Anthony? My baby is sleeping with an older man and you didn't think that merited a report to your only sister—me, her mother!"

"He's not an older man, Susan. You're the one looking at the picture. Not me."

Just then Eddy's phone buzzed with a text of the photo in question.

"Shit!" she yelled at her sister. "You just had to send me the picture. You can't leave well enough alone." She looked carefully at the photo. "How can you tell anything from this selfie? All I see is the side of his face and a lot of blonde hair and whiskers. Jesus, Susan, the front of his face is all smashed into hers."

"How much older is he, Eddy?" she was clearly concerned about the alleged age difference.

"He's not older than Beth," she said to quell her sister's fear of cradle robbery.

"See, you do know!"

"Susan, Beth was not overly generous with details."

Another lie.

"But he's her age?"

"Yes."

Eddy looked at the photo once more.

"He doesn't look Filipino," she said just loud enough for her sister to hear.

"He's from the Philippines? Oh Christ, I'll never see her again. They'll marry and move to the other side of the world. I'll never get to know my own grandchildren!"

"Susan, aren't you putting the cart before the horse? It's a long way from a fling to married with children living in southeast Asia."

"Is he a decent sort of guy?"

"Susan, once again, I never met the boy. The only thing I can tell you is that he read the Greek Classics in high school. Oh yes, he attended a private school in Manila."

"This is so exciting!" Susan exclaimed.

"Good night, Susan."

CHAPTER 39

COLONEL KATRINA SAAKADZE WAS working out of a temporary shared office space in the GRU Tower.

She hated it.

At the beginning of every work day, she reported to the work space concierge who assigned her to a work station. Her office for the day was a flat desk equipped with a power outlet and a high-tech office chair, one space of many in a large open expanse on the eight floor of the building. She'd open her laptop, connect to the network, and in full view of everyone else consigned to this flexible arrangement, she tried to work.

By mid-day, every work space was occupied. The floor was filled with the sounds of people listening to music and watching American cable news shows. Periodically, small groups would gather at a specific work space to discuss an issue or plan some strategy. It was like trying to work in the middle of an airport concourse.

She hated it.

By the day's end, she placed her laptop in a carrying case, grabbed her purse, and made her way to the elevator. As work spaces emptied, the ceiling lighting above each newly vacated desk dimmed.

God how she hated it.

* * *

THE ELEVATOR ARRIVED at her floor, but before she could walk into the cab, General Irina Rybolovlev strode out accompanied by a disheveled, bearded man who struggled to match her stride.

"Katrina! Good, I caught up with you before you left for the day."

The general was in a buoyant mood. She made the necessary introduction.

"Anatoly, this is Colonel Katrina Saakadze. Katrina, this is Anatoly—" and she stopped. "What is your last name?"

Anatoly turned to Saakadze, "Popov. I am Anatoly Popov, Colonel. It is my pleasure."

Saakadze nodded her head completing the introduction.

"Dr. Popov's team has some good news for us. Where is your office so that we may talk?"

Saakadze turned and gestured with her hand in the general direction of the work space that had served as her office for the day.

"My God," Rybolovlev said. "This is horrible. I will never understand why you younger officers prefer to work in this manner. Let's go back upstairs to my office."

∗ ∗ ∗

"NOW THIS IS an office, Katrina. Don't you agree, Anatoly?"

"Irina, you are a general in the GRU," Anatoly stated. "As a general officer you have an office those of us in your service can only dream of having one day. The rest of us share office space, breath the same air, and pretend not to notice those working around us. Is that not so, Colonel?"

Saakadze was uncertain how to respond. So she flashed a big smile instead.

She would kill for an office like this.

"Anatoly, Katrina is too cultured to complain to her superior about the obvious inadequacies of her current work environment. You, on the other hand, live for such moments. Do you not?"

Rybolovlev didn't bother to wait for his response.

"Let's have Sasha bring us some of her wonderful tea."

The general walked over to her desk and pressed a button on her desk phone. "Sasha, hot tea, please."

"Isn't Sasha gone for the day?" Popov asked.

"Sasha would never leave before me. Never."

Several minutes later, Sasha entered with the familiar Scandinavian tea set. This time with three cups.

While she poured the tea, the general encouraged Dr. Popov to make his report.

"When Lowandowski was still employed by the FBI, we traced some of his late-night hacking activities. Banking institutions use a minimal form of data encryption. We've developed algorithms to decode this encrypted data—"

He was interrupted by the general.

"Anatoly! I ask you for the time of day and you tell us how a watch is made. Please, cut to the chase, as the Americans are fond of saying."

Popov smiled and continued, "We found where he banks. Well, actually, one of his banks."

"So, we know where he is?" Saakadze asked.

"No, not yet. However, sooner or later he will transfer funds to a bank near where he is living. That is his past practice. We have no reason to believe he will change tactics now."

* * *

ANTHONY CHARLES WAS in a lecture when his cell phone received the text message which now awaited his reply.

Charles established a small number of corresponding bank relationships. He kept the bulk of his funds in much smaller banking institutions throughout the Caribbean, Cyprus, and Russia. He used the larger banks to surveil activity on the smaller banks that held his funds. The text message reported a balance inquiry had been received and processed by one of the banks holding his funds in Cyprus.

The script which sent him the text message was prepared to liquidate his holdings at the bank in Cyprus by distributing the funds in new accounts at still other banks. He keyed in the code to authorize the fund transfers and to close the account on which the balance inquiry had been made. The corresponding bank sprang into action and initiated the necessary transactions. By the close of business, the account in Cyprus would no longer exist. The funds it once held transferred to a series of intermediary financial institutions before landing in new accounts at different banks.

Charles did not know who made the inquiry. He couldn't afford to let the money remain on deposit to find out.

* * *

DR. POPOV STOOD before Katrina Saakadze looking like he'd lost his best friend.

"We lost him," he said. "We'll find him, again. One of these days he'll get sloppy. Then you can pounce."

Saakadze flashed Popov her best and biggest smile.

CHAPTER 40

"ARE YOU GOING HOME FOR Christmas?" he asked.

"Probably. Want to come with me?" Beth McFarland asked. "I'm certain my mother is dying to meet you. She'll even let us sleep together."

"Really?"

"Oh yes, that's my mother. Throughout high school, the nuns preached the evils of physical intimacy outside of marriage. At home, my mother encouraged me to have a fulfilling sex life before settling down."

"That sounds awkward."

"It was. That's one reason I insisted on attending university in Europe. It's too far away for my mother to jump on a plane, fly all the way here, and cheer me in the bedroom."

"She would do that?" he asked in disbelief.

"Figuratively, yes. Wait. Make that literally, yes."

"Strange," he shook his head.

"Your parents?" she asked.

"We would be sleeping in separate rooms, armed guards standing sentry."

"Enough said."

"Well, not really," he sat up in bed. "I'm going to spend the Christmas holiday in Aix-en-Provence. Would you like to join me?" He smiled and leaned back against the head board. "We could have fresh croissants and coffee each morning, read while a big fire roars in the fireplace, drink wine all day."

"That sounds wonderful," McFarland replied.

"What will you do? At home in New York that is."

"You know," she started, "I hadn't given it much thought. I guess I'll sleep in late—without you in my bed. Eat cold cereal with my dad each morning—without showering with you. Visit my friends and relatives—without sneaking off to canoodle with you."

"You make all that sound so…sad," he pursed his lips. "Canoodle, huh?"

"Yes, as in lots of," she smiled.

"I understand that canoodling is a popular past-time in Aix-en-Provence."

"Well," she said, hands on her naked hips. "Count me in."

"Won't your mother be unhappy?" he asked.

"Not if I tell her I'll be canoodling."

☆ ☆ ☆

THAT AFTERNOON, CHARLES Googled for the name of a rental agent in Aix-en-Provence. He sent the agent his specifications. By evening, his rental was arranged.

His landlord, Frau Meier, offered the use of her late father's Mercedes. She kept the old car under a tarp behind her home. Charles told Frau Meier he was driving to Bavaria for a ski vacation.

They agreed on the fee which he cheerfully paid in advance. He arranged to have the local repair shop check out the vehicle. The repairs weren't too expensive.

One week later, Anthony Charles and Beth McFarland departed for Aix-en-Provence following their last lecture period of the fall semester. While in Aix, they would study for their examinations—when they weren't canoodling, of course.

☆ ☆ ☆

THE DRIVE FROM Zurich to Aix-en-Provence was supposed to require between seven and eight hours. With ongoing construction projects, stops for diesel, food, and drink, Charles and McFarland didn't arrive until the dinner hour in Aix. In total, they spent nine hours on the road.

Charles' previous driving experience predated his adopted father's death when he was a high school student and known by his adopted name, Charles Lowandowski. Regaining his skills on the modern high-speed roadways while driving the massive land yacht was a breeze. By the end of the first hour, he had regained his self-confidence.

"Your driving was a bit sketchy back in Zurich," McFarland teased.

"I didn't drive that often in Manila. The drivers there are crazy mad. Everyone owns small sedans or motor bikes. The traffic signs are only taken as suggestions. Imagine the Roman Coliseum writ large."

For not having lived in Manila, his description was spot on.

"Back in the States, most kids can't wait until they're old enough to drive. As soon as you get your learner's permit, it's drive, drive, drive. On weekends, we used any excuse we could find to borrow the family car, pick up our girlfriends, and cruise. The independence of it was a joy."

"Did you ever drive a car like this?" he asked.

"No. My mom's cars were always official 'mom cars,'" she replied.

"What's a 'mom car'?" he was smiling.

"SUVs. The modern day version of the old family station wagon."

"What's a 'station wagon'?" he put forth his best cultural barrier.

"Oh, it's a U.S. of A thing. Not something a young man from a backward country like the Philippines would understand," she teased.

Charles refused to take the bait. He smiled instead.

"How about your dad's car?"

"My dad's this big-time corporate lawyer. So he drives high-end luxury sports vehicles. My mom calls them MLCV's."

"Okay, what's—"

She anticipated the question.

"An MLCV is a mid-life crisis vehicle," she said.

He put on his best confused facial expression.

"I can't even begin to parse that," was his response.

"It's another American thing, I guess."

They picked up the key to their cottage at the rental agent's office, parked the car, and walked the short distance to Place Ramus. The rental agent recommended an eatery favored by the locals during the off-season, Le môme. He called ahead to guarantee the young couple a seating.

The restaurant was a hit for McFarland. She hadn't read a menu in English since her arrival in Zurich at the beginning of the summer. The experience reminded her of an unexpected encounter with an old friend with whom she had fallen out of touch.

The Corsican food was outstanding. She even managed to forgo her otherwise required hot chocolate for two glasses of wine—one was her usual ironclad limit.

"If you're not careful," Charles teased, "I may take advantage of your drunken state and ravish you back in the cottage."

McFarland's response made him smile.

"Consider yourself fortunate that I don't throw my panties in your face right here and now."

* * *

THEIR COTTAGE WAS a relic of the past. It was located behind a larger home in town and was at one time the caretaker's residence. The current owners completely rehabilitated the structure adding the expected modern conveniences. During the high season, the cottage was always booked. During the winter months—since so few people preferred to see Aix in the dead of winter—it was usually available.

While Charles built a fire in the fireplace, McFarland toured the small abode. It was one large room with a private bedroom and ensuite. It more than satisfied her needs.

When she joined Charles by the fireplace, she couldn't help but laugh.

"You're watching a YouTube video on how to start a fire?"

"I was born and raised in the Philippines. Try to find a fireplace in Manila," was his defense.

In minutes, they had a raging fire. The chill in the cottage disappeared, although the heat in the bedroom was another matter.

Charles had no idea how to operate the home's central heating system. Neither Charles nor McFarland had ever lived in a home heated by a hot water boiler system. They wouldn't discover the temperature controls on the radiators throughout the home until the next morning.

They dove under the thick bed covers to stay warm. All in all, not a bad temporary solution.

* * *

THE NEXT MORNING, they awoke to a raging snow storm. The young lovers bundled up and made the trek to the local *boulangerie* where there was a sufficient supply of hot chocolate, croissant, and the best preserves McFarland had ever tasted.

They left with a shopping bag filled with breads, cakes, and cookies.

"We should do some shopping for meals," Charles stated as a matter of fact.

"Do you cook?" McFarland asked.

"Don't you?" he returned the question.

"Nope. At home, my mom did all the cooking. I ate, of course, but never had an interest in cooking. That was my older sister's thing."

"You are a lot of trouble," he said.

"Perhaps, but I'm worth it," she replied with a smile that warmed him from top to bottom.

CHAPTER 41

THE THREE ONLY HAD THE five weekdays between Christmas and the New Year off. That wasn't sufficient to fly back to the U.S. and then return several days later to London, Rome, and Zurich. Eddy O'Conner, Alice Linda, and Joe McRory decided to celebrate in Zurich instead. They were their own European family.

The embassy's consulate in Zurich graciously provided O'Conner and Linda their own one-bedroom flats for the duration of the holiday week. They took their morning repast on the first day together in a nearby *boulangerie*.

"I'm hoping to connect with my niece while I'm here," O'Conner said.

"We should all go to dinner one evening," McRory suggested.

"She's not going home for the holiday break?" Linda asked, pushing McRory's suggestion into the background.

"No. At our lunch in Rome she told me she intended to spend the time here instead."

"Do you have a picture?" Linda asked.

"Believe it or not, I only have one my sister sent me several weeks ago. It's a selfie with Beth and her new man."

O'Conner put air quotes around "man."

"Break it out," Linda politely demanded.

It took O'Conner a minute to fetch her phone from her purse, navigate through the screens, and locate the photograph. Both Linda and McRory were amused by her lack of comfort using the device. O'Conner took notice.

"Okay. I'm a digital immigrant. What can I say?" was her excuse.

"More like a digital idiot," Linda teased.

O'Conner passed the phone to Linda.

Linda examined the picture closely—without saying anything. McRory immediately noticed and leaned over to examine the photo as well. He grabbed the phone from Linda's hand.

"This is a joke, right?" McRory demanded. "It's a bad joke. But a joke, right?"

O'Conner, nonplussed, sat immobile.

"Eddy, this is Charles Lowandowski," he whispered across the small table.

O'Conner laughed, "No, it's not, Joe, Linda." Then she grew quite serious. "Is it? It can't be. It's Beth's young boyfriend, Charles Anthony. He's only eighteen, like Beth. He attended a private school in the Philippines, he reads the Greek Classics…." Her voice trailed off. She fell back against her chair. "Oh my God. Are you certain?"

"Trust me," Linda spoke just above a whisper. "I spent enough time with the kid. That's Charles Lowandowski. His hair is much, much longer, he's grown a rag tag beard, but that's Lowandowski."

"Are you certain," O'Conner was repeating herself now. She was in shock.

"Well, if you can produce him and I can strip him down, yeah, I can confirm it. Eddy, seriously," she said pointing to the phone, "that's Charles Lowandowski."

"Oh my God," O'Conner quietly exclaimed, "How could I have been so stupid?" Followed by, "Oh my God, Beth!"

McRory stepped in, "Eddy, it's cognitive dissonance. You weren't out in the field chasing him. You were with your niece in Rome when she told you about her new boyfriend. Who would ever connect 'new boyfriend' with the master criminal who gave us the slip in Vanuatu? Over lunch with your niece no less."

"You two recognized him immediately," O'Conner responded.

"Yes, Eddy, we did. I slept with him for weeks. Joe poured him one drink after another at the beach. For weeks, months, we both ate, drank, and slept Charles Lowandowski—pardon the 'slept.'"

All three sat there in shock while the business of the *boulangerie* continued unabated.

"Where is she now?" Linda asked.

⁂

"SUSAN, I HOPE I woke you up! Turnabout is fair play, you know."

"Eddy, what time is it?"

"It's six hours later here than it is there. So that means it must be 4 a.m. in your warm bed as you blissfully sleep next to your adoring husband."

"Eddy, it's a five-hour time difference, not six."

"Afraid not, big sister. I'm in Zurich."

"No!" she was wide awake now. "What a shame."

"Shame? What the hell are you talking about?"

"Beth is with her beau on a ski trip in Bavaria. She's canoodling, Eddy, with her beau, Anthony," her sister reported with more than an appropriate amount of glee.

"Where?" O'Conner pressed.

"What? Why? Is there something wrong? Oh my God, is Beth okay?"

"Susan, why shouldn't she be? She's canoodling, right? With Anthony?"

"Oh, thank goodness. Yes, she's *canoodling*!"

"Did she say where in Bavaria she might be staying?"

"She did. For the life of me—it's 4 a.m., Eddy!—I can't recall. It made me think of the musical, *Grease*. I do remember she's staying at a hotel with 'neck' in its name. Made me think of necking, and you know, canoodling," Susan sighed.

⁂

COLONEL KATRINA SAAKADZE watched Dr. Anatoly Popov make his way toward her. She had never seen a man move so lightly. It looked like he could float.

"Colonel," Popov formally addressed her.

"Dr. Popov," she replied smiling.

"I told you we would catch him. Sooner or later he'd make a mistake."

"I gather he did?" she asked.

"Yes. He wrote a check to a rental agent—an electronic check—which we can scan as soon as it is issued. Had he written a conventional check, it would have taken weeks to clear through the EU banking system. Even then, we can't always make an inference about the recipient unless we do a deep dive into the recipient's account—" His pause reflected her raised eyebrows. "I'm doing it again. Aren't I?"

"Don't give me the watch, Dear Anatoly. Just give me the time of day," she said playfully smiling. She didn't know why, but she found this man endearing.

"Lowandowski paid an agent in Aix-en-Provence for a cottage rental."

He handed her a brief written summary.

Without saying a word, Saakadze grabbed her purse and made her way across the crowded bull pen area. Destination: The elevator and beyond.

Popov stood and watched her move.

"I could watch that woman walk away from me every day, all day," he said to no one.

* * *

"WHAT DID SHE say?" Linda asked.

"Beth is staying in a town whose name reminded her of the musical, *Grease*. She's staying in a hotel that reminded her of necking." O'Conner threw both hands into the air.

"Well, it is 4 a.m. in New York," Linda offered the best excuse she could under the circumstances.

McRory looked up from his iPhone.

"They're in Lenggries. Probably staying at the Brauneck Hotel. There's a train leaving from the train station in forty-five minutes. You can transfer in Munich for Lenggries. It's a very small town.

194

It's a short walk from the train station to the hotel. Total trip is about five and one-half hours."

Linda stood.

"I'm going with you."

"What about me?" McRory asked.

"Joe, please stay here. I may need you here if we miss Beth in Lenggries."

* * *

"SUSAN, WHO CALLED at such an ungodly hour?"

"That was Eddy. She's in Zurich. She wanted to get in touch with our Beth. You know, do some aunt-niece things, I guess."

"I thought she was in Bavaria?"

"She is, Edward. She is. See the postcard she sent? It's in with the morning mail."

"Where? I don't see it."

"The mail is where it always is, Edward. On the table in the front hall."

CHAPTER 42

THE TRAVEL ARRANGEMENTS WORKED in her favor from Moscow to Paris. The train schedule from Paris to Aix-en-Provence was another matter altogether. The next two scheduled trains were cancelled due to previously announced track repairs. By the time Colonel Katrina Saakadze boarded the southbound TGV train, she'd spent over two hours at Gare du Nord trying to look more like a tourist and less like a senior GRU military officer.

A little over three hours later, she stepped off the train and picked up her rental car at the nearby Europcar rental office. A little over an hour later she parked in front of the rental agent's office.

"Good afternoon," she offered the agent a friendly greeting.

"May I be of assistance?" the agent's reply was somewhat less friendly.

"I'm trying to find my nephew. I believe you may have provided him a rental."

"Your nephew's name?"

"Anthony Charles."

"I'm afraid I cannot help you. He turned in his keys and left this morning."

"Did he say where he was going?"

"No, but I'm going to guess he was returning to university."

Saakadze exited the office and walked to the nearby café. Once seated with her tea and croissant she sent a text. Thirty minutes later, Dr. Popov reported new information: *No watch. Just time of day. AC entered Switzerland in May on new passport. Received a student visa in Zurich. Popov.*

THE BIG LOWANDOWSKI

* * *

ANTHONY CHARLES AND Beth McFarland hated to leave early, but they decided to tour Besançon on their return to Zurich and the university. They arrived late in the day. Based on the rental agent's recommendation, they stayed at the Le Repère des Anges, a short distance from the city—walkable only in the warmer weather.

The next day, the couple was responsible for a torrent of photographs. They snapped selfies from the ramparts of the castle overlooking the river valley. They became a spectacle at every venue they toured.

"Are you going to join me in this huge tub?" McFarland teased.

"I don't know," Charles teased her back. "It looks like I'd never fit."

He leaned down and captured the two of them in yet another selfie.

"Of course, you can. Come. I'll slide over and make room for you".

"It might work better if I undress."

Charles disrobed but not before placing his phone next to McFarland's. McFarland was good to her word. She cleared a spot for her lover. By the time Charles was covered with bubbles and hot water, all the photographs on his phone migrated to hers.

The hotel's Wi-Fi was as good, if not better, than advertised. Within minutes, McFarland's Instagram chronicled their day in Besançon, and now the Larnod District up the hill from city center.

* * *

EDWARD MCFARLAND JOINED his wife for dinner that evening. He had something to discuss, but didn't want to alarm his wife, Susan.

"I showed the postcard to the partners this morning," he started.

"Were they jealous?" she asked.

"How did we receive the postcard so quickly?"

"It's one of those apps Beth has on her phone. She snaps the photo, turns it into a postcard. It's printed and posted here in the States. Voila!

"Why?"

"It was just one of the questions the partners raised."

"There were others? Like what?"

"John Gillespie was convinced the cottage in the postcard was one he's been trying to rent for years—without success, I might add."

"Really? Beth and Anthony are students. I know exactly how much cash we send her every month. I can't speak for Anthony's parents. It seems unlikely the kids travel in the same circles as John Gillespie."

"Exactly," he replied.

"There's something you're not telling me. Isn't there?"

"Just one small thing."

"And that is?"

"The cottage John talks about is in Aix-en-Provence. Not in Bavaria."

"I'm sure he's mistaken," Susan added somewhat less than convincingly.

Susan McFarland called her sister.

"Susan! What is it with you and telephone calls in the middle of the night?" Eddy wasn't pleased. "We traveled all day to get here. The trains didn't run on time—in Germany no less. We're both beat."

"*Both* of you?" Susan asked.

"Don't get over your skis, Susan. I'm here with a colleague who graciously agreed to keep me company. Now why are you calling?"

Susan McFarland told her sister. She could hear Eddy relay the story to her "colleague."

"Susan, can you look at Beth's Instagram account?"

"Yes, I have it here."

The conversation shifted to the phone's speaker. Susan's husband, Edward, could hear everything.

"Is the same photo on her account?"

"Yes."

"Listen carefully. My friend Alice will tell you how to read the geotagging information for the photo."

Alice Linda provided the step-by-step instructions.

"Oh my God," Susan exclaimed. "John Gillespie was right. The photo was taken in Aix-en-Provence."

Edward chimed in, "She's eighteen. She's shacking up with her boyfriend. And, she lied to her mother about some of the details. I don't see a crime here."

He took his dirty dishes to the sink and walked out of the kitchen.

"Edward is probably right, Susan," I'm sure Beth will fill you in on the details—when she's ready."

"I guess," Susan still sounded miffed. "I feel badly I sent you on a wild goose chase to—where did I send you, again?"

"Lenggries and the Brauneck Hotel. Now good night!"

After Eddy ended the call her sister said aloud, "Lenggries and the Brauneck Hotel. Sounds lovely."

Before joining her husband for an evening of television and a warm fire in the fireplace, she navigated to her daughter's Instagram account.

"Yes, dear Beth, canoodle away." She was flooded with warmth.

* * *

SAAKADZE FOUND THE address of the rental the university unwittingly provided Dr. Popov courtesy of the rental car's GPS. The hour was late. Too late for a social call. So, she improvised.

"Yes? Who's there?" Frau Meier called through the door.

"Olivia Charles, Anthony's mother," Saakadze did her best to sound like the concerned mother.

"Just one moment, please." Miller turned on the porch light and opened the door. She was wrapped in a robe, her hair in rollers, and her feet in over-sized fluffy slippers. "You are Anthony's mother? Please come in Mrs. Charles. I hope you can overlook my appearance. I wasn't expecting any visitors at this hour."

"Yes, and please accept my apology for disturbing you this late in the evening. I haven't heard from my Anthony in weeks—more than a month, really—and I needed to know that he was, you know, okay." She played the role of the embarrassed helicopter mom to perfection.

Meier smiled, "You mean you don't know about Anthony's *friend?*"

Saakadze responded with a mixture of shock and dismay.

"Anthony has a friend? He's never said a word about a girl. It is a *girl*, right?"

"Oh yes, she's very much a girl."

Saakadze made the sign of the cross.

"Thank goodness. These days you're never quite certain what your child will drag home."

"You needn't worry on that count," Meier assured her. "Ms. McFarland comes from an outstanding family in the U.S. Your Anthony could do much worse. If you saw what I saw at the university, you would realize how fortunate you are. Your son is the consummate gentleman. You have much to be thankful."

Saakadze sighed and her whole body seemed to slump with relief.

Meier suddenly realized how concerned the woman was.

"Please excuse my manners. Come in. Let me pour you some good Swiss hot chocolate, or something stronger, if you'd prefer."

Saakadze accepted the invitation and joined Meier for the hot drink and a small pastry as well. Meier proved to be an easy interrogation. At the end, Saakadze had all the information she required.

"Ms. Charles—Olivia—I hope you won't find this imprudent, but Charles doesn't favor your side of the family. Does he?"

"No, he is the image of my husband's father, God rest his soul. To this day, whenever my mother-in-law sees him, she's convinced her husband has returned from the grave."

* * *

SHE SHARED THE details with Popov. In turn, he provided her with the reservation information for the hotel he'd arranged on her behalf. She hadn't expected such thoughtfulness. *This man is slowly working his way into my bed,* she thought.

"If you can get me the information, I can look through her social media accounts," she said. "These Americans chronicle every minute of their day on social media. When I lived in the U.S. I found this practice astounding."

"Now who's telling how a watch is made?" Popov teased. "I know exactly what you intend to do once I send you this information."

CHAPTER 43

JOE MCRORY SULKED ALONE in Zurich. The trip Eddy O'Conner and Alice Linda made to Lenggries was a bust. Nevertheless, he would have enjoyed joining them. Now that they were going to Aix-en-Provence, he was pissed. Aix was on his bucket list.

Since he was no longer under house arrest, McRory made his first attempt at a morning jog following the end of his incarceration.

He set his course to start at the U.S. Consulate offices, heading north along the lake toward the city center. At the apex of the lake, he followed the Limmat River until he saw the Marriott Hotel ahead. The total one-way distance was a hair less than two miles. Round-trip it was almost four. Not bad for his first run in weeks.

McRory decided to do his mid-point turn in the hotel's driveway.

That's when he saw her.

Colonel Katrina Saakadze was claiming her car from the hotel valet.

What the hell, he thought.

He walked toward the building passing the rear of Saakadze's car. As unobtrusively as possible, he snapped several photos of the car before entering the hotel lobby.

"Hello, Eddy," his breathing was not yet back to normal.

"Joe, is that you? Are you okay? It sounds like you're out of breath."

"I'm at the Marriott Hotel. Colonel Saakadze just drove away after claiming her car from the valet. I'm sending you the photos now."

"Just got them," O'Conner replied. She promptly sent the photos to Henley via text. Quick as ever, Henley returned the text, *I will call you within two minutes*, Henley.

Good to his word, O'Conner's phone showed an incoming call from "Private."

"Hello, Eddy, this is Henley."

"Henley, did you receive the photos I sent to you?"

"I have," he responded. "Unfortunately, the images of the alleged Colonel Saakadze are from the rear, and the car partially obscures her body as she enters the driver's compartment, to be specific. Under these circumstances, a positive identification is beyond my limits. Nonetheless, I will adopt Mr. McRory's working hypothesis the driver is Colonel Katrina Saakadze and act accordingly, to be specific.

"I have identified her vehicle. It was rented from Europcar in Aix-en-Provence at the TGV station, to be specific. The car is now overdue at the rental station. The rental contract does not permit Colonel Saakadze to drive the vehicle into Switzerland, to be specific."

"What actions have you taken?" she asked.

"I've notified the rental agent of the vehicle's location in Zurich along with the photographs you've provided, to be specific.

"Further, Colonel Saakadze's hotel reservation, originating in Moscow by an A. Popov, extends through this day with a departure tomorrow morning, to be specific.

"I have summoned backup from our offices in Bern. However, their ETA is normally one hour and forty-five minutes. I have authorized the payment of tolls to save travel time to Zurich. As a result, the revised ETA is one hour and twenty minutes, to be specific.

"I have also notified Interpol that Colonel Saakadze, a senior officer in the GRU, recently PNG'd by the U.S.A., is in Zurich. I am authorized to notify the Zurich authorities, if you'd like, to be specific."

"Yes, please do that, Henley," O'Conner said. "By the way, Henley, Alice Linda and I are in Lenggries, Germany. Only Joe McRory is in Zurich."

"Eddy, I am already in possession of these facts. Following an analysis of your after-action reports, I do not recommend a delegation of ground control to Joe McRory. His success rate is below the minimums, to be specific."

Linda heard this last segment and laughed.

"The same is true of Ms. Linda. However, my analysis of her phone's IP address suggests she is in your immediate presence, to be specific."

Now it was O'Conner's turn to laugh.

"I concur with your assessments, Henley," she said.

"Unnecessary, but thank you, to be specific," Henley replied.

Linda laughed again.

* * *

MCRORY WAS ADVISED by O'Conner that Henley would be forwarding additional intelligence. Moments later, Henley's text landed on all three phones.

NSA intercept of telephone call between Colonel Saakadze and A. Popov requests Popov to provide social media accounts for Beth McFarland, a U.S. student at the University of Zurich, to be specific. Next, NSA intercept originating from A. Popov to Colonel Saakadze provides the Instagram account for Beth McFarland (click here) to be specific, Henley (Part 1 of 3).

Most recent NSA intercept originating from A. Popov to Colonel Saakadze provides address of Beth McFarland's student residence in Zurich (click here) to be specific, Henley Part 2 of 3).

DNI has issued the following--

McRory's phone reflected only the start of the third installment. The bulk of the message was never delivered. His attempt to contact O'Conner failed, likewise, his attempt to contact Linda. However, when he pressed the *click here* hypertext in the second part of the multipart message, a Google Map for Beth McFarland's residence appeared in his phone's web browser. Pressing the Directions link and entering "Marriott Hotel Zurich," the phone displayed the walk to follow to navigate the 1.8 kilometers from the hotel to McFarland's residence.

McRory briefly considered the only question that mattered: What should he do?

* * *

COLONEL SAAKADZE CONDUCTED a complete tour of the small student flat. She found no weapons, no chemical sprays—in short nothing in the way of a defensive weapon.

Saakadze had not lived the life of a typical U.S. female teenager while growing up first in Gori and later in Kutaisi, both in Georgia. She was stunned to find so many creature comforts and clothing. Student life in Georgia was ascetic. What lay before her smacked of parental and self-indulgence where money was not an issue. The contrast with her bleak childhood room in Gori, where she had recently spent several weeks, could not have been starker.

This will be easy, she thought to herself.

She made herself comfortable under a pile of scented comforters to ward off the winter cold.

* * *

MCRORY'S PHONE WAS working only intermittently. During one period when the phone operated without incident, he was contacted by the backup team dispatched by Henley.

Wilhelm, an operative assigned to the U.S. Embassy in Bern, complained about cell phone coverage.

"Just outside of Zurich, I received a partial text message from that fucking android, Henley. Then nothing. We're in the dark here. Any suggestions?"

McRory was relieved to learn the problem with receiving text messages from Henley was not his alone.

"I had the same problem," he said. "The McFarland residence is just up the *strasse*."

"Let's go," Wilhem replied. He was eager to do more than make the drive from Bern to Zurich on such short notice. "Get in."

The car drove the kilometer distance to the apartment building. The three men from Bern, plus McRory, made their way into the building and climbed the two floors to McFarland's. Her flat was at the top of the stairs.

The floor was empty.

"Holiday break," McRory offered.

Wilhelm withdrew a leather zippered case which, when opened, contained a set of picks.

"I was a boy scout growing up in Switzerland," he boasted. He mock saluted McRory, "Always be prepared."

Uncertain how to respond, McRory nodded toward the lock.

In record time, Wilhelm picked the lock and opened the door. He gestured for McRory to lead the way.

"No, please, you," McRory returned the gesture. "You're the one always prepared. I feel like a third wheel here."

* * *

COLONEL SAAKADZE HEARD the voices through the door. She withdrew her service revolver from her purse and attached the silencer.

The flat was in the shape of the letter "L." The large rectangle making up most of the flat, the vertical stroke of the "L," contained a small kitchen and a common area combining a living space, eating space, and a student's desk. The somewhat smaller horizontal stroke held the sleeping space and compact ensuite.

Saakadze lay crouched on the bed covered in a large comforter. Hidden beneath the comforter, her gun was pointed in the direction of the four men—three of whom presented before her in a tight group, the fourth, McRory, stood somewhat off to the side.

McRory spoke.

"Gentlemen, it is my distinct pleasure to introduce you to Katrina Saakadze, holding the rank of colonel, in her country's military intelligence directorate."

Wilhelm spoke next.'

"Colonel, it is our pleasure. Please slowly remove your hands from under the comforter. Bring them out into the open—slowly, very slowly."

Saakadze smiled, "But of course. I am outnumbered by so many brave and handsome men."

She quickly fired three shots, from left to right. Because her weapon was resting in her lap, the trajectory of the bullets was low, striking each of the three at midsection.

McRory saw Saakadze's eyes flinch before she fired. By the time the first shot rang out, he dropped to the floor and reached for his ankle holster that extended below the cuff of his sweat pants.

Saakadze's eye and hand positions were synchronized. Following the first shot, her gaze and aim moved centimeters to her right, lining up with the middle of the three men. She fired again.

By now, McRory's hand grasped his pistol grip and he pulled the weapon from its holster.

Saakadze's eyes and hand moved yet another few centimeters to the right. She fired a third time. However, Wilhem, on the far right of the trio, started to move to his right, her left, and as he did he was no longer in the trajectory of the third bullet coming from the muzzle of Saakadze's gun. She was forced to abruptly stop the rightward arc of her movement and start a swing back to the left, the direction from which she had fired the first shot.

McRory now had his weapon out of the holster. His right arm was swinging into a shooting position, his left arm and hand swinging into place as well.

Saakadze fired two shots at the flying Wilhem. The first shot tore through his light jacket but missed his body. The bullet flew past Wilhelm and into the kitchen where it shattered a series of three bell jars, two of which held dried pasta, and one which contained small, wrapped chocolates. Glass, metal lids, pasta, and chocolate rained down from the countertop and onto the bright linoleum flooring.

Her second shot was fired further to Wilhelm's left, where his body had yet to appear. This caused Saakadze to jerk to the left to properly time the shot. Wilhelm's body moved directly into the path of the bullet.

By now, Saakadze had fired four bullets through the down comforter. Pieces of material and down feathers formed a cloud in front of her face. As she redirected her line of sight and her hand to the right, where McRory had been standing, she realized he was no longer where she expected him to be.

McRory was in a classic, crouched shooter's position. Saakadze's upper body was obscured in a cloud of white suspended in midair.

Saakadze had only a moment to reposition her weapon where she thought McRory must now be. Doing so under ideal conditions would have been difficult. The cloud of floating debris in front of her made her shot an educated guess, at best.

* * *

LATER, MCRORY WOULD recount what happened. After he fired, he was struck in his left hip at his pants pocket. The force of the gunshot pushed him back on his heels, the gun flying out of his hands and into the direction of the kitchen where it clattered across the glass shards, pasta, and chocolate covered linoleum.

The pain in his left hip radiated down his leg and up into his abdomen. He lost his wind and was unable to breathe. His vision blurred and the scene of the flat's ceiling was replaced by blurry stars and flashes of light.

He remembered drops of some liquid falling across his face and into his eyes further obscuring his vision. Then all he could recall was the quiet.

Minutes later, he regained consciousness as his lungs involuntarily took in a large quantity of air. The panic of not being capable of breathing subsided as his lungs slowly regained function.

He reached down to his hip in search of his wound, to gauge the degree of the damage from the gunshot. All he found for his efforts was his shattered phone in its advertised indestructible case. As he slowly moved into a sitting position, he saw his empty and now shredded pants pocket. What remained of the phone fell to the floor between his legs.

I'm not bleeding, thank God, he thought, but I'm sure as hell going to have one damned painful hematoma.

McRory shakily stood. His three comrades lay motionless on the floor. One quick look around the apartment, and with no telephone to be found, he searched Wilhelm's jacket for his phone. Not finding it, he bolted from the flat and descended the two flights of stairs to ground level. As he pushed through the heavy glass lobby doors to the outside, he faced three of Zurich's finest screaming at him in German.

McRory slowly raised his hands above his head in surrender. The screaming didn't stop. He dropped to his knees. Still the screaming didn't abate. He fell forward into the snow with his arms behind his back. Finally, the screaming ceased.

* * *

HENLEY CONTACTED O'CONNER to inform her the team was in transit to the university hospital and the Department of Trauma Surgery.

There was only one train station in Lenggries, and all trains to any destination outside of this rural segment of Bavaria went through Munich. Instead of transferring to a train for Aix-en-Provence in Munich, O'Conner and Linda made their way back to Zurich and the university hospital.

They found McRory sitting in the surgical waiting room.

"Joe, are you alright?" O'Conner asked as she took an adjacent seat.

Linda grabbed a shock of his hair using it to twist his head in a circle.

"Alice, what the hell are you doing?" O'Conner demanded.

"I'm looking for his head wound. Look at all of the blood on his forehead, in his hair, and all over his face."

"The hospital staff checked me out in the ER. They couldn't find a wound either."

McRory's actions were slow and muddled. His speech and reaction times lethargic.

"They told me I could clean up at home. Maybe it was the hotel. Oh hell, I can't remember," the words flowed from his mouth like a drying stream bed.

"What happened to the other three?" Linda asked. "You know, the backup team from Bern."

"They've been in surgery since the EMT's brought us in," McRory responded. "All three were gut shot. Not a pretty sight."

"So this must be their blood all over you," O'Conner stated.

"No." His reply was slow but deliberate. "It must have been her blood."

"You shot her?" Linda exclaimed. "Way to go, Joe!"

"I guess," he stammered. "Yeah, probably so." He took a deep breath. "I'm uncertain."

"Hell," Linda complained. "What do you know?"

"I got shot in the hip. Destroyed my new phone. And the case." He looked at them both. "My hip hurts like hell."

"Oh no, Joe," O'Conner laughed. "Not another hematoma!"

CHAPTER 44

THE PAIN WAS FAR WORSE than child birth. Colonel Katrina Saakadze was overwhelmed by the number of nerve endings in her badly damaged fingers and hand.

The gun shot struck her own weapon, bending back her hand past the breaking point of her wrist. The gun pressed back in her hand until she could feel the bone fracture in her palm and several of her fingers. At this point, she wasn't certain how many of her fingers were broken. Clearly, there was more damage to her wrist and below to allow her to make any use of it while driving.

Earlier, while surveilling the several blocks surrounding McFarland's residence, she passed the campus of a private clinic advertising twenty-four hour emergency access. Saakadze maneuvered her rental with one hand into the parking lot behind the large building. Standing beside the locked vehicle, she took a deep composing breath and walked toward the entrance marked for emergencies.

One of the clinic's specialties was orthopedic surgery and trauma to the neuromuscular system. The specialist who examined her recognized the severity of her injuries.

"How did this happen?" he asked.

"My building has a large dumpster in the parking lot. With great difficulty, I managed to push up the heavy lid. When I tried to place my trash inside, I lost my footing on the ice. The heavy lid slammed on my hand. I must have blacked out. I don't know how long I was hanging like that with my hand trapped."

"Well, that's certainly a new one. Who ever thought dumpsters could pose such a danger?" His concentration was riveted more to her injuries than her explanation.

Following the brief physical examination, he offered his assessment.

"I can tell from the extensive bruising and swelling, the hyper extension of the fingers, you've sustained multiple fractures. You're fortunate to have made it here so quickly.

"We're going to place your arm and hand into a cold ice bath to reduce the swelling before there is any longer-term nerve damage. Unfortunately, you must have surgery to repair the damage. We'll take a full set of x-rays once we get you under sedation in the operating theater. Otherwise, the pain involved would be unbearable.

"Did you have anything else planned for this afternoon?" The surgeon moderated the bad news with a bit of humor.

"How does surgery and recovery sound?" she returned the levity.

"Good," he said. "It's a date."

"Can you save my hand?" she asked.

"Oh, for certain," was his unflinching response. "It's badly injured, but you came to the right place. I'll set each of the broken bones. Now that the bleeding has stopped, I can see the extent of the loss of three finger nails. They should regenerate with time. In the interim, however, your manicurist may be missing some of her work."

* * *

HENLEY'S TEXT MESSAGE took much longer than usual to finish downloading on O'Conner's phone.

"What's the story with cell coverage here?" she asked McRory.

"Tell me about it," he said. "Both Wilhelm and I experienced the same problems."

The text finally finished downloading.

Eddy, there are no reports of injured parties receiving treatment for gunshot wounds in the immediate vicinity, to be specific.

However, these reports only cover the public hospitals and clinics in a ten kilometer zone from the city center, to be specific.

We will continue to monitor reports and enlarge the area of interest to twenty kilometers, to be specific. Henley.

"Come, Joe," O'Conner spoke. "Let's have Alice and I get you back to the Consulate where you can clean up and change your clothes. Then we'll treat you to a light dinner. What do you think about that?"

"I'm really sore," he said.

"Yes, we know," Linda replied. "That damned hematoma."

* * *

ANTHONY CHARLES AND Beth McFarland landed on her floor to find the door to her residence wide open. A trail of blood droplets and bloody footprints originating in the stairwell led to her flat's entrance. As she peeked around the door, she found the blood trail made its way to her bed and bed sheets.

There were also several pools of blood in front of her bed as well. The kitchen looked like a war zone.

"What the hell happened?" McFarland asked. "Look at my comforter! It's destroyed and there are feathers everywhere."

Anthony Charles had an idea of what might have happened.

What if they found me? What if they discovered Beth is linked to me?

"Charlie, are you okay? You look like you might puke."

"Beth, this scares the hell out of me. Are you safe here? Should you be going home instead?"

"Who said anything about going back home? First, I want someone to tell me what's happened? Why does my flat look like a war zone?"

"Where do you start?"

"I'll call the landlord. She'll know what to do. What about you?"

"I have to return Frau Meier's car. Check my mail. You know, the usual stuff."

"Go ahead, then," McFarland suggested. "Whatever happened here is long over."

* * *

CHARLES COVERED THE big Mercedes with the tarpaulin in its usual parking spot behind the townhome. Before he could finish, Frau Meier opened the back door of her home and walked gingerly over the packed ice and snow.

"How was Bavaria?" she politely inquired.

"It was great," he lied. "The Philippines don't offer much skiing. So this was a treat."

"And the car? How did it perform? Did you encounter any difficulties?"

"With the car? No, it was fantastic." He briefly glanced back at the covered vehicle. "I filled the tank with diesel."

"Good," she said. "Why don't you come in for some hot chocolate."

While they walked to the kitchen, Meier mentioned her recent visitor.

"You never mentioned you had so young a mother. And beautiful too."

Charles did his best neither to look dumbfounded nor dumbstruck. Clearly someone pretending to be his mother paid a visit to Frau Meier.

"How is my mother?" he inquired. "Did she look rested? Well?"

"To be candid, she looked stunning. The two of you do not look alike at all."

What to say in response, he thought? He elected to side-step the issue.

"I wasn't expecting her to visit. Did she say where she was staying? I'm eager to see her."

"What is it about men and their mothers? I've yet to meet one who can cut those apron strings." She teased him. "I offered my spare bedroom, but she declined. She's already checked in to the Marriott Hotel."

Charles was already planning his next move.

"And where is your beautiful girlfriend?"

"She's resting from the long trip. We'll have dinner later this evening, after I visit with my dear mother."

"See what I mean?" Meier teased again. "Mothers *before* girlfriends. You men are so predictable."

*   *   *

BACK IN HIS room, Charles packed the bare minimum in his back pack. Picking through the mail that arrived in his absence, he found the brown envelope postmarked several weeks earlier in Manila. He stuffed the unopened envelope in his bag, took one last look around his room, and left the home with a heavy heart.

*   *   *

SAAKADZE RECOVERED FROM anesthesia without any ill effects. Her right hand and wrist were heavily wrapped, but thankfully, without any pain or discomfort.

Before she underwent surgery, she contacted Anatoly Popov and briefed him on her current situation. She expected to see him in another two to three hours.

*   *   *

CHARLES PURCHASED THE one-way rail ticket to Vienna using his Philippines passport stamped with his student visa for Switzerland. A quick trip to the ATM machine permitted the withdrawal of almost his entire cash balance. For the immediate future, he would make every purchase with cash.

CHAPTER 45

THE SCENE BETWEEN BETH MCFARLAND and her landlord was unpleasant.

"Look at what you've done to my apartment," the older woman screamed. "You are a horrible, horrible tenant. You are a horrible American!"

"I didn't do this. I am not responsible for any of this."

McFarland's hand swept the room, emphasizing the damage in the kitchen and the blood coating the floor in front of the bed.

"I left for vacation before Christmas and locked the door. I returned an hour ago, and this is what I found."

"You can prove you were away?" the old woman was skeptical.

"Of course," McFarland was working hard to maintain her cool.

"And you let no one stay in your apartment while you were gone?"

"No, absolutely not."

The landlord was checking all possible explanations from her years of tenants, some good, some not.

"I have called the police. They should be here shortly. Then we'll see."

The woman crossed her arms. Her face took on a self-righteous demeanor.

Within minutes there was a knock on the open door. A young man dressed in business casual attire entered and introduced himself as the detective assigned to the case.

"I have the report filed by the officers who responded to the call," he started.

"Who called?" the woman interrupted.

"One of the neighbors on the floor above reported she heard gunshots in the building."

"How many shots?" the woman wasn't going to make the officer's explanations easy.

"The report doesn't say," was his response. "As I was saying," he continued, "officers arriving on the scene encountered an American—" when he was interrupted again.

"Ah ha!" the woman spat. Turning to McFarland, "I hold you responsible for all of this. Your American friends are all like cowboys with guns shooting everywhere."

McFarland briefly stared at the old woman in disbelief. Turning toward the officer she asked, "The name of this American?"

"A Joseph McRory. He is staying at the U.S. Consulate where he is employed by a U.S. contracting firm on government business at the consulate."

"I don't know a Mr. McRory. I've never met anyone by that name," McFarland insisted. "I've never even visited the U.S. Consulate."

She cast a triumphant look at her landlord.

The detective looked back and forth between the two women.

"May I continue?" he asked. Without receiving a response, he continued nonetheless. "There were three men found in the apartment. Each was seriously wounded." He pointed to the blood covered floor near the bed. "The three men are all Swiss nationals from Bern. At this point, we do not know anything more about them."

McFarland pointed to the floor where the men were discovered. "I don't know anyone in Bern," she insisted. Looking to her landlord, "Do you?"

"Yes, I have family in Bern," the woman answered tentatively. "Why do you ask?"

McFarland let loose, "You insist I must know this Mr. McRory because he is an American. You seem to believe all Americans know one another." She laughed once to convey the questionable nature of such a belief. "However, you have family in Bern—where I know no one. So these three men must be people you know."

"Is this true?" the officer asked.

The landlord was figuratively knocked back on her heels. "Who are these three men?" she asked the officer.

He looked at the report. "The men carried no identity papers. They are still receiving treatment in the hospital. I will not be able to interview them until tomorrow, at the earliest."

The three reached what seemed to be a temporary impasse. The detective chose that moment to continue.

"However, we did recover a vehicle in front of the building registered in Bern."

"To whom does the car belong?" the landlord inquired.

"The car is registered to the U.S. Embassy in Bern."

"Ah ha!" the old woman screamed pointing her finger repeatedly at McFarland. "I was right. You Americans have ruined my beautiful apartment. All you Americans are in league with one another. I want you out!" she screamed at McFarland. "Take your filthy American things and leave here at once."

"Where will I stay?" McFarland asked. "All of my things are here."

"Go home, then," the old woman said with more moral authority than circumstances suggested.

* * *

MCRORY INSISTED ON escorting Eddy O'Conner and Alice Linda to McFarland's apartment. As the three approached the building's lobby, McRory saw his impression undisturbed in the snow. He instantly recalled being forced to drop to his knees and then a face plant with his hands behind his back.

O'Conner noted his ashen appearance.

"Joe, are you up to this? Alice and I can go up alone while you wait in the car."

"No," he said. "I'll be fine."

He pulled open the large, heavy glass door allowing O'Conner and Linda to enter the lobby. They immediately noticed the spots of blood leading up the staircase and the bloody footprints running in both directions. McRory saw them as well. Standing at the foot of the stairs, he took a deep breath, and lead the way up.

Once the three had ascended to the second floor they heard the shouting. As they made their way to the next floor, O'Conner recognized the voice of her niece, Beth. She hastened her climb leaving Linda and McRory in the rear. Both looked at one another and picked up the pace as well.

O'Conner entered the apartment and took in the scene. She saw the older woman and her niece in a stand-off while the police detective observed from the sideline.

"What's going on here, Beth?"

* * *

"AUNT EDDY? WHAT are you doing here? Did my Mom send you?"

"Yet another of these horrible Americans?" the landlord said under her breath but loud enough to be heard.

Linda and McRory finally appeared.

"Even more Americans?" The landlord was overwhelmed. "Am I to expect the entire American cavalry? Are you here to take this horrid little girl home?"

The police detective suggested introductions would be helpful.

"This is my Aunt Eddy. My mother's sister. She's from San Francisco," McFarland stated. "I don't know the other two."

O'Conner made the balance of the introductions: "These are my colleagues, Alice Linda and Joe McRory."

At the mention of McRory's name, the old woman launched into a tirade.

"McRory!" she screamed. "You are the one responsible for the damage to my apartment."

McFarland looked at McRory, "Oh shit," she muttered.

McRory stood silent looking from the detective to O'Conner and back again.

"Say nothing, Joe," O'Conner directed. Turning to the landlord she offered an explanation. "We received a report that a Russian agent entered my niece's apartment without her authorization. She was waiting for my niece's return."

"Aunt Eddy, a Russian agent?" McFarland was thoroughly confused. Looking at her landlord, "I don't know any Russians. I've never been to Russia. Ever."

The landlord stepped toward McFarland, poking her arthritic finger repeatedly into the young girl's chest.

"You also claimed *not* to know McRory here. But what have we learned, huh? You *do* know McRory—or at least your aunt does. And you do know your aunt, do you not? So why should I believe you now? Why should I believe you don't know of this Russia person whom you let illegally enter my apartment?" Giving everyone in the room yet another self-righteous look, "Russians, Americans—a pox on both countries. You are all hooligans who do not know how to behave properly in polite society." Pointing to the damage in her apartment, she continued her rant using her finger like an imaginary weapon. "You are all cowboys and cowgirls with your shooting guns and your spurting blood."

"Old lady," Linda added her voice. "You are a fucking loon. As far as I'm concerned, this whole country is filled with Nazi sympathizers."

"Alice!" O'Conner silenced her colleague. "We don't need two people spouting inappropriate statements. You are not helping here."

"Yes, thank you, madam," the detective added. "My grandfather, born here in Switzerland, died fighting the Nazis."

"My country thanks your family for their sacrifice," O'Conner offered with solemnity.

"See!" the old woman launched into yet another tirade. "This one speaks for the American government, no less. Americans, Russians—they are all heathens cut from the same wretched cloth."

* * *

MCRORY AND LINDA stood by the car. O'Conner and McFarland walked along the sidewalk.

"Eddy, what's going on here? Who are your friends?" she asked pointing in the direction of the car. "And Russian agents, Eddy? I thought you were a nun. That you took an oath of poverty and spent your whole life working for your order. Is any of that true?"

"Beth, I'm going to share some facts about my life that no one, other than your late grandparents, my father and mother, knew. I'm going to do this, because I trust you. Can I trust you? Because you cannot tell anyone what I'm about to share."

McFarland nodded her agreement.

"For all of my life—even now—I worked for the U.S. intelligence community. Originally, I joined a religious order as a cover for my work with the Agency in what was then communist East Germany. About ten years ago, I retired, prepared to spend the rest of my life in an Abbey atoning for the many things I did for my government that weren't exactly following the teachings of our church.

"Then Alice, one of my protégés at the Agency, came to me for help. I'm going to spare you all the details, but I left the Abbey and retired from my order. Since then, Alice, Joe, and I have been working for the intelligence community."

"Eddy, I had no idea. I think what you did all those years was great. Really. But what does any of this have to do with me?" her niece asked.

O'Conner turned to face her niece. "Listen carefully to what I'm about to tell you. Don't react. Just listen. Okay?"

"Sure," McFarland was uncertain.

"Our company, Triple Play, was asked by the intelligence community to investigate the murder of a young FBI special agent, in Washington, DC. We found a young man at the center of a lot of bad that was going on. We originally thought he was a limited function adult. He was hired by the FBI to do low level custodial work in their offices."

"Okay," McFarland stated hesitantly.

"Long story short, this young man was putting on a brilliant act. He conned the FBI. The Russians found out and tried to use his fraud to steal FBI counterintelligence secrets."

"What happened?" McFarland found this compelling.

"Lucky for him, he skipped town. No one could find him. For a while, we weren't even certain he was still alive. The Russians have been known to bury their failures."

"That's horrible, Eddy."

"Yes, it is."

"Was this guy ever found again?"

"Joe spent several months working the case. He discovered the young man had some plastic surgery and adopted a new name and what we call a 'legend' in the intelligence business."

"So, that stuff actually happens?" McFarland was incredulous. "That's the stuff of the fiction we buy for Dad, you know, gifts for his birthday, Christmas, and Father's Day. He loves reading all about spies and secret agents."

"I'll grant you that it's not an everyday event in civilian life. But in my world, in the intelligence business, it's not unknown. And this young man moved to the Philippines, created a new family, claimed to attend a private school—"

"Eddy! No way! You can't be serious. Are you telling me Anthony is 'that' guy?"

O'Conner said nothing as she looked into her niece's skeptical eyes.

She took a shuddering breath before stating, "I don't believe you."

"Believe me," O'Conner said. "Somehow, the Russians tracked him here to Zurich. They spoke with his landlady, learned about you. The Russians believed they could get to him through you. So, one of their agents broke into your apartment to await your return.

"By pure dumb luck, Joe saw the agent leave the Marriott Hotel here in Zurich. Using backup—the three gentlemen from our embassy in Bern—they confronted her in your apartment. The rest, I think, you can figure out on your own.

"By the way, your young man's real name isn't Anthony Charles. It's Charles Lowandowski."

"Wait a minute, Eddy. What was Joe doing here in Zurich? Of all the places in the world to be, it sounds like you're not telling me everything."

"Beth, I won't lie to you. Under national security rules, I've told you too much already. But to answer your question: Alice, Joe, and I are on separate assignments in Europe. I'm in Rome, where we met for lunch. Alice is stationed in London. Joe is stationed here in Zurich. I proposed the three of us spend the time together between Christmas and the New Year here in Zurich. I planned to surprise you here in Zurich.

"Only then did your mother tell me you were canoodling in Bavaria. I made my excuses to Alice and Joe and traveled to Bavaria to surprise you. I stayed at the Brauneck Hotel in Lenggries.

"Your father figured out you were actually in Aix-en-Provence, but that didn't happen until after I made it down to Lenggries."

"No! How did Daddy do that?"

"All those photos you've been posting to your Instagram, Beth. You and Anthony—Charles Lowandowski—posted selfies from your travels to Instagram."

McFarland stopped, pulled out her iPhone and navigated to her Instagram.

"Holy shit! You're right," she exclaimed.

"Didn't you post those photos?" O'Conner asked.

"No. Yes. I mean, I think I know how that happened." O'Conner waited for the explanation. "It's not important," her niece confessed. "Here I thought I executed a bit of brilliant misdirection by convincing Mom I was in Bavaria when I was actually in Aix."

"Beth, that's what I don't get. Why go to all that trouble? Your Mom knows you have a boyfriend. The 'canoodling' is what most young women would try to hide from their parents, but yours already knew."

"Eddy, you don't know Mom. I was afraid that she'd jump a flight to Bavaria—with or without Dad—to track me down and share in all my joy. My relationship with Anthony was mine. I didn't want to share it with Mom. Do you understand?"

"Beth, to be candid. I don't understand your Mom at all, and she's my sister. We grew up together. And I can assure you your grandmother wouldn't understand, or condone, any of this."

CHAPTER 46

LEWIS GINZER, A U.S. CITIZEN, formerly Anthony Charles, formerly Charles Lowandowski, was too preoccupied to enjoy the bright sunny Swiss landscape as his rail car made its way to Vienna.

Ginzer's fraudulent passport reflected a visitor's visa stamp issued by Switzerland. The only problem was that Ginzer had overstayed the visa's 90-day validity. Explaining to the border authorities in Austria why he hadn't extended the visa would be awkward and entail payment of a fine. The Swiss were highly efficient where visas were concerned.

He could cross the border as Anthony Charles instead. Charles' passport had a Swiss student visa. What he didn't know—and couldn't risk—was whether the border authorities were looking for Anthony Charles.

Ginzer elected to leave the train in Buchs while still in Switzerland. Buchs was within a casual two hour walking distance of Schaan in Lichtenstein. He was unlikely to be challenged by border officials from either country. Once in Lichtenstein, Ginzer could travel east by rail to Feldkirch, Austria—and beyond.

* * *

DR. ANATOLY POPOV reported to General Rybolovlev's office before departing to Zurich.

"Popov," Rybolovlev started, "please give the colonel my best wishes for a speedy recovery. I just spoke with her surgeon. He expects to release her from the surgical ward day after tomorrow. I have arranged her physical therapy with the sports ministry department that put our athletes to rights."

Popov grimaced at the thought of the colonel at the tender mercies of the physical terrorists in the sports ministry. Rybolovlev sensed his concern.

"Don't worry, Popov. The colonel comes from tough stock. She'll manage the rehabilitation with flying colors. If it were me, I'd do everything I could to have the sports ministry manage my care. They may be task masters, but the results they achieve are astounding."

"Yes, Irina, I agree. Nevertheless, she will not have what the American's refer to as a picnic."

They both produced a gallows laugh.

"Now, Popov, let's be clear about the outcome you will produce in Zurich. The decision by the executive committee is that you bring Mr. Lowandowski back here, or that you terminate him in Zurich."

Popov started to object.

"Anatoly, I know you have no experience with wet work. And this Lowandowski matter is not an appropriate assignment to lose your virginity, so to speak. So I have requested the Spetsnatz Group to assign a companion for your trip."

"Spetsnatz?" Popov asked. "Aren't you taking a risk sending someone to Zurich who looks like, and acts the part of, a special forces operator? Especially as my 'companion,' he'll stick out like a sore thumb. I might as well wear a t-shirt stating 'The Killer Is With Me.'"

"Always the comedian, Popov? No, I'm not sending a walking billboard for murder and mayhem as your companion.

I've asked the Spetsnatz to dig into their archives for someone with some antiquity. Not some doddering fool, mind you, but someone just as capable today as he was in his prime."

"And whom would that be?" Popov asked.

"His name is Igor Kuznetsov. He cut his teeth, and lord knows what else, in Afghanistan. The Spetsnatz hierarchy reveres this old soldier. They have him lecture at their academy. I've been assured that Igor will get the job done."

"He understands your preference to bring Lowandowski here, alive?"

"Of course, Popov, of course."

Rybolovlev dismissed his concerns by fluttering her hand above her head to emphasize he was needlessly worrying.

"So, go, Popov. Go see your girlfriend. Give her my best but tell her to get her pretty ass back in the office by the end of next week."

"Irina, she's not my girlfriend," Popov protested.

"No? Well, maybe not, yet. But I see how you watch her, Anatoly. Everyone does," she said smiling. "If it happens, it will be good for you both."

Popov, not knowing what to say, said nothing.

As he turned to leave, the general added one more thought.

"Popov, the colonel is not to be involved in this operation. Make certain she knows she's not supposed to come anywhere close to what you and Kuznetsov will plan."

* * *

THE PRIVATE CLINIC in which Colonel Saakadze was recuperating had a *private* policy regarding the use of opioids following surgical procedures. Unlike public health care facilities where opioid use was being curtailed as a matter of public health policy, Saakadze's orthopedic surgeon was free to prescribe opioids throughout Saakadze's recovery and her otherwise painful rehabilitation.

When Anatoly Popov arrived to visit with his colleague, he was relieved to find her free of pain and discomfort. She was clear headed and more than capable of participating in the impromptu tactical discussion General Rybolovlev had instructed Popov to hold in Zurich with Saakadze.

Popov was accompanied by a distinguished older gentleman. Looking like a member of the British aristocracy, his grandfatherly appearance belied both his feral and lethal tendencies.

Popov was not normally a fearful person, but Kuznetsov scared him.

CHAPTER 47

LEWIS GINZER STOOD ONE HUNDRED meters from the Swiss border with Austria. He reached into his backpack and withdrew the brown shipping envelope containing his newest passport. He tore open the seal and withdrew the document. A folded note fell from the passport onto the ground.

Ginzer looked at the note as it fluttered in the light breeze. His first instinct was a sense of foreboding. Retrieving and reading the missive provided confirmation.

"We know who you are and where you are. We'll be in touch shortly. It is in your best interest to cooperate. Do nothing stupid!"

He quickly did the math.

Ginzer immediately understood there was no hiding with either of his passports.

Returning from the direction in which he'd come, he made his way back to Buchs and from there to Zurich.

* * *

"WHERE IS THE boyfriend?" Alice Linda asked Beth McFarland.

"Frau Meier said he left her home several hours ago," she responded.

"He's gone," Linda stated.

"Maybe. Maybe not," McFarland replied in a small voice. "You don't know him like I know him."

Linda laughed. "Yeah, only if you don't count biblically."

"What?" McFarland exclaimed. "I know what 'biblically' means. You do not know Anthony in that way."

"'Anthony Charles,' no. Charles Lowandowski, yes."

The two women engaged in a staring contest, each determined not to blink.

Linda spoke first.

"You can thank me any time you please."

"Thank you? For what?"

"The sex. I bet it was good, wasn't it?"

"He had a lot of sloppy habits I had to change," McFarland parried. "You know what they say about bad habits?"

"I do," Linda thrusted. "Virgins don't have any and don't know any better."

"What's your point?"

"The blind don't lead those with sight. He has experience. You? None."

"You don't know that," McFarland's voice was petulant.

"Sure, I do. I know all about you."

McFarland's phone rang. She rose from the couch in McRory's flat and stood by the large living room window for added privacy.

"Hello?"

"Beth, where are you?" Charles asked.

"Anthony, are you okay? Where the hell are you? Where have you been?" She was beyond exasperation.

"Can we talk?" he asked.

"If you want to meet me here."

"Where's 'here'?"

"I'm at one of the flats in the U.S. Consulate compound in the city."

"What are you doing there? Why aren't you at your apartment?"

"Are you kidding me!" her voice was much louder now, attracting attention of the others. "Did you see my apartment? Besides, I've been evicted."

"The Consulate gave you an apartment?"

"No, I'm staying with a friend of my aunt who's working at the Consulate. If you want to meet, then you'll have to come here."

"Okay, I'll come to you."

"Ask for Mr. McRory's flat. He'll escort you from the reception area."

"McRory? Would that be Joe McRory?" he queried.

"Do you know Joe?"

She was incredulous.

"What else have you not told me?"

She was shrieking now.

* * *

MCRORY FOUND CHARLES standing in front of the fireplace in the lobby reception area. He was staring into the fire. The firebox was surrounded by floor to ceiling windows on both sides elongating the scale of the image. Charles looked small, defeated and framed by the windows and fireplace.

McRory approached from behind and tapped Charles on his shoulder.

"Charles Lowandowski," McRory saw no need to use any of the young man's aliases.

"How long have you known?" He asked without turning away from the fire to face McRory.

"From the beginning," was the response.

"And Linda McRory?" he asked.

"Her real name is Alice Linda. I think you two originally met in the FBI Office."

"No!" he exclaimed. "I would have recognized her."

"I'd say that's incorrect," McRory chuckled. "Or maybe you were too focused on seeing her naked and you forgot to carefully look at her face."

Lowandowski mentally ran through the video loop of his time on Vanuatu.

"Is there a nun here?"

"You must mean Sister Evangeline O'Conner, or Eddy, since she left her order. And, yes, she's upstairs as well. I think she's the only one you haven't slept with—well, including me, of course."

Lowandowski pivoted to face McRory. He looked like he'd seen a ghost.

"Oh, it gets much worse," McRory added chuckling yet again. "Your latest conquest, Beth McFarland, is Eddy's niece." McRory paused to enjoy the kid's chagrin. "Did I mention that Beth is Eddy's favorite niece in the whole wide world?"

"How screwed am I?" Lowandowski asked.

"Well, let's run with that analogy—or would it more appropriately be a metaphor? In any event, if you were a screw, your head would now be below the surface of the wood. In short, you have been sunk and countersunk."

McRory was enjoying himself.

Lowandowski took a deep breath.

"If I understand the lay of the land, there are three very unhappy women waiting for me in your apartment."

"Charles, in the short time I knew you on Vanuatu, I never thought of you as given to understatement. That, just now, was an extraordinary understatement."

"Well, lead the way," Lowandowski soberly suggested. "It's time to face the music."

"More like the entire orchestra," McRory added unable to help himself. His smile, however, quickly disappeared as he saw the older gentleman standing at easy rest across the street.

They walked toward the elevator.

* * *

KUZNETSOV WAS WEARING a hounds tooth pants and matching sports coat, a scarf around his neck. No gloves, no jacket. A small 35 mm SLR camera hanging around his neck.

The temperature in Zurich was almost thirty degrees warmer than Moscow. And it was an order of magnitude more tolerable than the mountain ranges and desolate plains of Afghanistan in the winter. He would never forget the horror of that country. It was a place where surviving the climate was no more than the buy-in price of a high stakes card game.

Survival among the tribal heathens of Afghanistan was far from a certainty. The Soviets were better armed, better clothed, and better equipped than the Afghanis. But his boys—and they really were still children—were not as tough as the locals.

Every time he sent a squad out of their encampment to patrol their perimeter, he started to write the letters of condolence for the mothers and fathers waiting at home. Too often, the patrol never returned. When they did, the survivors were often so shaken, so unnerved, he had to send them back to the larger bases.

He went out alone in the early morning hours to find what was left of the bodies. He lost count of the times he could hear the screams as the women finished the job their men had started. The older women, in particular, were especially skilled with their curved knives. They, as their mothers before them, disemboweled the wounded to watch their final agony.

That's when Kuznetsov started his personal war on the women of Afghanistan. He matched their cruelty, and often went well beyond, to send a message to their families.

When the Soviet forces completed their withdrawal in early 1989, Kuznetsov was one of the last to leave. His superiors were well aware of his atrocities, but the indignity of their defeat at the hands of the comparatively primitive Afghanis was used to keep Kuznetsov in place as he butchered one local woman after another.

He could watch the consulate building all day, if need be. The weather didn't matter. He didn't operate on that level.

And now he knew where to find Mr. Lowandowski.

CHAPTER 48

JOE MCRORY FELT LIKE HE was escorting Charles Lowandowski on the condemned's last mile. Unfortunately for Lowandowski, there was a fate worse than death. And, it was to be found just beyond the door to his apartment.

Beth McFarland joined Lowandowski by his side. They held hands.

"Aunt Eddy, this is Anthony Charles. Anthony, this is my Aunt Eddy."

McFarland blushed.

"Where are my manners. The gentleman who escorted you here—"

Lowandowski interrupted.

"—Joe McRory, and," pointing to Alice Linda, "Alice Linda, although I knew her as Linda McRory."

McFarland was confused and lapsed into silence. She also dropped his hand.

O'Conner spoke next.

"Charles Lowandowski, how are you? Were you followed here?"

"Aunt Eddy, why would he be followed. It was my apartment they broke in to," McFarland remained confused.

Her aunt was about to make matters worse.

"Beth, the person who entered your apartment is yet another of our acquaintances, Colonel Katrina Saakadze of Russian Military Intelligence."

"Eddy, what would someone from Russian Military Intelligence want with me. I don't have any state secrets."

"The colonel didn't want you, Beth. She wanted Charles Lowandowski," O'Conner said pointing to her boyfriend. "She was prepared to take you hostage and use you as leverage to get to him! She wanted Charles Lowandowski!"

"You're the second person to call him that name. I don't know who Charles Lowandowski is. But, I do know this man," she pointed to Lowandowski. "And his name is Anthony Charles. Tell them, Anthony."

Lowandowski took another one of his deep breaths.

"She's right, Beth," he slowly started. "And so is Alice Linda. My real name—actually, the name given to me by my adopted parents—is Charles Lowandowski."

"You were adopted?" she quietly queried. "I thought your parents were from Europe."

He stopped. The number of lies he had told her were about to be undone.

"Tell her, Charles," O'Conner nudged.

"My adopted parents were killed in a driving accident while I was still in high school. They left me a lot of money. Well, it seemed like a lot at the time. The probate court in Maryland assigned a financial guardian who encouraged me to get a job. I needed the benefits and an annual income."

"Your guardian made you drop out of school to get a job?" McFarland quizzed.

"No, I dropped out on my own. I wasn't a good student. Actually, I wasn't any kind of student," he said.

O'Conner sought to move the confession along.

"Beth, he posed as a limited function adult to gain a low level custodial job with the FBI. He conned everyone into thinking he was a—"

"Retard," Linda interjected.

O'Conner gave Linda a death stare.

Lowandowski looked into McFarland's eyes. "Beth I wasn't a nice person back then. I did things I shouldn't have done," he confessed.

"I guess I'll have to get used to calling you Charles Lowandowski," Beth smiled.

"Oh my God," was heard from everyone else in the room—including Lowandowski. "Beth, dear, you can't be seriously considering remaining with this person?" O'Conner was beyond bewildered.

"Eddy, I fell in love with the person Anthony—I mean Charles—has become. I didn't know, I don't know, anything about his earlier life. In fact, I don't care about what he may, or may not, have done to others before we met."

McRory pulled at Lowandowski's back pack. Once freed from the young man's shoulders, he dumped the contents onto the dining room table. Two passports spilled out into the open. McRory opened both.

"This passport states you're Anthony Charles of Manila in the Philippines. This next passport states you're an American citizen from Coeur d'Alene, Idaho by the name of Lewis Ginzer. So you were Charles Lowandowski, then you became Anthony Charles, and now you were prepared to skip town and assume the identity of Lewis Ginzer."

"Where were you going, Charles? Tell my niece you skipped out on her after dropping her off at her burgled apartment with blood on the floor and the colonel in the wind."

Beth asked in her small voice, "Is this true?"

Lowandowski started to cry.

"Oh, don't fall for the crying routine, Beth. Take it from me, those crocodile tears are designed to free you from your panties. I know."

Linda's "help" wasn't.

McFarland sneered at Linda and said in her best adult voice, "You are so vile."

* * *

THE DISCUSSION CONTINUED for another hour. Whatever outcome O'Conner thought they'd achieve, she was surprised to find that arguing with her niece was really no different than the many exasperating disagreements she had with Beth's mother, Susan, throughout the years.

Lowandowski, surprised to find he'd survived the confrontation with his relationship with Beth intact, insisted on making amends with his former landlady, Frau Meier. It was agreed that McRory and Linda would escort him.

The three left the consulate compound walking the short distance to Lowandowski's rented room.

* * *

IT'S SAID THAT you can't hear approaching electric vehicles. Certainly, none of the three heard the panel van come up behind them. They did hear the side door slide along its track as the van stopped beside them.

From the doorway, Anatoly Popov shot the tranquilizer darts into the buttocks of McRory and Linda. They each reacted to the sting by grasping and pulling at the dart. Meanwhile, Igor Kuznetsov ran toward them from behind. He spread both arms around Lowandowski and closed them like a vise while at the same time lifting the young man's body off the ground and into the open doorway of the panel van.

Kuznetsov landed on top of the boy and held him pinned to the floor of the vehicle. Popov pulled at one of Kuznetsov's pants legs to clear the track as he slid the door closed.

The van quietly accelerated from the scene.

O'Conner was watching from McRory's apartment.

So was her niece.

CHAPTER 49

WITH ASSISTANCE FROM THE CONSULATE security staff, and her niece, Beth McFarland, Eddy O'Conner recovered the limp bodies of Joe McRory and Alice Linda. Both McRory and Linda received prompt medical attention by the local physician on call. The physician examined the two tranquilizer darts and offered the opinion that a strong animal sedative was used.

Both Linda and McRory were slowly emerging from their torpor with the aid of large doses of strong Swiss coffee.

Linda was squinting and shielding her eyes.

"Whatever they hit me with has left me sensitive to bright sunlight," she complained.

"Beth, dear, would you draw the curtains closed, please," O'Conner requested.

McFarland was not thrilled with the prospect of providing any assistance to Linda and even less when it came to her comfort, but she complied nonetheless.

"Bitch," she muttered under her breath.

"Hey, it's my eyes that hurt. There's nothing wrong with my hearing," Linda responded.

"How are you, Joe?" O'Conner inquired. "You've had a rough two days."

"I have a horrible headache," he complained. "And the bright light is a killer."

McFarland placed a cold compress across his eyes. "Does this help?" she asked.

"Yeah, a lot. Hey, Alice, try one of these cold compresses. It provides immediate relief for the eyes."

"Okay," was her answer.

McFarland made no effort to prepare a compress for Linda.

"I'm still waiting here," Linda complained.

"Bitch."

⁎ ⁎ ⁎

O'CONNER RECEIVED THE text message from Henley: Based on an earlier report to the DNI, the NSA has intercepted message traffic between GRU HQ and geo coordinates corresponding to the Russian Federation's Consulate in Zurich, Switzerland, to be specific. Operatives A. Popov and I. Kuznetsov (photos to follow) will escort C. Lowandowski to the Russian Federation Embassy in Bern, Switzerland, to be specific. Date of travel is tomorrow, to be specific. Departure in the morning hours, to be specific. The DNI has authorized your intervention. Henley.

O'Conner, Linda, and McRory requisitioned vehicles from the consulate's motor pool. All three vehicles took up position on the A1 motorway beyond the toll plaza for traffic originating in Zurich.

Anatoly Popov and Igor Kuznetsov drove the same panel van. The distance from Zurich to Bern was well within the range of its battery powered propulsion system. Charles Lowandowski sat restrained in a chair with a hood over his head. As the vehicles approached the toll plaza, the CCTV system captured the images of Popov and Kuznetsov. O'Conner, Linda, and McRory received notification.

The panel van accelerated out of the toll plaza and quickly reached the posted speed limit. The three vehicles abandoned their standing positions alongside the roadway.

The vehicle driven by McRory accelerated past the panel van and signaled to enter the right lane occupied by the van. He was approximately 100 meters ahead. Linda's vehicle accelerated until she was in a shadowing position of the van. O'Conner's vehicle in the center lane pulled alongside the panel van. On O'Conner's signal, McRory's vehicle slowed and the panel van rapidly closed the distance. Linda narrowed the already small distance separating her vehicle from the van.

The van was effectively boxed in.

Popov drove the van. With the exception of this assignment, he was not an active field operative.

"Anatoly, we're boxed in!" Kuznetsov barked.

Popov maintained his composure.

"Tell me something I don't know, Igor," he calmly replied.

Without warning, Popov swerved to the right. The van left the high quality pavement for the rougher right shoulder.

"Accelerate, Anatoly! Faster! Faster!" Kuznetsov yelled.

The electric propulsion system immediately responded.

"Pass the lead vehicle, Anatoly!"

Snow and ice that accumulated on the roadway had been plowed throughout the night and into the morning hours. While the three lanes of paved highway were almost dry, the right shoulder was a slurry of ice and the salt brine applied to clear the roads.

The torque produced by the electric wheel motors forced the van's wheels to turn far more rapidly—virtually all at once. The tires on the van were unequal to the demands of the propulsion system on the wet and slick surface. The van swiveled rather than traveled along the shoulder in a straight line. Popov tried his best to counteract the forces moving his van toward the guard rail.

O'Conner issued the order: "Move the box to the right. Keep it tight. Leave him no room!"

McRory's vehicle responded first. The van's front bumper made contact with McRory's rear bumper.

"Slow it down, Joe!" O'Conner barked.

Linda's vehicle made contact next.

"Maintain contact, Alice! Keep the front of your car right up his ass!"

"Right up his ass," Linda repeated while smiling. "I never thought I'd hear those words from Eddy."

Once McRory and Linda formed a three vehicle conga line, O'Conner positioned her car to make contact at the left rear wheel. When she was ready, she swerved sharply right. The tire on the van disintegrated with tire tread flying in all directions.

Popov attempted to oversteer to correct for the van's rear end movement toward the guard rail. The right rear wheel of the van struck the guard rail and started to climb, its rear now higher than its nose. O'Conner took the opportunity to wedge the right front of her vehicle under the climbing van, in effect, nudging the van to flip over the guard rail onto the snow filled right of way separating the motorway from its property boundary.

The van was suddenly airborne. Its forward progress, originally a climb, slowed and the van's trajectory brought the front bumper into contact with the ground. The rear followed as the van rolled, its rear over front, two times before coming to a stop. The van lay on its roof. The wheels continued to spin.

Without the weight of the vehicle to moderate the speed of the wheels, they continued to accelerate as if Popov had floored the accelerator. As the wheel motors reached their rated RPM, they started to emit a high-pitched squeal.

O'Conner was already out of her car, weapon drawn, as she approached the supine van.

Kuznetsov was strapped by his seat belt, upside down in the passenger's seat. He released the belt's locking mechanism and fell down into the roof of the vehicle. This gave him the freedom of movement to pivot on his rear. He kicked the door window. It shattered into pebble-sized pieces into the snow and ice.

Quickly, Kuznetsov emerged through the opening as he withdrew a knife from his ankle holster. He drew back his arm to throw the knife but lost his footing in the snow and fell backward. He quickly repositioned and drew back his knife one more time.

"Don't do it!" O'Conner screamed. "Stand down or I'll shoot."

Kuznetsov smiled in response. Convinced he could throw his knife before O'Conner could gain position for her shot. He had greater faith in his knife skills than he did O'Conner's ability to fire with accuracy while on the run.

He was almost correct.

O'Conner, knowing she lacked the opportunity to take a proper firing stance, fired anyway. The bullet was slightly wide to the left and low. Instead of striking Kuznetsov dead center in his forehead, the bullet caught him high on his right shoulder knocking him further toward the madly spinning rear wheel.

Kuznetsov's head struck the spinning tire. The effect reminded O'Conner of the time she saw a large deer struck crossing a high-speed road. Instead of deer fur flying through the air, pieces of Kuznetsov's scalp and silver hair took flight above him.

O'Conner couldn't understand how, but Kuznetsov's head snapped back toward the tire instead of continuing to move toward her from the force of contact with the spinning tire. His neck scarf was grabbed by the rubber tread. The effect was to garrote Kuznetsov. His head was completely severed from his body, his heart continuing to pump blood spray into the air and the spinning wheel. The snow forward and rearward of the tire were colored a darkening red hue.

Linda and McRory took up positions in back and front of the vehicle.

McRory vomited at the sight before him and fainted.

"Holy shit, Eddy," Linda said with reverence.

CHAPTER **50**

"**E**DDY, WHERE ARE YOU?" Susan McFarland inquired.

"I'm *still* in Zurich," she answered.

"'Still'? The last we spoke, you were in that small village in Bavaria—with your female friend."

"Lenggries."

"Yes, that was it, Lenggries. So, now you're back in Zurich?"

"That's what I said, Susan. I'm in Zurich."

"Are you with your friend?"

"I'm with both of my friends."

"You have two friends, Eddy? Most people would be satisfied with just one friend."

"Susan, what the devil are you trying so hard not to say?"

"Eddy, what you do with your life is your business."

"A fact about which I am well aware."

"Let's change topics."

"Okay, change the topic."

"Have you seen Beth?"

"Yes, Beth and I have spent a lot of time together, since I returned to Zurich."

"Well?"

"Well, what?"

"Have you met Anthony?"

"Yes."

"That's it, 'yes'?"

"Yes, it is."

241

"What's he like? Are they good together? Are they, you know, canoodling?"

"Oh, for Christ's sake, Susan. If you want to know about your daughter's sex life, why not ask her?"

"You're my sister."

"Yes, I am your sister. I'm not your daughter's chaperone. I am her aunt and her friend. I am not a squealer, Susan. I never was. I am not now. I won't be one in the future. Are we clear?"

"Geez, Eddy. You are so touchy! I thought since you now had a *friend*, you'd be more mellow."

"Goodbye, Susan."

"Wait, Eddy, I still—"

* * *

"PLEASE CALL YOUR mother and answer all her questions about Charles," Eddy said to her niece while they sat in the hospital's surgical waiting room.

"What do I tell her, Eddy?" Beth McFarland asked. "That I fell in love with a man who's several years older than I thought? Who duped the FBI, possibly stole state secrets, and then skipped the country on a fraudulent passport? That he pretends to be a Filipino who graduated from a private school in Manila, but in reality, he's a high school dropout from the Washington, DC, suburbs?"

O'Conner gave the matter some thought.

"That's not a bad start," she replied.

"What did you tell her?"

"I can't tell your mother a thing. She believes I'm romantically involved with Alice Linda and that we were canoodling in Lenggries."

O'Conner shook her head in frustration followed by a sip from her coffee cup.

"Yuck," her niece said quietly. "You and Linda? How gross. You are way too classy for someone like Alice Linda."

"Thank you, I think?" O'Conner responded. "You do know that some female couples are older-younger or younger-older, not every couple is of the same age?"

"Eddy, it's not the age difference between you and Alice that bothers me. It's Alice Linda that bothers me. You can do so much better."

"You, too?" O'Conner was incredulous. "Alice is my *business* partner. We are not romantically involved."

"If you say so," her niece hid her face in her coffee cup so O'Conner would not see her smile. "I mean, you two do hang out a lot."

"Of course we do. We're business partners. Business partners work together."

"Eddy, when people my age hang out together it's usually because they're involved."

"First, my darling niece, you and your friends are university students. You don't have jobs. You don't have business partners. Second, if I wanted to have a romantic relationship with Alice—and I don't—then I certainly wouldn't be ashamed to admit so."

"If you say so."

"I say so."

O'Conner found the two conversations—first the mother, then the daughter—to be beyond maddening and tiresome. She stood and walked out of the waiting room.

"You are so like your mother," she tossed the words over her shoulder.

"I am nothing like my mother!" McFarland said with a bit too much conviction.

"Oh, my darling niece, you are so much like her."

* * *

JOE MCRORY'S COLORING was not yet normal. He still looked pale. By contrast, Alice Linda was ebullient.

"Eddy, may I borrow your phone?" McRory asked. "Mine was damaged yesterday and I haven't had the chance to replace it. I need to call my mom. If she doesn't hear from me once each week she worries."

"That's very thoughtful, Joe. Certainly."

O'Conner handed over her phone.

"Eddy, you are such a bad ass," Linda gushed.

"Alice, for the last time. I didn't plan Kuznetsov's—" she searched for the right word, "—demise."

"Can we change the topic?" McRory was clearly queasy. "How is Lowandowski?"

"Yeah, how is that little shit?" Linda added.

"The surgeons say he broke his right clavicle and ruptured his spleen. The clavicle they can't do much about. He'll have to wear a sling for one, maybe two, months. But at his age, they're not expecting he'll need rehabilitation or suffer any lasting effects.

"The spleen is being surgically repaired as we speak. That is, if it can be repaired. If it can't, then they'll remove it. Either way, they expect he'll remain hospitalized for the next week or so."

"So, what happens to the little shit after he's discharged?" Linda asked.

"Good question," O'Conner wearily responded. "The DNI doesn't want him back in the U.S. The Russians are apparently willing to go to extreme lengths to get their hands on him."

"If the U.S. doesn't want him back, then why did we risk our butts to save him?" McRory was aghast.

O'Conner said nothing in response. She met, and held, the stares from both of her colleagues.

"We were supposed to, you know, kill him?" Linda suggested.

Again, O'Conner said nothing.

"We were. Oh shit," McRory stated.

"My niece's involvement makes matters somewhat more challenging."

"What? Why?" Linda was alarmed. "She's still very young. She can find another guy like that," Linda snapped her fingers to emphasize the point.

"Alice were you never that age? That much in love?" O'Conner inquired.

Linda said nothing in response.

McRory, however, wasn't going to miss this opportunity.

"Your niece and Alice have something in common. Lowandowski was their first," he said smiling.

"What? My ass, McRory!" Linda was indignant. "My bedpost had so many notches people thought it was termite infested."

"That's hardly a point in your favor, Alice," O'Conner scolded. "I'm still trying to figure out a way to ease Lowandowski out of the picture without hurting Beth."

"By the way, Alice. Beth thinks you and I are an item."

Linda stood silent and stung.

"Oh no, Eddy. I can do much better than that."

CHAPTER **51**

DR. ANATOLY POPOV SPENT THE entire morning sitting outside of General Irina Rybolovlev's office. It was almost noon before Rybolovlev's assistant, Sasha, ushered him into the inner sanctum.

"Popov! Look at you," Rybolovlev criticized. "You are bruised, the scabs haven't had time to form on your wounds, and you're walking like an old man.

"I send you to Zurich for a simple snatch and grab. I give you one of the best retired officers the Spetsnatz had to offer. This whole operation should have taken place without a hitch. Instead, you conduct this simple business as if you worked for the American intelligence community.

"Worse yet, Kuznetsov is dead—beheaded no less!

"Do you know that no one in this building can recall an operation where one of our own was beheaded? Not a single one. That's how many.

"I can't even order a bowl of borscht at the Spetsnatz HQ cafeteria, if they consider inviting me to visit. And trust me, I'm not holding my breath waiting for that invitation."

"Irina—" he started before she cut him short.

"General Rybolovlev! You may not conduct the business of your career with the respect it deserves, you may not give the GRU the respect that it deserves, but you will address me by my rank and surname, Anatoly!"

Popov took a calming breath to steady his nerves.

"General, Kuznetsov and I successfully grabbed Lowandowski off the street. Right in front of the U.S. Consulate I might add. The problems did not begin until the next morning as we prepared to deliver Lowandowski to our colleagues at the Embassy in Bern."

"What is your point, Popov?" Rybolovlev face was crimson and contorted. "I have read your pathetic report. I know what happened. I know what didn't happen. And I certainly know what could have been anticipated.

"With all we know about this O'Conner woman, and her two idiots, you should have anticipated some hair brained scheme to wrest Lowandowski from your control would take place. Did you not stop to consider this possibility?"

Rybolovlev walked around her desk to stand face to face with Popov.

"You should have requested reinforcements, backup from the consulate, and failing that, the embassy. And I don't mean the U.S. consulate and embassy. I mean ours!"

She emphasized the last point by poking Popov's chest with her index finger for each word she spoke. Unfortunately, Popov's chest injuries from the van's steering wheel caused him to flinch with each stab of her finger.

"Good!" she exclaimed. "It should hurt. You should never forget the dishonor you have brought on this office."

"Yes, General Rybolovlev," came his defeated response.

"You are to go to Kuznetsov's family. They do not know of his death. It is your task to deliver the news. Be certain to explain how your ineptitude contributed to his death. And, if they ask about the details, you are to omit nothing! Nothing! Do you understand?"

Sasha entered the office and handed a folder to Rybolovlev. She read the enclosed one page report.

"Ach! As if it can't get any worse, Popov."

"General?" Popov inquired.

"I just received a one page memo from the Foreign Ministry. The Swiss have formally declared you to be *persona non grata*, Popov. You may never visit Switzerland again. You cannot even transit through the airports or their train stations. For you, Popov, Switzerland is kaput!"

"I am deeply sorry, General."

"Yes," she replied. "You are indeed."

Rybolovlev returned to her normal position behind the desk. She pressed the intercom.

"Sasha, come retrieve this despicable waste of trash from my office. And contact Colonel Saakadze. Let her know I will join her at the Marriott. She is to disregard my earlier order to return to Moscow."

"General," Sasha responded. "Colonel Saakadze's return flight departed Zurich almost thirty minutes ago."

"Ach! Everything you touch turns to shit, Popov!"

Turning her attention back to her assistant.

"Sasha, get me on the next flight to Zurich, reservation at the Marriott. Have my car meet me out front."

Rybolovlev stormed out of the office leaving a diminished Popov in her wake.

CHAPTER 52

"THE WEATHER ISN'T GOOD IN Moscow, I'm afraid," the ticket agent offered.

"Believe me, it seldom is at this time of year," Colonel Katrina Saakadze glumly replied.

Her injured wrist and hand didn't throb if she used the sling and the large supply of opioids the private clinic's pharmacy provided as a departure gift. As an added benefit, the opioid provided a nice buzz. It helped offset the unattractive prospect of returning to Moscow mid-winter.

Saakadze made her way to the departure gate for Aeroflot flight 2393 to Sheremetyevo International Airport. She took the opportunity to do some window shopping in the small stores along the walk. She made several small purchases from the duty-free store: Chocolates for General Rybolovlev's personal assistant, Sasha, a bottle of extraordinary American scotch for the General, and some condoms for Dr. Popov.

The purchases would be delivered to Saakadze as she boarded the aircraft.

As she stood before the security screening area, Saakadze paused. If she made her way through the checkpoint, then her assignment in Zurich would be a failure. Given her recent deportation from the U.S.A., Saakadze grew concerned that two failures in a row would be a blight on her otherwise outstanding record.

* * *

THE MONK'S ROBE and hood was raising welts all over his body. His face was flushed. His cheeks so puffy that his eyes were mere slits. He was quickly becoming unrecognizable.

He never would have worn the rental garment without first having it laundered. Unfortunately, he found the costume store at the last moment and there wasn't time to have the garment cleaned.

The eleven-minute train ride from the city to the airport provided Joe McRory the time to spot Saakadze before she cleared security. Unfortunately, once beyond the checkpoint, she was lost to him forever.

* * *

WHAT THE HELL, she thought. I'll show up in Moscow a day or two later than planned. I won't be labelled a failure. Not if I can help it.

Saakadze turned away from the checkpoint and walked in the direction of the escalators that led to the train station below.

* * *

MCRORY'S HANDS WERE so inflamed he couldn't stop scratching. The scratching only made the itch worse.

His fingers had swollen to the point that making a fist was becoming difficult.

When Colonel Saakadze turned in his direction, he panicked.

Shit! He thought. Now that I have a shot, my body won't cooperate.

He quickly ran through a list of possible interventions. Almost all involved a level of dexterity his hands could not deliver. Then it hit him. As the colonel stepped onto the escalator tread, he took off at a dead run.

As the escalator carried Saakadze down to the train platform, she was quickly dropping from sight. After McRory landed on the first tread, her head disappeared below the floor.

McRory leapt from the tread to the partial wall surrounding the opening in the concrete through which the escalator descended.

There was a parapet on the top of the wall holding a curved glass half-wall to prevent anyone from falling into the pit. There was just enough space on the parapet for McRory to land one of his shoes.

He had to move quickly along the narrow purchase to keep up with Saakadze. When the drop separating them was large enough, he jumped into the pit.

Saakadze enjoyed the descent, undoubtedly due to the buzz of her painkillers. Her whole body was relaxed.

And she never saw it coming.

McRory spread his feet while in midair. He managed to position each foot so they were aligned with each of the colonel's shoulders. As his feet made contact, Saakadze's upper body rapidly bent forward. Her own feet transitioned from a flat position on the metal escalator tread to the balls of her feet, and from there her feet failed to serve as an anchor for her own body.

She was in a state of free fall. Her good hand was still by her side. Her injured hand remained in the sling. She did not put her hands out in front of her falling body to break its descent onto the lower metal treads of the moving escalator. In fact, she didn't react at all until she heard the young girl scream.

Coming up the opposite escalator was a young mother holding the hand of her young child. The faces of both reflected the shock of seeing a flying monk descend through the opening in the ceiling to land on the shoulders of the colonel. The little girl screamed at the dissonant image.

By this time, Saakadze's body was now parallel to the train platform below and she disappeared from view of the opposing escalator carrying mother and daughter up to the airport's departure and arrival areas.

The scream drew McRory's concentration from the task at hand. Instead, he stared at the two people moving up and in the opposite direction. As they passed, the mother looked into McRory's eyes. She would later tell the police she had never seen such an evil face with slits where the eyes should have been and the swollen, blotchy, bright red complexion. Surely she had seen the devil.

Saakadze finally started to move her hands forward of her falling body. It was too late. Her face landed on the separation between two adjoining metal treads, each at a different height.

The weight of McRory above her forced her jaw to land on the zig-zag of the tread's imprint. The skin on her face tore in a pattern matching the tread's edge. The teeth on the left side of her jaw separated from the bone which shattered.

Her nose suffered lacerations as well.

She lost consciousness.

As Saakadze's body completed its forward fall, McRory launched toward the bottom of the escalator. His right foot contacted the bottom metal plate surrounded by the concrete floor of the train platform. He brought his left foot forward onto the platform proper and continued his sprint toward the waiting train.

Before reaching the first car, McRory heard the train chime announcing the closing doors. He managed to lodge one hand into the opening as both doors met. The obstruction sensor aboard the train issued the command to open the doors, and McRory fell inside.

Given the late hour, he was the only passenger in the car.

As the train exited the station, McRory opened the seat window. The cold winter air felt good on his face. By placing his hands on the stationary part of the window, the cold air streamed across his inflamed hands. The relief the cold temperature provided was immediate.

As the train accelerated, the cold air started to numb is face and hands. He nevertheless maintained his position letting the cold air mitigate the swelling and reduce the angry, red welts.

Payback's a bitch, he smiled.

* * *

"ALICE, HAVE YOU seen my phone?" O'Conner asked.

"Oh shit, yes. I forgot," Linda answered. Joe asked me to give the phone back to you.

O'Conner powered on the phone and checked for voice mail and text messages. That's when she saw it.

Henley, let me know when Colonel Saakadze checks out of her hotel, O'Conner.

Followed an hour later by a response.

Eddy, Colonel Katrina Saakadze checked out of the Marriott Hotel forty-two minutes ago, to be specific. A reservation on Aeroflot flight 2393 to Moscow in her name is scheduled to depart the Zurich airport at 10:45 p.m. local time, to be specific. A reasonable inference: Colonel Saakadze is returning to GRU HQ, to be specific. Henley.

Linda saw the concern register on O'Conner's face.

"What's wrong?" she asked.

"Joe's freelancing, again."

* * *

THE ELEVATOR OPENED into the consulate building lobby. Just as O'Conner and Linda exited the cab, a monk entered the lobby. The security staff member on duty challenged the visitor.

"Excuse me, sir."

McRory stopped and drew back the hood of his costume. While the swelling had abated, his face and hands were still inflamed. He was barely recognizable.

"Mr. McRory, is that you?" security asked.

"Yeth," he responded. "My tongue is thwollen, and I don't thound like me. But it'th me."

Linda bent over at the waist in hysterics, slapping at both knees.

"It'th not funny," he insisted. "I have an allergic reaction to thith damned cothume."

Turning to the building reception desk, O'Conner asked, "Can you have the consulate medical officer come to Mr. McRory's apartment?"

CHAPTER 53

IT WAS STANDARD POLICY FOR the city hospital. Whenever a foreigner was admitted, the patient's consulate was notified. The consulate, in turn, notified General Rybolovlev's personal assistant, Sasha. Unfortunately, Sasha could not notify the general until her flight landed in Zurich.

Rybolovlev's first reaction was anger.

"Sasha, you told me Colonel Saakadze was already enroute to Moscow!"

"That's what she reported in her text message, General. Is the Colonel okay? The consulate didn't have any information about her injuries. Just that she was admitted and in surgery."

"Ach!" Rybolovlev spat. "In surgery, again?"

"Yes, General."

☆ ☆ ☆

FOLLOWING A BRIEF visit to the Russian Federation Consulate, Rybolovlev made her way to the hospital. The physician charged with Saakadze's treatment briefed her on the extent of her subordinate's injuries.

"Katrina sustained the majority of her injuries to her face," Dr. Bachman reported.

"The majority?" Rybolovlev followed. "There were other injuries—beyond her face, I mean?"

"Well, yes. Apparently, Katrina was discharged from a private clinic in the city earlier today. According to her physician at the clinic, Katrina sustained fractures to several fingers, her hand, and her wrist.

"When she fell on the escalator, she reinjured her fingers. The hand and wrist repairs by her orthopedic surgeon remain intact.

"Then there are the contusions to both her shoulders. Whatever struck her, did so with significant force. Fortunately, the damage is temporary—mostly soft tissue injuries, although those tend to be quite painful."

"What about her facial injuries, Doctor?"

"Her jaw was severely fractured from the force of her fall onto the metal escalator tread. Again, the force was substantial. When she was admitted to the emergency ward, the imprint of the metal tread could be clearly seen on her face.

"I looked in on Katrina prior to your arrival. If you look carefully, you can still see the outline of the jagged edge of the tread. I expect the bruising will take several weeks to fade.

"We wired her jaw together, but we were unable to save the teeth that were dislodged. Our maxillofacial surgeon has inserted a spacer to properly align her jaw. Once she has recovered, Katrina will require substantial restorative dentistry.

"And then there was the laceration."

"How bad was it, Doctor?"

"As lacerations go, it was shallow. There was no muscle or tendon involvement. Katrina was fortunate in that regard. She will regain complete control of her facial gestures."

"Do I hear a 'but' in that statement, Doctor?"

"Yes, you do," he responded. "While the laceration was shallow, it was long. It spans the distance above her ear to the bottom of her jaw.

"Our plastic surgeon is one of the best in the Zurich. He worked very hard to minimize the scarring. However, he is concerned that with her fair skin a permanent remnant is possible. Whether or not that comes to pass, whether Katrina will require additional surgery is not yet known."

"May I see her?" Rybolovlev asked.

"She was briefly conscious following surgery. I spoke with her in the recovery room where I described her injuries as tactfully as possible. Unfortunately, her reaction causes me concern about her mental and emotional health. I ordered a sedative. We will likely maintain her sedation for the next several days. I am not eager for her to see her image in a mirror. And I certainly do not want a visitor's reaction to her injuries to cause further distress.

"I must ask: Why are you here to visit? Does she have parents or family nearby?"

"Her parents are infirm and unable to travel the long distance involved. Katrina is their only child, and under the circumstances, it is probably best that they not see Katrina in her present state. When she is better, of course."

"Yes, but it is unusual for an employer to act as family in these situations, Ms. Rybolovlev."

"We are much more than supervisor and subordinate, Doctor. Much more."

Bachmann gave Rybolovlev an appraisal.

"Yes, of course," he responded. "Is there anything else I can tell you?"

* * *

EDDY O'CONNER, ALICE Linda, and Joe McRory reached an impasse.

O'Conner was unable to persuade either Alice or Joe that acting on their own in company matters was unwise for any number of reasons.

"Joe, I appreciate your need to seek retribution for your injuries," O'Conner tried one more time.

The injection of epinephrine administered by the consulate's physician reduced his swollen face. His speech returned to normal.

"Not just my injuries, but what they did to Alice. The slate of slights and indignities was too extensive to overlook, Eddy."

"I don't often agree with Joe, but in this case I do, Eddy," Linda insisted. "This team of Russian GRU types pushed us too far. If we don't push back, they'll steam roller us whenever they please.

"Back in the day, when you were undercover in East Germany, would the agency let an injury or death to one of their own pass?"

O'Conner sensed the futility of pressing the issue further. She changed the topic.

"How seriously did you injure the good colonel?" she asked Joe.

"I gave as good as I got," was his response.

O'Conner's face suddenly turned ashen.

"Do you think they took her to the hospital?"

"I'm certain of it," McRory answered. "Why?"

"Charles is still there. Beth is with him non-stop."

* * *

GENERAL RYBOLOVLEV LEANED against the wall outside Saakadze's room. As she contemplated the colonel's injuries her anger with the Americans developed into a burning white hate.

It was the dinner hour. A hospital employee pushed a cart with meals down the hall. As the cart rolled by Rybolovlev she saw each meal was labelled by patient and room number.

"Lowandowski!" she said aloud.

"I'm sorry," the employee asked. "Were you speaking to me?"

"Yes," she was improvising. "I'm here visiting two of my friends, Katrina Saakadze and Charles Lowandowski."

"You have two friends in the hospital at the same time?"

"What are the odds?" Rybolovlev remarked.

* * *

O'CONNER WALKED THROUGH the lobby of the university hospital toward the elevators. As the doors opened, a stylishly dressed woman exited. O'Conner gave way, letting the woman pass.

There was something about the woman. O'Conner did not know her. She also did not *not* know her, or more precisely, her archetype.

As she walked away from the elevator and O'Conner, there was something about the woman's posture and her stride that was familiar. O'Conner decided to follow.

The woman exited the lobby and made her way to the sidewalk where she paused. Removing a phone from her clutch, she made a call.

O'Conner watched one side of the telephone conversation from the warmth of the lobby. The woman was clearly excited. She punctuated her comments by jabbing a finger into the air. Her warm breath produced a series of small clouds with each point she made. Clearly, someone was getting an earful.

O'Conner sent a photo of the woman as an attachment to a text. She awaited the response. She didn't have to wait long.

Eddy, with a probability of sixty percent, the subject in the photograph is General Irina Rybolovlev of the GRU, to be specific. Checking the Zurich Airport's CCTV surveillance, I've identified a passenger on an arriving Aeroflot flight last evening with similar clothing, height, and weight, to be specific. The same person checked into the Marriott Hotel one hour and fifty minutes later, to be specific. Will check with the NSA if their surveillance shows a telephone call at this date and time with geo coordinates for the university hospital. Henley.

O'Conner texted Linda and McRory:

Get to hospital as quickly as you can. Come prepared.

* * *

EDDY O'CONNER EXITED the elevator and rapidly made her way to Charles Lowandowski's room. As she turned the corner and the corridor came into view she saw a priest leave Lowandowski's room. As they passed one another, O'Conner greeted the cleric, "Father."

She walked into the private room to find her niece Beth McFarland holding hands with Lowandowski.

"We're married!" McFarland squealed.

CHAPTER **54**

"**Y**OU CAN'T BE," AN incredulous Eddy O'Conner responded.

"We are," gushed the bride.

Charles Lowandowski smiled and affirmed the deed was done.

"How did you satisfy the residency requirements?" O'Conner asked.

"Charles went on-line and whipped up the bureaucratic stuff this country demands." The bride was still gushing. "Isn't that romantic?"

"Well, it's certainly resourceful—and very illegal, Beth," O'Conner was deliberately raining on her niece's parade.

"In any event," Beth McFarland-Lowandowski retorted, "the priest made it all official. In the eyes of the Church, we are united as man and wife."

She flashed her new engagement ring and wedding band.

"How did you arrange for the rings?"

"Charles did it all!"

"Let me guess. He did everything online. All of this—" O'Conner gestured with her hand to include the flowers, the rings, and the departed priest, "—was done using the internet and *your* hacking skills." The last comment was directed at her new nephew.

"Well, I've been tied up in the hospital recovering from my surgery. How else did you expect me to get all of this done?"

"Not at all!" O'Conner insisted. "I'd prefer that you didn't do any of this," again with the hand gesture. "This is all wrong, Beth. And you're too young to be married. There's so much of life you have yet to experience. And look who you picked to be your husband."

O'Conner was on an unfiltered roll.

"Hey," a wounded Lowandowski interjected. "I'm laying right here, you know."

"Oh please," O'Conner dismissed the wounded feelings of her latest nephew. "You're a criminal. You're a thief. And lord knows what else."

"Aunt Eddy, I love you dearly and I'm touched by your concern. But Charles is my husband now. You need to accept my decision— our decision."

McFarland-Lowandowski took her husband's hand in her own.

"What about your parents, Beth? What is your mother going to say about this? What about your father?"

"They'll be here tonight?" was her response.

"They know?" O'Conner's incredulity returned. "They approve?"

"Charles contacted them yesterday and sent them first class tickets to fly here and help us celebrate." She looked adoringly into the eyes of her husband. "Daddy's going to treat us to a big wedding supper as soon as Charles is discharged from the hospital."

* * *

ALICE LINDA AND Joe McRory took the stairs to the fourth floor rather than wait for the elevator to arrive. By the time they entered Lowandowski's room, they were winded. And confused.

The room was filled with flowers. McFarland and Lowandowski were grinning like idiots. O'Conner, who sounded the alarm summoning them to the hospital, sat dumbfounded in a chair staring into space.

"What the hell is going on?" Linda asked.

"We're married!" screamed the bride.

"No shit, girlfriend," was Linda's shocked response. Looking toward O'Conner, "Is this true?"

"You are not my *girlfriend*, bitch," McFarland hissed.

McRory found his voice, "Beth you have to lose the hostility toward Alice."

"Wives don't like the women who've slept with their husband," was her petulant response.

"I wasn't his girlfriend," Linda said pointing to Lowandowski.

"All right, wives don't like their husband's whores!"

"Enough!" O'Conner screamed.

* * *

THE THREE TOOK their conversation to the nearby waiting room.

"Eddy, you do realize that the three of us are now responsible for protecting the bride, the groom, and her parents from the crazy Russian GRU general who wants us all dead?" McRory queried.

"It's become a nightmare," Linda dryly observed. "How are you going to explain this to the DNI?"

O'Conner removed her phone from a coat pocket and started texting.

Henley, please inform the DNI that my niece, Beth McFarland, has married Charles Lowandowski, Eddy.

The response was immediate.

Eddy, please correct typographical errors and resubmit, to be specific, Henley.

"So the android has a sense of humor?" McRory added.

Henley, there was no error. Eddy.

The next response was a bit less timely.

Eddy, upon a review of the historical record, this marriage should have been recognized as possible—probable, in fact, to be specific. The DNI has cancelled the termination of Charles Lowandowski, to be specific. The DNI has instructed me to state the following on his behalf: "He's your problem now," to be specific. Henley.

* * *

MEANWHILE, A QUIET observer stood around the corner, hidden from view. The voices coming from Lowandowski's room were easily overheard from her vantage point.

CHAPTER 55

SWISS AIR FLIGHT LX15 LANDED at Zurich's airport at 10:50 a.m. Edward and Susan McFarland were among the first group of passengers to thread their way through immigration and customs. Susan still wore the corsage her new son-in-law had delivered for the mother of the bride.

Neither of the McFarland's had slept since receiving the telephone call from their youngest daughter announcing her forthcoming marriage. They knew very little about Charlie, except his name wasn't Anthony Charles after all. Nevertheless, they had flown more than 3,900 miles to meet the young man who had so captivated their daughter in so little time.

As the McFarlands passed through the final doorway separating the secure area of the airport from the general population they were welcomed by the hundreds of greeters present to claim their own arriving friends and family.

"Edward, I don't see them. Do you?"

"Susan, I don't know a 'them.' I know my daughter when I see her, but I've only seen the kid from photos where they were connected at the mouth."

"You are so cranky pants, when you fail to sleep through the night."

"I'm not cranky, Susan. What I am is worried about my youngest daughter. The thought of her spending the rest of her life with a boy we know nothing about—change that," he said, "we do know he met her under false pretenses—does not warm a father-in-law's heart."

"Edward, let's be realistic. Shall we?" his wife started. "If this marriage works out, then fine. You've worried about nothing."

"And?" he followed with more than a little doubt in his voice.

"*And*, if it doesn't, then they'll separate and divorce. Beth will have another chance to meet the right guy."

"That thought is supposed to make feel better, Susan? Honestly, there are times I wonder if I know you at all."

He was too tired and worried to sound exasperated, but he was.

"Edward, listen to me. I am the mother of the bride. I'm wearing a mother's corsage. A corsage my new son-in-law purchased for me—not the new father-in-law. So not only is it official, but I won't listen to you try to ruin my day."

"Susan, news flash: You're not the bride. The day isn't yours."

Susan ignored his last remark when she saw the driver carrying a tablet with their name in large letters.

"Oh look, Edward, Charles has arranged for a driver to take us to the hospital."

"We're the McFarlands," Edward announced to the smallish woman dressed in driver's livery.

"Please follow me," the driver responded.

The McFarlands had to rush to keep up with their driver.

"Shouldn't she be pulling our luggage?" Susan whispered to her husband.

"Maybe not, Susan. This is Europe, after all.

The driver passed through the lobby doors and out onto the sidewalk where the other drivers' vehicles were parked. She stopped at a small, black BMW sedan. A two door vehicle. There was a ticket under the wiper blade.

"Is this our car?" Susan was bewildered. "Aren't limos supposed to be larger?"

"Madam, this is the land of smaller cars. You are not in America. By the way, this is a rental. Our regular vehicle is in the shop for repairs."

The driver pulled open the passenger door and folded the passenger seat forward. The McFarlands became contortionists as they bent and swiveled their bodies to make their way into the rear seats. She slammed the door shut.

"Limo drivers here border on the rude. Don't you think?" Susan asked.

"Well, Susan, like she said, we aren't in America anymore."

They could hear the driver struggle to fit the two large suitcases into the cramped trunk. After positioning and repositioning the luggage more than several times, she finally succeeded and slipped into the driver's seat.

"What is your name?" Susan asked.

"You may call me Irina," she replied.

* * *

ALL FIVE REMAINED in the private hospital room. McRory borrowed additional chairs from nearby rooms. Beth McFarland laid, fully dressed in a stylish, large cardigan sweater with deep pockets, and her boots, on top of the blanket next to her new husband.

Everyone was uncomfortable by the close quarters.

Charles Lowandowski's phone rang. His new bride answered.

"Hello, yes it is. No, he cannot. I'm his wife," she smiled. "What do you mean they didn't arrive?"

Eddy O'Conner shot out of the chair and grabbed the phone from a stunned Beth McFarland-Lowandowski.

"This is Eddy O'Conner. I'm Susan McFarland's sister. Edward McFarland is my brother-in-law. What's going on?"

She listened to the voice at the other end.

"We know they landed. My sister texted me after they cleared immigration."

Another pause on O'Conner's end of the conversation.

"Well, why didn't you say so initially? Did you have them paged? Did anyone respond to the page?"

One final pause.

"Yes, please have your driver go back and make one more try. I'm sure they're still in the airport."

O'Conner gave the phone back to her niece.

"That was the limo company—" she started before her niece interrupted.

"Eddy, we know that. We could hear. Where are mom and dad?"

"The driver returned to the airport to give it another try," O'Conner hid the concern from her reply. "They were probably in the restroom and missed the driver." Then she added, "Oh yes, the driver arrived late. He had an unexpected flat tire."

"Are flat tires ever *expected*?" Lowandowski's attempt at humor went unappreciated by everyone except his new bride.

"You are so smart," she said as she snuggled closer.

Alice Linda pantomimed vomiting.

"I saw that, bitch."

* * *

THEY STOOD OUTSIDE the room in the hallway.

"I'm sorry, Alice," O'Conner began. "I had no idea my niece could be so rude."

"She's still very young and insecure," Linda countered. "You don't need to apologize for her. She's responsible for her own actions."

"Eddy, I don't like the sound of the 'late driver missed his pickup'," said Joe McRory.

"Normally, Joe, I'd be worried. However, this is my brother-in-law we're talking about. Edward McFarland considers himself to be an accomplished urban orienteer. He lives for making his own way in strange cities. It would drive me crazy, but it's one of the things my sister fell in love with."

They heard the phone ring.

"That's probably them now."

Then they heard Beth McFarland-Lowandowski scream.

* * *

IT TOOK O'CONNER several minutes to restore her niece's sense of calm.

"What did the caller say, Beth," O'Conner asked.

"It was a *she* not a *he*. She had an accent," her niece began. "She said have Charles Lowandowski sitting by the curb in a wheel chair—alone—if we want to see the McFarlands alive." Then she added, "Eddy, the accent was Russian, I think."

O'Conner began texting.

Henley, have the NSA trace a recent telephone call to this geolocation. Let me know the originating telephone number and location. Eddy.

"What are you doing, Eddy," her niece complained. "This isn't the time to start texting your significant other."

Linda turned to McRory and silently mouthed the words, *Significant Other*.

McRory shrugged.

✳ ✳ ✳

TWO MEMBERS OF the consulate security staff were stationed in the room with orders from O'Conner to shoot Lowandowski or her niece if either made an attempt to leave. They wouldn't, of course. But the newlyweds didn't know that.

McRory changed into the standard hospital pajamas in the bathroom. To guard against the cold, he also pulled on his hooded sweatshirt.

Linda commandeered a hospital wheelchair from the lobby. McRory sat in the chair with a blanket covering his lap and yet another around his shoulders.

He looked like a Druid.

O'Conner pushed the wheelchair through the hospital and out onto the curb in front of the hospital. Before departing, she left him with strict orders.

"Shoot first. Ask questions later," she said.

"You mean if there is a 'later.'"

Linda and O'Conner sat in an unmarked consulate vehicle across the street from the hospital.

"He looks cold," O'Conner said.

"Nope. That's fear," Linda corrected. "That's a good thing."

CHAPTER **56**

THE PANEL VAN CAME to a stop in front of the university hospital. The van blocked their view. Neither Eddy O'Conner nor Alice Linda saw Joe McRory's planned abduction. The lack of knowledge made them both nervous. In Linda's case, her ability to make silly and inappropriate statements increased when she was nervous.

"This is Joe's first voluntary abduction."

The silliness of her remark was matched by O'Conner.

"Want to take odds he suffers a hematoma?"

The van pulled away from the curb. Both McRory and the hospital wheelchair were gone.

O'Conner pulled away from the curb. She followed at a respectful distance.

* * *

THE VAN WAS manned by two of the security staff from the Russian Federation Consulate. They took the time to make proper introductions.

"I am Ivanov," the taller one announced.

"Call me Stepanov," the heavy set one announced.

McRory was dumbfounded. His training told him that once the identities of the captors became known to the captive, the captive was as good as dead. But neither of these two gentlemen looked lethal.

"Would you like a pastry?" the heavy set one asked.

"Sure," McRory responded. "Who wouldn't?"

McRory's fingers pushed the pastries around the box until he found one to his pleasing.

"I've been kidnapped twice," McRory offered, "and not once did any one offer me something to eat, and certainly not a selection of fine pastries."

He smiled at his captors.

"Did you say 'kidnapped'?" Ivanov queried.

"Yes, kidnapped," McRory responded.

The two Russians spoke in their native language. While McRory didn't know Russian, it was clear from the conversation both gentlemen were confused.

"You do know this is not a kidnapping?" Ivanov volunteered.

"It isn't?" McRory answered.

"No," Ivanov said, "it isn't. We're here to give you a lift to the consulate."

"The Russian Federation Consulate, right?" McRory pressed.

"Yes, the Russian Federation Consulate. We're both Russians. This van belongs to the consulate. We work at the consulate."

Ivanov and McRory regarded one another with suspicion.

"So you mean this isn't a kidnapping?"

"No, it most certainly is not."

"Here's La Fonte," Stepanov called from the driver's seat.

He pulled the van in front of the restaurant, put the van in park, left the motor running, and exited the vehicle. From the back of the van McRory could not tell where he was going.

"How do you like this van?" Ivanov asked.

"McRory looked around.

"It's a van. Nothing special."

"You should have seen the van we used to have. It was electric. Ran very quiet. A great radio and sound system. I loved that van. I drove it all over Zurich."

"What happened to it?"

"Some Americans forced it off the road. Flipped over onto its roof. The van was a total loss."

"Sad to hear that. What happened to the person who drove?"

"A guy named Popov from Moscow. A real douche as you Americans like to say. And nothing happened to him. Nothing at all. Do you believe it?" he asked. "If Stepanov was driving, or I was driving, we'd be demoted and sent back to Russia in disgrace. But this guy Popov, he got banged up a bit, but he walked away from any responsibility, the douche." He paused. "That was a really nice van."

McRory decided to press his luck.

"Anybody seriously injured in the accident?"

Just then, Stepanov slid the side door open and passed in the pizza boxes. Ivanov spoke quickly to Stepanov, again in Russian, and Stepanov started to laugh while he closed the door. As he walked around the van McRory could hear his laughter continue.

"What's so funny?" McRory asked.

"There was one passenger. An older dude. Supposedly some deadly killer in the Spetsnatz. If you ask me, the only thing he ever attacked was a full bowl of borscht!"

Stepanov heard Ivanov's statement about Kuznetsov and puffed up his chest—apparently mocking the old soldier.

"You could say he lost his head," Stepanov added still laughing.

"Is he okay?" McRory played it dumb.

"No, not really. When I said he 'lost his head,' I meant he really lost it!" Stepanov drew his finger across his throat.

"He was decapitated?" McRory continued the dumb act.

The two Russians debated in their native Russian the meaning of the word "decapitated." At the end of their discussion, Ivanov turned away from Stepanov and toward McRory, "Yes, he was *decapitated*."

Stepanov drove the van away from the restaurant.

"We stopped for pizza?" McRory asked pointing to the two carryout boxes.

"Yes, of course," Ivanov said. "We were told you liked pizza. Is this not true?"

"Pizza's okay," he stated. "Where are we going now?"

"We're going to the Kunsteisbahn Oerlikon," Stepanov called from the front.

"The skating rink?" McRory asked.

"Yes, you know of it?" it was Ivanov's chance to ask.

"I went to an outing there recently. Went with some of the people in my apartment building."

Stepanov looked at them both through his rear-view mirror.

"Ah ha, so that's the connection," he said triumphantly. "We were instructed to take you to the Kunsteisbahn Oerlikon, feed you pizza, and watch the women skaters. After that, the consulate."

"Really?" McRory responded.

*   *   *

O'CONNER AND LINDA pulled into the parking lot at Kunsteisbahn Oerlikon. O'Conner parked on the opposite side of the lot and substantially away from the van.

"What are they doing?" O'Conner asked.

Linda was looking through the small field glasses she took everywhere.

"They're eating pizza," she said.

"Pizza?" O'Conner responded. "Shit!" she screamed. She started the car, pulled wildly out of the parking stall and sped through the parking lot toward the exit.

"What the hell, Eddy," Linda held on to the dashboard for stability.

"We were tricked, Alice."

*   *   *

EDWARD AND SUSAN McFarland followed their driver into the hospital.

"Irina, it's not necessary for you to accompany us to our children," Susan offered.

"Ms. McFarland, my orders were clear. I was to pick you up at the airport, bring you to the hospital, and deliver you to a specific room," the driver reported in clipped tones.

"Did that include driving us all over Zurich as well?" Edward smarmily asked. "The route you took was hardly direct. I am an amateur orienteer, and I know that you drove us all over hell's half acre. Probably to pad your bill, no doubt."

"Edward, Susan punched his arm, "there's no need to be nasty. We're here. The ride was lovely. That's all that matters."

"In a pig's eye," he muttered.

"Ignore him, Irina. Mr. Smarty Pants here didn't get a full eight hours of sleep last night and he's very cranky."

CHAPTER 57

THE MOTB, AND HER LESS than thrilled husband, swept into the hospital room pushing aside their limo driver.

"Beth, Charles!" she swooned. "The newlyweds!"

She crossed the floor and climbed onto the hospital bed, her daughter the bride on one side of her new son-in-law, she on the other, and Charles Lowandowski in the middle of the family sandwich.

Beth McFarland eased off the bed and ran into the arms of her father.

"Daddy, we're so glad you're here."

His daughter's affections melted away his fatigue and ill humor attributable to the long ride from the airport.

"Hello, sweetheart," he smiled and hugged his daughter. The hug lasted just long enough to make the other members of his family uncomfortable—especially his new son-in-law. "Why don't you introduce me to the young man who stole you away from me."

"Edward, Charles didn't steal her away. She'll always be our daughter. He just laid a large claim to her heart," Susan McFarland was chiding her husband, hoping to move his approach to his new son-in-law to a better place.

Edward McFarland strode to the hospital bed. The deliberate stride filled Charles Lowandowski with some concern. This was his first meeting with his father-in-law, a meeting most fiancés and husbands faced with at least some degree of caution. Lying prone in a hospital bed did not better prepare him. His father-in-law held the higher ground—both figuratively and literally.

Edward made the first gesture.

"Welcome to the family, Charles," Edward said absent the warmth of a genuine welcome.

"Edward," Susan McFarland chided, "give him a hug."

Beth McFarland-Lowandowski returned to husband's side.

Their driver found the family reunion a fascinating display of American culture and values—until she had enough. She closed the door and turned the lock.

The sound of the locking mechanism engaging was loud enough to cut through the family drama and capture everyone's attention. Everyone turned toward the driver.

"Edward, honey, did you tip our driver?" Susan McFarland asked.

"A tip isn't necessary," Lowandowski responded before his father-in-law could, "I made all of the necessary arrangements, including the gratuity."

"Shut up you twits!" Irina Rybolovlev shouted.

"Excuse me," Edward McFarland demanded, "I will not tolerate anyone speaking to my wife in that manner. Your conduct will be reported to the limo company. And, if you ask me, I believe this time tomorrow you will be searching for another job. You aren't very good at it judging by the route we took from the airport to the hospital."

Rybolovlev pulled her jacket aside and withdrew a small caliber pistol from a side holster. From her pocket she extracted a silencer. She attached the silencer to the gun.

The room suddenly grew quiet.

"We haven't been properly introduced," Rybolovlev followed in a saccharine voice. "I am General Irina Rybolovlev of the Russian Federation's Military Intelligence."

"No you're not," Susan McFarland offered in her most helpful voice. "My dear, you are the driver for the limo company that picked us up at the airport." Pointing to Lowandowski, "And my son-in-law made the arrangements for you to be our driver."

"Russia doesn't have women generals," Edward McFarland stated authoritatively. "They are very misogynistic." He turned to his wife, "I saw that on *Front Line* two, three weeks ago." Then he turned to Rybolovlev, "Listen, I'm sorry if my behavior was unacceptable and I offended you. Here, let me provide you with a gratuity—in addition to what my son-in-law may have already arranged."

"Bravo, Edward," Susan McFarland congratulated her husband for his generosity. Turning to her daughter and son-in-law, "Now that's the man I married. He's been cranky this morning. He didn't sleep well on the flight over."

"American idiots! I can't believe you brought the Soviet Union to the brink of disaster."

"Actually," Edward McFarland added, "We brought them to the brink, and then we pushed them over the edge." Looking back to his wife, he pantomimed the act of pushing an imaginary person over the brink. Looking back at Rybolovlev, "If you check, I think you'll find I'm right."

Rybolovlev had enough. She aimed the gun at Edward McFarland's right foot and fired.

Rybolovlev's aim was less than perfect. The bullet's trajectory skewed to the left of center and entered the shoe just above and to the right of his small toe.

"You shot my foot!" he exclaimed.

Rybolovlev misinterpreted McFarland's reaction to the missed shot for shock. She expected the pain would quickly prove overwhelming for him.

She was wrong.

Edward McFarland launched himself at Rybolovlev who was unprepared for the injured man to physically assault her, but he did.

The disparity in their physical sizes provided McFarland with greater leverage and strength. He immediately grabbed for her gun. The two of them struggled. Rybolovlev managed to bring the weapon alongside McFarland's head.

"Let go, you idiot, or I'll fire into your head," she screamed.

A member of the nursing staff politely knocked on the locked door.

"Hello, Mr. Lowandowski. You are not permitted to lock your door without a member of staff in the room with you. Please open the door, now."

McFarland made an exaggerated gesture of putting his hands above his head. He slowly backed away from Rybolovlev.

"Mr. Lowandowski, please open the door now. If you fail to do so, I will summon our security staff to unlock the door. There will be consequences, Mr. Lowandowski."

Rybolovlev turned her head to respond to the demand. When she did, Edward McFarland threw himself at her, again.

This time, Rybolovlev successfully fired her weapon. Edward McFarland took the round in his left shoulder.

The combination of the wound, the lack of sleep, and the effect high adrenaline levels had on his depleted reserves caused him to fall forward on to Rybolovlev pinning her against the door. He wrapped his right arm around her neck.

Edward McFarland outweighed Rybolovlev by at least fifty pounds. Fifty extra pounds of dead weight and gravity conspired to slowly drag Rybolovlev to collapse to the floor with McFarland on top of her.

The two deadlocked bodies blocked the door.

"Mr. Lowandowski, security is here to unlock the door."

They could hear the locking mechanism disengage. Security was unable to push the door open. They could hear a hurried conversation on the other side, although only Rybolovlev who spoke German could understand.

"Hurry, help me lift your husband off of me," Rybolovlev addressed his wife.

"A muffled, "Don't you God damned dare, Susan," came from the injured husband.

"Edward, there's no reason to use such language. Especially to me!" came her response.

"Listen to me, you fucking twits," Rybolovlev was beyond furious and contempt, "either pull him off or I will kill him."

Susan McFarland clucked at the spate of inappropriate language hurled at her from the far corner of the room.

Beth McFarland-Lowandowski calmly disentangled her body from that of her husband, stood on the floor, and walked over to the door and the two intertwined bodies blocking any egress or ingress. She reached into the pocket of her cardigan and withdrew a Glock semi-automatic weapon. She bent over her father's body and placed the muzzle in the middle of Rybolovlev's forehead.

"You so much as fart, old woman, and I will blow your God damned head off," she threatened.

"Ach! You stupid little girl. You don't know how to fire that weapon," Rybolovlev countered.

Beth disengaged the release.

"Do you care to test that thought, bitch!"

Susan McFarland looked at her son-in-law.

"Such language," she apologized. "I'm afraid she takes after her father."

"God damned right she does, Susan!"

"Edward!"

✲ ✲ ✲

EDDY O'CONNER AND Alice Linda returned to the hospital to find the unbelievable scene played out in Lowandowski's room.

Beth McFarland-Lowandowski continued to hold Rybolovlev at bay with a drawn weapon. Edward McFarland was being hustled onto a gurney for a ride to the emergency ward, an IV bag already sending fluids into his body.

Later, after the police arrived, Rybolovlev was taken into custody, and statements were taken, O'Conner pieced together what took place in her absence. There was one question remaining.

"Where did Beth get that gun?" she wondered aloud to Linda.

Linda reached under her coat to the holster affixed to the small of her back.

"I think I know the answer," she offered.

"Do you mean we raced after Joe and both of us were unarmed?" O'Conner asked. "What would have happened if we made a move to rescue Joe."

"From what I could see," Linda responded, a smile on her face, "they wouldn't have had enough pizza to share."

It was the last time Linda would smile for the remainder of the day.

* * *

JOE MCRORY'S CAPTORS dropped him at the hospital entrance following an afternoon of eating pastry and pizza—and watching the many fetching fräulein at the skating rink. He was quickly brought up to date.

"What will happen to Rybolovlev?" McRory asked.

"Probably nothing more than a gentle slap on the wrists by the Swiss authorities," O'Conner hazarded her guess. "Henley texted she entered the country on a diplomatic passport."

"Does this ever end, Eddy?" Linda asked as she examined the Glock. "I forgot to load it."

O'Conner smiled.

"I won't tell Rybolovlev, if you won't."

"It's not Rybolovlev I worry about," Linda quietly responded. "It's your niece. She already hates my guts."

"Yeah, about that, Alice. The two of you need to make the peace."

"Eddy, why? We'll be leaving soon. I doubt I'll ever run into the new Mr. and Mrs. Lowandowski anytime soon."

O'Conner became uncharacteristically quiet.

"No, Eddy. They're coming back to San Francisco with us?" Linda was dumbstruck.

"What?" McRory added. "Why"

"This thing with the Russians will never end if I leave Beth here. She won't agree to leave her new husband. He's not safe anywhere, unless I can keep him on a tight leash."

"Let them live with your sister and her husband," Linda insisted.

"Edward and Susan have absolutely no idea what's been taking place. Both of them refuse to believe Rybolovlev is military intelligence. They really do think she was their limo driver."

"You can't be serious," McRory was aghast. "Did they not just live through this horror?"

"They're citizens, Joe. They don't live in the same world the three of us do. Besides, the DNI has made me an offer I can't refuse."

"Which is?" he asked.

"I'm to finish debriefing my new nephew on his many criminal activities and turn the report over to him. He'll make the necessary arrangements with the Department of Justice. After Lowandowski pleads guilty—and he will plead guilty—the judge hearing his case will delay sentencing and place him under my direct supervision."

"Beth and Charles are going to live with you?" McRory was incredulous.

"Well, Joe, I certainly have the room. The company might not be too bad. She is my favorite niece, after all."

O'Conner paused to let her brain grapple with the scenario she just described before she continued.

"Beth can continue her studies at USF."

"What about him?" Linda asked.

"Well, there have been times when we could have made great use of a hacker with a criminal mind. Now I have one. For a nephew no less."

"He'll be a partner?" McRory asked.

"No, he'll always be on probation. One misstep, and off to a Supermax prison he goes."

"Does he understand that?" McRory continued the line of questioning.

"If he doesn't today, he certainly will tomorrow."

THE END